For Nothing

By
Nicholas Denmon

This is a work of fiction. Names, places, incidents are a product of the author's imagination, and any resemblance to any persons, living or dead, events or organizations is coincidental.

For Nothing

Copyright © 2011 by Nicholas Denmon

ISBN 978-1463567835

To my family, friends, and Jen. A special thanks to the city of Buffalo and those on both sides of the law who helped contribute to this novel.

For Nothing

By
Nicholas Denmon

An Upstate New York Mafia Tale

Chapter 1

He could see it happening. It was too fast. He told himself to step aside and reach for his pistol, but he heard his doom, and then he saw it.

The firing mechanism clicked, creating a chemical reaction that bottled up behind the bullet. The fiery reaction, trapped behind the bullet, groaned in protest at the delay the projectile was causing. Then, all at once, the force became too much for the bullet to hold back. With a roar, the bullet emerged from the chamber and exited out the muzzle of the cold .45 caliber pistol. The flames of the gunpowder explosion followed soon after, enveloping the bullet for a millisecond before it reemerged from its heated escort. The ball hurtled forward, burst through the leather material, through the cotton of the shirt below, and penetrated into soft flesh.

He stumbled with the impact.

As the bullet traveled, it displaced the blood in its cruel path and shattered the bone of the breastplate. The impact as the projectile splintered through that protective bone caused the tempered metal of the bullet to flatten into the size and form of a nickel. With the speed of light it split a seam between the pulsating heart on its right and the unmoving spinal column on its left, shredding a lung as it sped past. With less ease than it entered, the lead blasted out the rear, taking the newest layer of skin and a small fragment of the breastplate along for the ride and ripped another, larger hole through the back side of the cotton shirt and leather jacket. The ball proceeded forward for about a foot until it blasted into the brick of a building and came to rest, lodged into the sturdy masonry.

The hole that appeared in his back kicked him forward and threw Jack to his knees. His back throbbed, but the impact on his knees hurt worse, and he rolled over, feeling the cold, wet gravel on the side of his face. Jack tried to draw a breath. He opened his eyes and saw nothing, blinded by the light of the street lamp. He felt them strain as he realized the air wasn't coming. He tried again, still nothing. Only it was worse. Again. Nothing. Again. Worse. Warm water came out of his mouth.

Damn it, he thought, it was air he wanted. *Air, damn it.*

The incident took less than a second. One second to send Jack's blood pouring into his lungs and send his body crumpling to the ground. He gasped for a breath that would never come. His chest seized. Jack wanted to sit up, to get help, but his body couldn't respond to his pleas for action. He thought it ironic that here on a city street, so far from the nearest body of water, he felt as if he were drowning. The simple irony of it all left as fast as it came. He wheezed for air. The effort sent a spout of blood shooting from his mouth in a gurgled gasp. One second. One second was all it took to send twenty-eight years of moments, his life, flashing before his eyes, quicker than he could grasp and hang on to them. As this latest incident slipped past his scattered and fading memory, Jack slipped into eternal darkness.

*

The lone assassin stood there a moment, contemplating the kill. He killed scores of men, and some women, but it never ceased to amaze him how he could take life with such ease. This last one was a joke. Jack should have been prepared. He knew the rules that they lived by. He knew the rules that they, in the end, died by.

Rafael Rontego took another drag on his cigarette. He knew that time was not an issue in this particular district, but nevertheless he didn't want to take a chance. His employer owned the police, but he hadn't survived this long by leaving things to luck.

Witnesses. He laughed at the notion, but took a cautious look around at the windows that overlooked the street. Drawn blinds greeted him. No one would be so foolish as to get involved with a hit. They too knew the rules. Besides, Rafael chose this district for just those reasons. The slum of this neighborhood did not even begin to show up on the "We give a shit" radar of the Buffalo city police. Witnesses were not an issue here.

He looked down as the body of his latest victim twitched. It looked somewhat eerie to the killer, splayed as it was, under the lone street lamp of Walden Avenue. For a moment Rafael thought perhaps Jack survived the shot to the chest, center mass. He flicked the ash from the tip of his cigarette and peered at the body with more intent.

No. This one is dead.

A chuckle slipped past his thin lips along with the exhalation of his favorite smoke, as he realized that the twitch was just the nervous system's response. But Rafael hadn't survived this long by leaving anything to fate, God, chance, whatever people called it. He stood over Jack and discharged a second bullet into his chest.

He pulled once more on his cigarette.

God bless Sobranie smokes.

Rafael's boot extinguished the last flickering of flame from the butt of the cigarette as he ground the filter into the sidewalk. The assassin's head snapped up. His dark eyes followed the brim of his felt hat as he peered into the darkness. His ears focused with the precision of the trained killer he was. The dull echo of hurrying footsteps far down the city street greeted his ears. A block, perhaps two, from the direction of Genesee Street, down Stuart Avenue.

He glanced below one last time at the crumpled form at his feet.

Too easy.

With a resigned sigh Rafael Rontego spun about,

his trench coat twirling behind him, and vanished into the darkness.

Chapter 2

Jack came to him just forty-eight hours earlier. The last two days seemed like an eternity as they both worked out the details to protect Jack during the meeting. Jack was not very specific when he asked Alex Vaughn to help him; just that he needed some security with a meeting that was going down in a couple days. Alex was never one to pry; besides, if Jack wanted to divulge the specifics, he would have. Alex, of course, agreed to help him set up security. All Jack needed to do, all he ever needed to do, was ask.

They settled things as they always did, with a beer at the Old Irish Pub down the street. Alex liked this place—quiet locals, cheap beer, and information if one needed it. Jack had some Southern Rock playing on the jukebox before Alex even arrived. Jack was always the first one there, wherever they met. But this time, when Alex arrived, there was nothing playing on the box and he noticed two empty shot glasses in front of Jack. Something was wrong. The explanation he got was that the guy he was meeting with was "not someone to be taken lightly" and that "he wanted some backup to ensure his safety." Alex told Jack that in the particular area where they were meeting this informant they would need at least half a dozen personnel to cover all possibilities.

Jack was adamant that there would not be anyone besides the two of them on the operation.

"Six people?" he asked with obvious dismay. Though he tried to hide his anxiety, the uncomfortable shift of his weight gave him away.

"Listen Jack, you wanted my help to set up a safe meeting and I'm telling you it can be done with no fewer than six people, maybe five but that's stretching it. There are too many alleyways and side streets." Alex looked him straight in the eye to hammer home the point.

Again, the uncomfortable shift in weight. This time, though, it was accompanied by a slight grimace.

"It has to be just the two of us Alex. The situation is too tenuous for me to bring in anyone I don't absolutely trust."

And that was that. Even though Jack asked Alex for his help, he didn't intend to listen to his advice.

"What the hell, I'm just an undercover cop, what the fuck would I know about security on a damned urban street?" he thought with not just a small hint of sarcasm.

With Jack's unwillingness to bring in others on this mysterious op, there wasn't much Alex could do. He gave Jack a two-way transmitting earpiece so that they could hear each other, and waited about four blocks from the meeting place in his newest speedster, a rusty, faded blue '97 Ford Taurus. Jack was armed, that was good. He carried his police-issued revolver. Alex never left the house without his 9mm Beretta, the envy of beat cops carrying popguns. With the little assistance he could offer, Alex hoped the situation Jack was in didn't go awry.

Only it did.

At first it was just technical things—the earpiece was getting some sort of static. Alex first started to notice it when Jack was a few blocks away. He couldn't figure out what could be fucking with his damned earpiece. The range on it, he knew, was five miles. A few blocks should have no effect on the signal. That's when he noticed it. A low airplane flew in from the west.

"Damn."

How could he be so stupid, how many times had he worked this district? Buffalo Niagara International. He knew the right frequency to avoid air traffic control interference.

Alex tried to call Jack in to fix the frequency, "Hey Jack, if you hear me, switch the channel on your earpiece to five."

6

"I..nt......essed...static." was all he got from Jack in reply.

"Fuck!" Alex hated this shit.   Jack could be no more than a few blocks down, maybe if he ran down to him and told him before he reached the rendezvous. He slipped his butterfly knife into his right ankle strap and pulled his jeans over his brown boots. Winter in Buffalo is harsh.

Alex turned off his car feeling the biting frost of negative degree weather and pulled his brown leather jacket in close, flipping his collar up to break the swirling wind. As an afterthought while he hustled down the street, Alex patted his Beretta on his left hip. Alex had a draw so fast it promised death and even deadlier aim; he graduated in the top of his class at the academy. Patting the firearm, snug on his hip, he felt reassured. Alex hurried west on Walden Avenue, passing a boarded-up liquor store on his left and a burnt-out building on his right.

"Lovely," he whispered to himself.

Alex was gaining on Jack. He knew it because the earpiece was coming in clearer now and Alex was only three blocks away from the meeting. Alex stopped. He now heard another voice on the earpiece. Jack must have already made contact with whomever he was meeting. Alex slipped into an alleyway to his right and there he waited to see what was going down. Both the voices sounded muffled.

"Damn it all Jack, turn up your volume," Alex pleaded, hoping that Jack could hear him.

He crouched in the alley for what seemed like an hour, though his watch revealed to him the truth of the matter. A mere five minutes went by. He edged his head around the corner trying to get a good view of the street. That's when he heard it; through the static he heard it, the unmistakable whoosh of a muffled blast. Alex leapt out of the alleyway and ran down the street. It all seemed surreal to him and he felt like his legs were weighed down by lead.

God, let that have been Jack's gun, he thought.

Even as he thought it, he knew that he was wrong. Jack had no silencer. What came through the earpiece next was unmistakable. Jack's voice came through. Even though it came in as a gurgling mess, Alex knew Jack's voice anywhere. Still running, Alex's face drooped into a frozen grimace. He needed to get to the rendezvous.

As Alex neared the meeting point he almost let out a sigh of relief. There, in the street light, he was able to make out the form of a man under the-not-too-distant street lamp. Beyond that, the one thing on the street was an old white van parked haphazardly half a block down.

When Alex got closer to the street light though, his muscles tensed and his jaw clenched as he realized that the figure silhouetted under the glow was not Jack. Now aware of his own fast-falling footsteps, Alex slowed his pace down. The shadowy figure before him let out a breath into the gloom; the warm puff mingled with the frigid winter air. Alex trailed his gaze down to the pavement and his heart fell to the pit of his stomach. Alex knew it was Jack's crumpled form.

Throwing caution to the wind, Alex ran forward, quickening his pace, and snapping his head up to face his newfound adversary. With a start, he realized that his adversary was already on the move. All he glimpsed as he neared the horrific scene was the twirl of a coat rounding the corner up ahead.

After what seemed like hours, Alex made it to the spot where Jack lay sprawled on the sidewalk, his blood flowing onto the soft white snow beneath the prone form. The warm lifeblood of Jack was melting the snow and causing a slight steam to rise up from the tainted purity of the white winter freeze.

Alex knelt next to Jack, knowing the futility of it, yet he pushed his fingers up to Jack's lifeless wrist with all the tenderness he could muster. No pulse.

"Aw, Jack. What mess have you gotten yourself into?" Alex asked.

As he spoke, he touched Jack's face and wiped the blood that dripped from his mouth with the sleeve of his jacket. Alex's jawbone became taut as he attempted to hold his emotions from brimming over and the tears that begged to pour out, within.

With a sudden ferocity, Alex sprang up. It might be too late for Jack, but he'd be damned if it were too late for him to put a few lead holes through this bastard that committed the vile deed.

He took off around the corner. Running as fast as he could, he tried to think of where someone would stash a getaway car in this district. Alex knew where to go. Three blocks down there was an alley that was all but hidden from the main highway. It was the perfect spot.

He accelerated faster than even he thought was possible. Alex pushed himself to look past the burn that found its way into his legs as he ran past one block, then two. As he neared the third block and rounded the corner to come into the alley, he was brought to a sudden halt.

The headlights of a car were right in his face, assaulting his eyes that became accustomed to the night. Blinded by the glare, yet realizing that the car was speeding towards him due to the roar of the spinning wheels, Alex hurled his body behind the corner of the street. Inches. That was all that separated Alex from becoming mush on the windshield of the speeding automobile.

A quick flash of a bug splattered across his car front shot through his mind. With a shake of his head, Alex threw off the blindness now that the car's lights sped off down the road. He tried to peer at the fleeing car's rear bumper, hoping to see the license plate of the car before it was out of his vision.

"Fuck!" Alex said, realizing that the car was too

far for such a stroke of luck. With all the bottled rage spilling out, Alex let out a primal scream.

With a rush of adrenaline, he swung at the brick of the building next to him. The sturdy masonry did not give. His hand did, and the bones in his hands made a loud 'pop' that sent a sudden wave of pain into Alex's frayed nervous system. Alex flexed his hand; it was hurt, but not broken. Already, he could feel the blood rushing into his hand swelling his knuckles. He tried to grab his cell phone from his pocket but he couldn't get his swollen knuckles into the jeans. He reached in with his other hand and flipped the screen open. No service. With a grunt he shoved the cell back into his pocket with his injured hand.

Blinded for the second time in the evening—this time with the searing agony pulsating up from his swollen hand; Alex began to make his way down the deserted street. He needed to return to the body, to find some sort of evidence as to what transpired in the crucial moments between Jack's arrival at the scene and his subsequent murder.

On the way, he spotted a telephone booth and decided that he would use the payphone to call in the incident. After all of this, the cavalry would be a welcomed sight. He began to reach into his jacket, oblivious to the biting chill swirling on the winter winds. Plucking change from his pocket, he picked up the phone and shoved it between his cheek and shoulder. Damn his stupidity for injuring his hand.

Even this call is a hassle with one appendage out of commission, he thought. Dialing into the precinct, Alex composed himself enough to explain to the switchboard patrolman the situation.

Letting out a deep breath that trailed out in a wisp of whitened smoke, he walked up to the place of Jack's last gasps. Jack stopped bleeding; at least the flow stopped. Gentle swirls of falling snow began to cover up the footprints that were scattered in on the sidewalk. Fresh flakes settled on the bloodstained snow shifting the macabre spectacle one flake at a time. As Alex stood looking down at the scene, his knees became weak and gave out on him altogether. With the adrenaline drained from his body, Alex could no longer find the strength to stand and collapsed onto his knees, half melting into the snow at Jack's side.

With fresh falling snow now blanketing the bloodstained scene below, he thought it odd that Jack looked asleep. Alex held his head. He needed the familiarity, the solace, of shielding his eyes from the sight before him. He stayed like that for a long moment.

Summoning control over himself once again, Alex let out another cleansing breath and dropped his hands onto the chilled body of Jack and rolled him over. He noticed with interest that the bullet shot right through Jack's back. That meant the shot must have been close. Judging by the fact that Jack's weapon was not even drawn meant one of two things. Either he did not see the danger coming, didn't expect it, or perhaps the assailant was just that quick.

Just that quick...couldn't be. No, it had to be that Jack just didn't see it coming and didn't expect it. Alex had to believe that no one could be that quick. He knew that Jack was not a novice with a firearm.

Shaking the thought from his mind, Alex focused on the situation at hand. The sounds of distant sirens began to drift to his attention. As if that sound snapped him out of his fragmented thoughts, he reverted to his instincts.

Glancing around at the scene, Alex noticed a half-buried cigarette butt in the snow. It was a curious thing. Instead of the normal yellow speckled ass-end of a cancer stick, this thing was as black as the tar residue it was doomed to leave in your lungs. The filter sported a thin gold wrapping encircling it, but for the most part it was of the flat Black Russian variety. Interesting to say the least.

It was the one thing he saw of any material value.

As the sirens became louder, Alex weighed the possibility of letting the homicide unit cover the case; after all he had a conflict of interest.

Fuck it, he thought. *Personal conflict be damned.*

Jack meant a lot to him. For Christ's sake, the best man at his wedding to Charlotte was Jack. With a grunt, Alex leaned over to the cigarette and scooped it up and slipped it into his jacket. He eased upward and shook the numbness from his frozen legs. The veteran undercover agent maintained enough connections out here on the streets to rustle up some information. Favors could be called in easy enough.

No, he decided with a satisfied grimace. *This one is personal. The conflict is real.*

Alex wanted to taste the sweetness of revenge. Rules be damned.

*

Rafael Rontego walked up the narrow and dim stairway that led up to his one room flat. The apartment building itself was not much to look at, and the inside of Rontego's room was even less aesthetic in its appeal. Rafael pulled his room key out from the hidden compartment in his left boot.

The assassin kept a small knife or handcuff key there. It worked wonders if an unsuspecting cop was so kind as to handcuff him in the front. And if he wasn't, Rafael practiced many times the maneuver which enabled him to pull his shackled hands over his feet and to the front of his body in one fluid motion. After all, one could never be too prepared.

Silently, he slid the key to his apartment into the lock and shifted the bolt. He pushed the door open. Before stepping inside, however, he knelt down and peered about six inches above the door. The small breakaway thread he tied across the doorway was still intact. Rafael rose back up and stepped over the string.

All is well on the home front.

He walked over to the center of the room and glanced about. He hated this place. In the center was a mattress with no box spring. To the left was a small kitchen area that grew dusty from disuse. Cooking was best left to others of more...domestic persuasion. To the right of the bed was a lazy-boy which was a faded red due to age. Further to the right of that was a small closet and through the closet, toward the back, was a small bathroom.

With a cough, the assassin moved forward, pushing the door closed behind him. Rontego pulled a chair from the corner of the room around to face him. With one fluid motion he removed his black felt hat, his tribute to the gangster days of yore, and sent it swirling on to the chair. He took his black trench coat off of his shoulders—shoulders deceptive in their slenderness—and tossed it onto the chair's back. Hanging from both shoulders was a leather holster, which contained his weapons of choice: silenced pistols.

With a prudent look toward his lone window right above his mattress, Rafael took his weapons off and tossed them on top of his jacket. He walked over to the window and pulled up the blinds. From here he had a good view of the street.

Exactly the room he wanted. The previous tenant didn't want to give up this abode, but everyone could be persuaded where the assassin was concerned. He made sure the bolt locking the window was in place, and then pulled the blinds back down. Prying eyes were not welcome here.

Passing through his closet, he pushed open the door that led to the bathroom. The door itself was a nice touch to the place. Rontego added it himself. The door was the same color of the wall and, in the dim light of the interior of the closet, nearly impossible to find unless one was mentally on his toes.

Once in the bathroom, Rafael pulled the light string dangling down from the ceiling and stood in the swinging bulb's shifting light. He leaned on the ancient, shoddy porcelain sink, contemplating his reflection in the mirror. A lesser man would not be so bold as to look too long, lest he become disgusted with the view.

Rontego, though, had the unnerving ability to do just that. He could look time after time at himself and see nothing wrong. In fact, he liked what he saw. He saw a man who was the best at what he did, and Rontego never frowned upon success, even success like his. After all, he *was* the best at what he did. Nothing less was acceptable. He didn't even dislike the people that opposed him, if they were good at it.

Take Jack for example, Rontego thought to himself as he studied his face in the mirror. Jack was damn good at what he did; he knew him to be a decent cop. Jack just got careless. In this business carelessness was sure to end your tenure at the top. To be lazy was not a luxury one could afford when dealing with the likes of those on the dark side of society. So Rontego's boss had to clean up and Rafael did the deed quick, clean, professional. One shot, one kill.

With a satisfied grin, Rafael looked into the mirror. He shaved already once today, but the five o'clock shadow that followed his cheeks to his chin never seemed to lessen. His dark hair was perfect and combed backwards. His gray eyes could even be considered appealing, if not for the fact that there existed in them no humanity, no divine spark. He splashed some cold water onto his face and grabbed a small towel off the rack to his left.

Drying his face, he left the bathroom and walked toward the kitchen. Perhaps there was some leftover Chinese in the kitchen. After all, he worked hard tonight.

This was a well-earned meal. Rafael was hungry, and when he was hungry, he always ate.

Chapter 3

Alex pulled into the driveway of his townhouse apartment. The apartment looked dingy on the outside and had the look of a place where people stayed on their way to somewhere else. If the outside didn't look like much with its peeling yellow paint, then the inside didn't look much better.

Alex walked inside; his only thoughts were bent on finding his bed. He was so tired that he was almost sure that the nasty spring that poked into his back night after night wouldn't bother him.

Though the apartment was not dirty, it was not a place of frequent use, or dusting. The inside was bare. Internally, the place consisted of three rooms on the floor that was Alex's rent. There was a kitchen/small living room right in front of the entryway with a card table that Alex used to take his meals whenever he had a chance to dine in. Other than the two chairs pushed in at either end of the structure, no more furniture graced the room.

Who needed more furniture than that, Alex thought. Both chairs could be pulled into the living room and used as a couch or love seat.

The living room end of the kitchen was just a milk carton crate flipped over with an eleven-inch, black and white television holding on to a precarious perch atop it, in the corner of the room. Alex hated the damn thing but every now and then it would come in handy for a Sunday football game.

"God bless the Buffalo Bills" was Alex's Sunday motto. It used to be his motto anyway. Time, as of late, became a factor.

Alex tossed his keys on the card table with a deep sigh. It'd been a long day. He tossed his jacket onto one of the chairs next to him and put his hands onto the small of his back, arching upward and tensing his back. With a satisfied smile, Alex heard the crack as his vertebrae released the air in between their joints.

His underarm holster seemed to throw his back out a bit to the left, he was sure of it. Thinking of the Beretta, he slipped the holster off and walked to the wall left of his television. There in the wall was a nail wedged into a beam behind the wall. Alex hung his holster on the nail; he then bent down and lifted his left pant leg. Strapped to his ankle was a one shot Derringer. He unstrapped the ankle holster and hung that too on the nail. He unhooked the butterfly knife from his right ankle and slipped it into his back pocket. He turned right to head down the three-foot hallway that led to his bathroom.

Alex looked to the right of the bathroom entrance. There was a picture there of Alex, a woman, and a small child. He pushed past the picture and went into the bathroom. Alex flicked on the light and turned on the bath water, turned the nozzle to warm.

Damn pipes take forever to warm up in the winter, Alex thought with irritation.

Alex undressed and put his hands on each side of the sink. Looking into the mirror in front of him, he glanced at his reflection.

He needed to shave but then again, what was the point?

Alex's brown hair was long, just a few inches above his shoulders. His cheekbones, though prominent, were hidden by mud and blood that caked onto him, yet were visible in patches where tears had streaked the mottled artistry.

Steam rose in white puffs from behind the shower curtain. Inch by inch, as Alex peered into the mirror and let his mind wander, the fog clung onto the glass and Alex's face disappeared.

Alex pulled back the curtain and stepped into the scalding hot water. Water, which was Alex's purification.

Day after day, it was this burning hot water that cleansed more than Alex's body. It seemed to somehow, for the moment, cleanse his soul.

The water pounded on his skin, refusing to relent, yet Alex seemed to not notice, to disregard the heat. Face turned upward toward the showerhead, as if to ask why, Alex began to relax in his own private meditation. For a long time, Alex stood there and felt the grime wash away. He began to drift into a trancelike sleep.

All at once, he stood at the scene of Jack's death. Sure enough, there was Jack, lying on the snow, lifeless. Alex, in a dreamlike drift, got closer to the body. Jack was cold, as was apparent by his bluish-white complexion. Jack's face rested on a slight drift of snow and faced Alex. As Alex drifted closer he studied Jack's face. It looked as if Jack were asleep.

As he got even closer to his friend's face he noticed a shift in the temperature, a sharp decrease in the frigid air's already less than warm embrace. As the freezing air encircled him, a shiver found its way and crept along the length of Alex's back. As the shiver leapt off of his tailbone, Alex noticed he drifted too close to Jack's face. He began to retract from the body, and with one more glance at Jack everything stopped.

The air seemed to stop swirling, its biting cold gone for a split second. The blood that dripped from Jack's mouth stopped mid-drip and hung suspended in the air. Alex strained to get a better look at this phenomenon. And that's when he noticed it.

Jack's face, more important, his eyes, snapped open. They pierced into Alex with a stern ferocity. Alex willed himself to retreat, to run from this misadventure. But Alex could not move, could not close his own eyes. Everything, including him, was frozen as much as the air was before time stopped.

Alex pulled away with all his mental strength. He

pulled away to keep his sanity, to hide from his friend's piercing gaze. The unblinking eyes poured into Alex like nothing he knew. With all of his mental energy he strained.

"Wake up Alex," he heard. "Wake up!"

With a start Alex awoke half-leaning, half-kneeling in his shower.

How long have I been in here?

The water was now running cold. Alex shivered.

*

Rafael woke up at dawn. He always woke up at dawn. His bed was right in line with the sun as it too woke from its slumbers. He had an alarm clock. Ages passed since the alarm woke him up. His daily wake routine always began with Rontego deactivating the alarm of the clock shortly after the rising sun announced the new day's arrival.

Rontego rolled out of bed and grabbed a glass of water. He felt the cool liquid go down his throat and couldn't help but enjoy it as the water refreshed his throat, parched from the hours of sleep.

Rafael suspected that he slept with his mouth open. He never asked anyone if it were true. Perhaps it was too personal of a thing to know. He'd once been told that his legs kicked with a spastic twitch while he slept. He kicked the whore out of his place. He didn't believe in mixing the personal with business.

Never liked her anyway, he thought.

Slamming his cup down, Rafael wiped the sleep from his eyes and wandered toward the window. He checked the street below his flat.

"Good," he muttered to himself.

Nothing was below except the newspaper stand where he often picked up the most recent headlines. Every now and then he liked to read the advice columns. One time an associate of his asked why he read 'those damned things'.

Even though he hated being interrupted, much less by some jerk reading over his shoulder, Rafael answered "I like to see how fucked up everyone else's lives are. It amuses me and lets me know I'm the most normal guy I've met."

Normal. What an interesting word. Rafael led a life that most would consider the antithesis to normal. He often contemplated what it meant to be 'normal.' To him his life was normal, structured, and routine. Sure, he did things on the fringe of society, things that other's dubbed 'illegal' or even 'cruel'. He didn't dwell on the issue long.

He seldom dwelled on anything long. He came to the conclusion that 'normal' was accepting what the weak constructed to stave off the strong, to impede the takeover of the elite.

It was a numbers game. The weak had more of 'em so took the necessary precautions to ensure their safety, at the detriment to the few strong ones out there with any balls. Every so often the weak could trick a strong one on to their side, often through money and brainwashing them on the value of a moral society; moral in the eyes of the weak. This meant protecting those little bastards at the expense of your own time, sweat and blood.

No, Rafael thought, *I am the normal one, taking what's mine*.

After all, wasn't it Herbert Spencer, a man of considerable mental strength, who coined the phrase 'survival of the fittest'? Darwin's "natural selection" at its finest. The weak tried to berate him into silence too; his ideas tore apart their notion that there was a creation. A creation that a God would have made with equal love for all.

Rafael was not sure of God's existence, neither did

he deny one. Hell, he witnessed too many people call out His name either moments before or during their own actual trip to the other side.

Perhaps one day, he too would find this God waiting for him on the other side of some cosmic journey on the coattail of whatever soul he had.

More than likely, Rontego mused with a morbid sense of serenity, *he would just become worm food in some anonymous hole in the ground.*

Rafael shook the thoughts from his mind. Today was not a day for such morbid thoughts. He leaned over and stretched to his toes. He always enjoyed a good stretch. With a grunt Rafael jerked up and began getting ready for the day.

Today he was going to talk to his boss. The boss. Rontego never dealt with anyone but the boss, though he ran into a lot of the old man's associates when he was getting an assignment or collecting his cash. He always dressed nice when going into 'the office'. After all, he was a professional.

Minutes later, Rafael Rontego was walking down the streets of Buffalo. The office was a mile or two down the road and the cold invigorated the assassin.

From top to bottom, he was dressed in the finest quality clothing. Atop his jet-black hair rested his trademark hat. A gangster-style, black felt hat that brimmed outward from his head several inches in circumference was traced by a black ribbon that was almost flush against the felt. The hat was perfect and round except in the front where it indented as if to allow a forefinger to sweep from the wearer's head.

He wore a black Giorgio Armani suit measured to perfection and lined by smooth gray pinstripes. Tucked into his jacket was an elegant Gianni Versace silver tie. His white cuffs trimmed the outside of his suit and his silver French cufflinks appeared and reappeared in time with his brisk gait.

If you were lucky enough to get a close view of his cuff links, your death was probable. However, if one could speak from the grave, they would tell you that the letters engraved on the links were S and M. Rumor had it that Rafael might be a sadomasochist. Rafael ignored the absurdity of the claim. He'd be damned if he ever told what those initials stood for.

Rontego stopped. He tucked his most recent purchase, a copy of the Buffalo News, under his arm and stooped over to tie his Gucci wing tips. Rafael continued his walk to the office.

A block later he reached inside his long overcoat and pulled out a wad of twenty-dollar bills. Without breaking step, he snatched one out of his money clip, reinserted the wad, and folded the twenty into a smooth crease. As he rounded the corner of the block there was an old beggar. *Predictable*. The man sent his cup up to Rafael. Rontego dropped the twenty into his cup and started to walk away.

I don't shit where I sleep, he thought.

As an afterthought, Rafael turned around and grabbed the man by the collar of his welfare duds. With a quick yank, Rafael stood nose to nose with the homeless man.

"Take that money and eat something for fuck's sake! I swear to whoever you call God that you will meet him if I catch you buying a drink with that twenty."

Before the startled man could nod, Rontego let go of the beggar's lapel and moved on. Wiping his hands on the folds of his jacket, Rontego entered the club in front of him. The parking lot was all but deserted at this hour, yet he knew that inside there were at least half a dozen guys.

Rumors was a nice enough place, for people who went out.

Chapter 4

Alex awoke to the alarm's incessant beep ringing in his ears. He rolled over to turn the damn thing off and let out a groan. His head was pounding and the infernal spring in his back was always a pleasant way to greet the day. Alex rolled back the other way toward his nightstand.

"God, what the hell was I thinking," he groaned aloud to no one in particular.

The bottle of Jim Beam smirked down upon him, Alex Vaughn, its latest trophy. Alex rolled into a sitting position and shook his fist at the bottle. It won this round.

Alex cleared his throat and looked back at the clock. It was 9:00 a.m. He grunted again; his captain would be pissed. Lucky. He was between undercover gigs or this would ruin everything. Alex picked up the phone and dialed in to the precinct. They wouldn't mind him taking a few days off; after all this was a personal tragedy. It was about to get a lot more personal too.

After a brief conversation with the desk sergeant, Alex hung up the phone and went into his travesty of a kitchen. Still in his boxers and plain white tee, Alex mixed together some instant coffee, extra caffeinated. He saw his answering machine blinking. Twelve messages and one guess what they were all about. He ignored the blinking red light.

He threw on a pair of jeans, his snow boots, took his weapons off his nail in reverse order and put on his brown leather jacket.

Still, the blinking light assaulted his eyes. He picked up the phone and looked at the caller I.D.; *she* called. Twice. He flipped open his cell phone. She was one of very few people who had that number. She called there too.

Charlotte.

One message. Her voice sounded musical, as it

always did.

"Alex, I heard. Jesus Alex I heard. If you don't want to go tonight, that's fine. I don't even know if it's a good idea. I mean, what are we doing anyway? We should be moving on. Christ, I hate voicemail. Call me."

He looked out his window. It was beginning to snow, and with an annoyed huff Alex went into his bedroom closet and grabbed a pair of brown leather gloves and his brown beanie.

He flipped open his cell and hit a button to return the call. She answered on the second ring.

"Hello?"

She sounded even better in real life.

"Charlotte, it's me Alex."

She gave a nervous giggle. "I know Alex; it says it on my phone. How are you? I'm so sorry."

"I'm alright. It wasn't me that was shot." The words sounded hollow. He knew she wasn't fooled either.

"Okay? I just wanted to let you know it's okay if you don't want to go tonight."

Alex felt his grip tighten on the phone. "No, it's okay. I've been trying to get you to meet me for weeks now."

Alex walked over to his nightstand and pulled out the two tickets to Shea's Theater. Bribing her with tickets to a musical was the only way she would agree to see him, even on her birthday.

"I'm still not sure it's a good idea."

"I'll see you there at seven."

Alex hung up before she could protest. The truth was he needed to see her. He felt numb. He studied the tickets for a moment and then put them in his jacket.

Alex looked around. He was forgetting something. He glanced at his nightstand one more time and a Saint Christopher medallion hanging on a silver chain, tossed over his bottle of Bean. Not only had the bottle smacked him down, the damn thing looted him while he was in his sleep as well. Alex Vaughn walked to the bottle and grabbed his chain.

"Mine," he said.

Alex stepped out of his bedroom with the chain safe, tucked under his jacket and white T-shirt. The coffee was ready. In a whirl, Alex grabbed his steaming mug and walked out of his townhouse apartment.

He got into his Ford Taurus. After two attempts at getting the engine to start, it rolled over with a moan. Alex drove through the city streets; he was heading back toward Walden Avenue, the scene of the crime. He already knew what he had to do, with a smirk he reached into his coat pocket and pulled out the cigarette butt from the scene.

"Ah, *MY* latest victim," he said with satisfaction.

This little baby was going to give some information to work with. This was a rare cigarette, Vaughn was sure of it. All he needed to do now was go into some convenience stores and ask around, ask who knew a guy that had a very particular taste in nicotine. Once he found out whom, it would officially be on.

*

The assassin stood still in the gloom of the night club. His eyes needed a moment to adjust as the blackened double doors closed behind him. As his eyes came back into focus he noted the familiar surroundings.

Off to the left was a bar that came out into the center of the room in a semicircle. In front of the gunman, extending outward from the bar was a dance floor that was settled underneath a twirling disco ball. At the head of the dance floor was a DJ booth that was enclosed by a metal cage on three ends. On the right, after two doors leading toward separate gender restrooms was a door that led to a manager's office.

Rafael Rontego swept his hat from his head and tucked it under his arm along with the newspaper he purchased earlier; with his free hand he brushed his hair back from his face.

Two large men came out of the back office, but with one look at Rontego, they nodded their heads and went back inside. Rafael walked up to the office door and raised his hand to knock on it.

Before his hand could lie to rest on the sturdy oak door, he heard the expected "Come in," from within.

The assassin eased opened the door and slipped inside.

"Hello Rafael. I have been waiting for you," said an old man at the desk.

The man was slender but had strength built into his frame that age developed. The veins that stretched tight under his thinning and aged skin obscured his corded muscles. He wore a suit, but the jacket was hung over the back of his large mahogany chair and his white shirtsleeves were rolled up to the elbows. His right hand was somewhat yellowish in color and the large cigar that was half smoked in the ashtray explained the discoloration.

"I supposed as much Don Ciancetta. However, the business of which you and I discussed previously is now complete." As he spoke to the Don, Rafael tossed the newspaper on the old man's desk.

Circled in black ink on the lower right hand column of the front page was a headline that read *Local Cop Slain in Shooting.*

"Hmm, I see our little friend is no longer a problem." The Don shifted the paper and started reading the caption under the headline.

As he read it, Rafael studied the old man's eyes. Though his eyes were a light green and might even be considered kind, Rafael knew the deception hidden beneath that gaze and marveled at the contradiction. Those green orbs of his were set deep into the angular features of his face. He was always clean-shaven but Rafael was almost positive that it was because he didn't want the gray of his beard to show. Speckled into the Don's slick black hair were patches of gray that brought a distinguished look to the boss.

"Because of the nature of the target's position and the inevitable fallout surrounding its completion, I am going to have to ask for double my usual rate," Rontego said as a matter of fact.

With a cough, Ciancetta looked up at him. "Of course, my friend. It is a well earned twenty."

He reached down under his desk, into a drawer at his side. Rafael heard the drawer slide open. Ever the soul of caution, Rafael shifted his weight so that he could angle sideways toward the old man; even as he shifted he dropped the hand behind his hat backward toward his hip, until he felt the cold steel of his pistol brush up against his palm.

At that instant there was a rush of air at the assassin's back. With a quick and fluid motion, Rafael spun around, pistol in hand. His gun was level right at the forehead of the interruption.

"Holy Shit!" said the young man with his arms raised wide at his side.

Rontego recognized the youngster as the son of Ciancetta, and with a death-cold stare at the boy, holstered his pistol.

"Jesus, Rontego!" yelled Don Ciancetta. "Here's your fucking paycheck", he said as he tossed a bundle of cash at Rontego.

The assassin caught it in the air, even as he finished holstering his pistol with his other hand.

"Damn, you are fast man," stammered Joseph Ciancetta as he let out a long breath of air.

"Just be careful who you're pointing guns at

Rafael. My boy should be viewed as if he were me," Don Ciancetta said. His voice flat and even, his way of issuing a threat.

Rafael hated when the old man threatened him, the vein in his head throbbed along his jaw line with an unnatural pulse. He was afraid that one day it would burst, then all the other Guido's in the place would pin the death on him and then he would have his hands full.

"I understand, Don. I just always watch my back, comes with the territory." Rafael tucked the money away into his jacket and flipped his hat back onto his head. "Now Mr.Ciancetta, with your permission, I take my leave."

"Sure thing. Rontego, I have something I want to talk to you about, later." With that Don Ciancetta stood up and extended his hand.

Rontego took the Don's hand and felt the expected foreign object embedded in his palm. He grinned with the realization of that feel, relished its implications. With a deft motion, Rafael slipped the object into his own palm and brought his hand into his pocket.

With a nod and a quick tip of his hat, Rontego pivoted and left the room. As the door shut behind him, the assassin quickened his step and with a flourish, was out the entrance and back onto the quiet city streets of Buffalo. He checked his watch. He had a play to catch.

Chapter 5

Alex drove for about three miles, down into the heart of East Buffalo. Walden Avenue wasn't much to look at during the day, and at night it was a downright nasty place to be. The need for survival oftentimes turned on the predatory switch that caused some human beings to treat other human beings like crap.

Alex did a stint as an undercover narcotics officer in this district several months back. At the time he went by the name of Victor Garducci. When Alex was about one key piece of evidence from being able to get an indictment against the Mafia crew in which he was embedded, they yanked him from his post. He found out later that there was an unsubstantiated rumor that his cover had been compromised.

Vaughn was displeased. In the name of 'Alex's safety' the higher-ups decided this was the correct course of action. Alex felt that it was all politics. The force could ill afford another undercover agent to be revealed and executed.

A string of deep agents were discovered as of late and the Internal Affairs people, as well as the Feds, were all over the situation but came up blank. Years of posturing, maneuvering, gaining the confidence of several gangsters all resulted in wasted time and free information for the lucky soul that inherited Alex's case file.

Alex pulled up to a Gas and Go convenience store. He grabbed his cigarette butt that was now in a Zip-Lock baggy and entered the store with a RING as the door chimed to announce his entrance.

On the right of the inside were rows of various goods that the gas station sold, with a freezer in the back for beverages. In front of Alex was a fountain machine for soda and on the left was the clerk counter where cigarettes and lottery tickets were sold.

Alex walked up to the fountain machine and filled up a large cup with root beer then proceeded to the counter. There, he encountered a large and round Haitian man with a jovial face and a pair of thick spectacles that hung around the tip of his nose. The man had curled gray hair and wore a yellow T-shirt with "Gas and Go" in bright red letters. His name tag read 'Enrique'.

"Hey there...Enrique," Alex said, reading the man's name tag, as he leaned on the counter.

The clerk was preoccupied adjusting some things beneath the counter. Without looking up he said, "Hey yourself, what can I do you for?"

Alex reached into his back pocket and pulled out his wallet. He wanted to get this man's attention. With a flip of his wrist he tossed out the back flap on his wallet, revealing his metallic police badge, ID number 4977.

"Just have a quick couple questions and a pop that I want to buy."

Enrique glanced on the counter and saw the badge, he stopped in mid business. Still paused, the clerk moved his eyes upward from the badge and looked at Alex Vaughn.

"What kind of questions?" he asked.

"The kind that need answers, it will take just a moment," Alex said as he replaced his wallet in his back pocket.

He continued, "I need to know where I can find a cigarette like this." He pulled the Zip-Lock containing the cigarette butt from his side and tossed it on to the counter in front of the clerk.

Enrique picked up the bag and held it up to the light. "Well, officer, I hope you don't need any of this right now," he said with a chuckle as he peered along his nose and through his goggled glasses.

"Why's that Enrique?" Alex asked. His interest was piqued now. He felt his list of targets was about to narrow in drastic fashion.

"Well sir, to be honest, there are just two places that sell these, if my eyes serve me right. This cigarette you have yerself here is a Sobranie. The only two places you can get these is Smoke 'n Stuff over in the village of Hamburg. And the other place is a specialty shop downtown."

Enrique put the bag back on the counter and looked with triumph at Alex. He was milking the attention like a weatherman that knew the forecast. Alex indulged the man, however.

"And good sir, what might the name of this specialty shop be?" Vaughn put the baggy in his coat pocket.

"How'd I know you were going to ask that?" Enrique laughed. "The name of the shop is Inhaled Imports and is about five-ten minutes north of here. Go down Genesee a bit I think."

"Thanks Enrique, I know the place. You have been a tremendous help." With that Alex turned to leave the store. He had business to attend to.

Alex was interrupted though; hand on the door, with a cough from Enrique. Alex, tired of the clerk's games, turned around and with an undertone of annoyance questioned, "Yes?"

"That'll be a dollar six sir," Enrique said with his eye on the root beer in Alex's hand.

Alex, more than a little embarrassed, pulled a five out of his pocket and put it on the counter. "Keep the change, man."

With that Alex got in his car and pulled out of the gas station. His mind was abuzz with these recent developments.

He knew of this place called Inhaled Imports. It was a Mafia owned business. It was right next door to the pool-hall that he frequented while undercover.

It was the same pool-hall that contained members of Old Joe Falzone's crew.

Falzone was the consigliore, or advisor, of Papa Leo Ciancetta and was the current underboss of Leonard Ciancetta Junior, the current Don. Old Joe held a lot of power in the Buffalo-Niagara underworld. The least of this power was not in the local unions. Hell, Local 210 in Erie County was about as corrupt as a union could get.

The power that Old Joe Falzone held due to this Local was quite significant and was a base of power that, in the hands of an 'aspiring' underboss, could very well undermine Don Ciancetta. The fact that Falzone was allowed to operate that particular union, unchallenged, showed one of two things. It either showed Ciancetta's faith in Falzone's loyalty, or it showed a covert power struggle of sorts with Ciancetta not being able to harness enough power to wrest control of the union from Falzone.

Interesting possibilities in either case.

This was the very crew that Alex attempted to infiltrate. When he was pulled off assignment, a few undercover cops in other operations dropped the hint that he left town, to sources known to report to Old Joe.

The word on the street was that 'Victor Garducci' owed an unhealthy sum of money to an old associate out in New Mexico and would be gone for several months. The higher-ups in Alex's precinct figured this would give the Buffalo crews enough time to either forget Victor ever existed or enough time for whatever trail remained, leading to Alex, to vanish.

Well, just maybe, it was time for 'Victor' to come home. First he had to meet Charlotte.

*

Rontego walked towards Shea's Theater. The building stood just a bit off of the boardwalk and off-white stone with carved dramatic faces rimmed large arching windows. Perpendicular to the street, a sign read "Shea's" at the top and the word, "Buffalo" ran the length of the thin sign from top to bottom. The green sign was lined with bright white lights that cut through the crisp evening. Rontego shoved his hands into his pockets as he approached a group of huddled patrons in their long jackets and thick coats shuffling inside. Rontego pushed past them. He wasn't here to catch a show. Tonight was all business.

Without a glance to either side, he walked into the building, where an usher greeted him, but upon recognizing him, let him pass. Rontego kept his hat tilted forward and he hunched his shoulders, looking at the ground as he walked. He hated large crowds. Not the crowds so much, just the people. Ignoring the beautiful interior and the plush carpets that lined the marble floors, he bound up a flight of stairs covered with a red trailer. He knew where Muro Lucano sat. The brute never missed a show. Always, he sat in the same seat. Rafael Rontego shuffled through a door that led to the main balcony overlooking the stage, and sure enough, he saw the large man's back. He reclined in a seat facing the stage, and only a few other people dotted the balcony. Rafael took a seat behind the set of broad shoulders. He saw the pinstripes that rolled downward and the jacket draped over Muro's lap. He opened his mouth to speak, but Muro beat him to it.

"Rafael. How are you, old friend?" Rontego saw something shuffle under the jacket on Muro's lap, and Rontego's hand drifted inside his coat out of habit.

"Well enough. I've been conducting business." Rafael felt himself smile. He knew the grizzled veteran would understand what he meant.

"So I hear." Muro threw the words. It seemed as if it was just another thing to say, but Rafael felt the weight.

"You hear much. I left something at the scene. Do you know if the boys in blue found it?" Rontego thought to his cigarette. It bothered him a bit, but not much. If he could get it out of evidence, though, he would.

"I hear more than you know. More than I want to know." Still, Muro didn't turn to face Rafael. Rafael studied the stubble on the man's jaw line. The mandibles flexed as Muro continued. "Relax about evidence. Word is, they found nothing. Some cop mucked up the scene real bad anyway. Some friend of your guy." Muro paused, and then switched direction. "We've known each other a long time. We have been fortunate to be on the same side of these things in the past. But Fortune, she is a crafty bitch."

Rontego didn't know what Muro was yapping about. But he didn't like being in the dark, and he disliked Muro's cryptic conversation even more. On visits like these, in the past, there was banter, a few tidbits about the reasons such business was conducted, and life went on. Rontego liked that flow to the order of things. This was something different. He decided to take some of the power back.

"Well, if she is such a bitch, I could change her mind. I could take you out. If I wanted. Right now." Rontego smiled. He had no intention of shooting anyone in a crowded theater. But Muro and he enjoyed a different way of communicating. "You know better than to keep your back so open."

Rontego lifted his eyebrow in surprise when Muro smiled and shook his head back and forth. "I know better. But you don't know what I know Raf. Look under the seat." Rontego placed his hand under his seat. His fingers groped, blind, until he touched a bulky object. He felt the tape and smiled as he pulled it from under him and Muro continued. "You think I don't have my gun pointed at you under my arm right now? Maybe you're stupid enough to believe bullets don't go through chairs."

Rontego pulled the carved wooden piece onto his lap and tugged the masking tape off of it. The chess piece lay in his palm, the pawn gazing up at him.

Rafael smiled again and stood up, placing his hand on the back of Muro's seat. "Til next time." He started to turn away, when he felt a hand clamp down on his. He turned back and looked at Muro who finally spun around, his brick hand holding Rontego's to the seatback.

His eyes held Rontego's for a moment. "Til next time."

Muro released Rontego's hand and looked back at the stage. People began to file in, and the curtain on the stage lifted. Rafael Rontego went up the stairs, his hands back in his pockets, rolling the pawn between his fingers. Something about Muro's face alarmed him. What it was, he couldn't tell. He filed the look away, and picked up his pace. He had to get out of the theater before the damned singing started.

*

Alex and Charlotte walked through the theater in silence. She seemed to enjoy the play and they seemed to get along as the night went on, but they always got along when they didn't have to talk. They got along when they could bury their concerns with distractions. That was how they operated for so long. Alex didn't know any other way. He glanced around the theater as they made their way towards the exit.

"We should talk."

She said it soft and quiet and Alex tried to ignore her. He knew what talking meant. He looked at the ornate ceilings with their decorated tray crevices. The theater, a baroque masterpiece, was recently renovated.

Worth every penny.

Surrounded by the awe-inspiring theater and the

35

mix of French Rococo and bits of Spanish architecture, he couldn't help but look at her. She outshone all of it.

"Fine, let's talk."

He held the door open for her as a crowd shuffled by on their way out. The cold blast of Buffalo's night air hit them as they exited. Charlotte shivered, but Alex didn't know where to put his hands. So much was off limits these days. He watched her shiver again, and made to put his arm over her. He did it a thousand times in the past. This time, like the last time, she shrugged him off. The heat rose to his face despite the swirling winds.

"Alex, you know what I want."

Alex looked at the ice on the sidewalk. "You know I can't Charlotte. I mean, now, of all times."

Charlotte turned to look at his face. But he still stung from her shrug, and refused to meet her eyes. "You can do whatever you want."

Alex looked past her. His irritation was palpable. She wouldn't let him touch her. Jack was dead.

She won't let me touch her. He felt his hands tremble, the emotion boiling to the surface. He heard his voice lift. "I catch bad guys Charlotte. It's what I do."

"Don't give me that crap. You choose what you want to do. You always have. You know what; I guess we don't have much to talk about after all." Her voice got louder to match his.

Alex knew where this was going but it was like a play he had seen a thousand times and was powerless to avoid. He played his part perfectly.

"Well then I guess we don't." He felt the sentence come through his throat louder than he intended and people turned to look. He felt the heat in his face compound. "You're so damned selfish Charlotte."

""I'm selfish? I'm selfish?" She said it twice and Alex knew it was a done deal. Anytime she said anything twice he knew to brace. "You're the one who does whatever he wants. Just remember, Alex, you choose your life and everyone else just has to hope for the best. Well, I'm done hoping. *We're* done hoping Alex."

She turned to walk away, but spun around after a step. "I'm selfish? You're just a little boy Alex. Why don't you grow a pair and grow up." Her eyes watered and Alex wondered how they didn't freeze to that cold face of hers.

He hated her tears, always had. But he couldn't help himself. It just came out.

"Go fuck yourself Charlotte."

He spun around first this time and walked away as people swerved around him in pairs, some shaking their heads at him as he passed. He couldn't remember when having the last word felt so terrible.

*

Rontego walked down the street back towards his apartment. The snow began to fall now. The assassin lifted the collar of his suit jacket and lowered the brim of his hat to shield himself from the frozen falling droplets of water. Those same droplets resulted in an odd mixture of hard, tiny hail and a flurry of soft snow that melted as soon as it landed on your heated frame. With a grunt, Rafael fumbled inside his Armani suit pockets and pulled out a cigarette.

"Maybe this will keep me warm," Rontego mumbled as he let out a puff of warm breath.

The hit man glanced down at his feet as he burned the tip of his cigarette and felt the taste of the smoked tobacco fill his mouth, then his lungs. His pants were getting wet in the slush that was left behind from the nasty snow.

As Rafael Rontego stumbled onward to his apartment, he let his mind wander a bit and he took in what transpired at the meeting with Don Ciancetta and with Muro. He rolled the pawn between his fingers again. The first time he met Muro, when he was learning how to do a hit, Muro gave him the pawn. Rafael stared at it, unsure what to make of it. He never played chess, and he was pretty sure you needed a whole set anyway.

Muro laughed at his confusion. "It's a reminder."

"A reminder for what? Rontego asked.

"That these," he lifted his jacket showing his gun holster. "These make it so even a pawn can take out a king."

Ever since, the two of them traded the pawn when they wanted to make a point. This time, Rafael was unsure what point was being made.

Shaking his head, he revisited his meeting with the Don. He was amused that Leonard Ciancetta had become the new boss in Buffalo. Things changed in the last few years. Rontego remembered back when leadership in Buffalo was consolidated. He had never known many years of peace since he entered the services of the organization. The last real years of 'peace' ended when Rafael was just a young boy.

The best he could remember, it was back when he was about four or five years old. He met the man who held the reigns to Buffalo's underworld for over fifty years. His dad introduced them. The man was Don Magaddino. Rontego remembered the awe with which his father spoke of the man. When he met Magaddino he was nervous and he did not even know why.

The man was old, but his strength, unmistakable. When he looked into the old man's eyes he saw a sort of tiredness and a look as if he were contemplating something that he could not change but desperately wanted to. More than that, though, he remembered the Don's hands. They were large and encompassed the entirety of his hand when the man reached down and shook his. When he shook hands with this grown up, this powerful adult, he felt as if he were being treated like a man. That feeling stuck with him for a long time. But that was in a time since passed. Magaddino was the last man to hold things together, and it was before Rontego's time. He did however, have that meeting as a claim to fame.

Rontego walked with a brisk trot. The cold began to bite at him as the wind snaked around and grazed against the sides of his neck. With a puff on the tobacco, he let his mind continue along its course so long as it was not focused on the weather enveloping him.

He thought back, the times with Magaddino were the 'good times'. Like all good leaders though, his success at running the family spoiled some capos, and they began to bemoan the power that the Don held. They forced the old Don into retirement. It was about this time that the family began to have a shift in power.

That was before the Pieri brothers and Fino fought the Cammilleri wars. Before Crazy Fino's own son betrayed him and sided with the Pieri brothers. Whereas Magaddino led the family for fifty years, now they would go through three bosses in twelve years.

It was during these wars that Rafael Rontego earned his stripes. He earned a reputation most men would have to die for. With skill, he maneuvered himself on both sides of the war and made a killing on hit contracts. The assassin kept out of the spotlight and left the politics to whoever paid him the most. It paid off in more ways than one, too.

At first, the Pieri brothers seemed to win the war. Sal, 'The Eye', Pieri even claimed the title of boss for a while. If Rontego came out on the winning side, he would have been short lived, because less than a year later, it was Crazy Fino that got the upper hand and ousted 'The Eye'.

That victory lasted for four years, so Rontego got a little comfortable and it became a suspicion when one of the Pieri brothers, (this time 'The Eye's' younger brother Joseph), resumed controlling interest in the Buffalo Empire.

Through some sleek maneuvering, once again, Rafael was able to scratch a living running a gambling ring and making hits when things became chaotic enough to cover his tracks.

About six years into Joey, "The Blade", Pieri's reign, the assassin made a near fatal mistake. He carried out a hit for Old Ciancetta against an upstart Pieri associate. The word traveled fast and a hit was out for Rontego. Scared for his life, Rafael barricaded himself in his apartment.

It was a very tense time.

Fortunate for Rontego, Old Man Ciancetta moved quicker than the hitters and within a week the hired guns sent to take out Rontego were dead and Joseph Pieri was abdicating the Buffalo throne to the Ciancetta factions.

In that time period Rafael became a cold-blooded assassin. With the exception of his first hit, he felt very little remorse, a rare ability that worked in Rontego's favor in these particular situations. It wasn't that Rafael was unable to feel guilt, it was that he was able to switch those feelings on and off at will.

But that was a while ago. Now with Old Ciancetta semi-retired in Florida, Little Leo was in charge. Little Leo was no longer little though, and an aging man himself. He was now responsible for Rontego's primary income. Still, Little Leo was a shifty boss.

He sent Rafael out on a lot of hits, which was fine by Rontego, but there was something in his demeanor that often made recognizable blips on Rafael's danger radar.

Rafael served Old Leo with loyalty, a sort of thank you for saving his life. However, it was no secret that Rafael Rontego considered his debt repaid with the Old Man's retirement.

Now, the new Don Ciancetta was fair game. Perhaps, that was why he kept Rafael busy. For Little Leo, it was a win-win situation. Either Rafael stays busy and takes out the Don's dirty work, or Rafael gets pinched and spends the next three hundred years in jail, or Rafael gets a bullet in the gut and all that he knows dies with him. Still, he felt as if the man wanted to do the deed himself, as if Rafael was too successful and he was uncomfortable with such a person holding the keys to so many doors.

Oh well. Rontego was doing well under this arrangement, as was the new Don. He used Rafael's contacts a lot as of late, and as long as Rontego was useful, he did not see any reason to worry about things not in his control.

A strong gust of wind brought him from his inward contemplation. Rafael was burning low on his smoke and tossed the butt onto the embankment along the curb. He brought one hand to his hat as the gust of wind threatened to lift it off of him and send it swirling into the vast, impenetrable whiteness that built up all around him.

With a glance upward along the brim of his hat, Rafael squinted and saw he was about fifty paces from the shelter of his apartment. In a burst, Rontego sprinted onward, across the intersection in front of his place, and into the black metal door that led into the warmth of the narrow stairwell that led to the heat of his home.

Chapter 6

The 1997 Ford Taurus squealed into the parking space in front of Alex Vaughn's townhouse. The faded blue rust wagon's squeaking brakes were the only telltale sign of Alex's excitement. He never liked the fact that he was yanked from his old case. His mind was made up now.

Alex entered his apartment and without hesitation, grabbed the phone hanging on the wall of his kitchen. He punched in seven digits as quick as he could get his fingers to move and he felt the chill leave his body as he became accustomed to the heat coursing through his home. Several rings later he heard a familiar voice, gruff but not impolite.

"Hey, Vincenzio here."

Alex's friend Ryan Slate was also an undercover agent. He was going by the name of Ricky Vincenzio as of late. Right now he was just an associate to the younger Ciancetta. A friend of Joseph Ciancetta, the new Don's son. Alex needed a favor, and lucky for him, Ryan Slate A.K.A. Ricky Vincenzio was in a prime position to deliver.

"Vaughn here, I need a favor, Victor Garducci is reactivated. Leak of his return via New Mexico immediately. Contact me again at seven o'clock PM."

He hoped that Ricky would understand and get on with the favor. He had faith in his friend though; Vincenzio was not an unintelligent bastard.

"Yeah sure thing Papa, I'll get right on that. Look, I am a little busy right now; can I call you later tonight?" Ricky was covering his ass and not letting on to the conversation.

Alex knew that this was his way of agreeing, and letting Alex know that now was not a good time.

"Sure thing Ricky; thanks a lot. I'll be expecting your call."

Alex hung up the phone. So far, so good. Alex

went into the bathroom. It was time to mob himself out. He looked at his face. His long brown hair would be fine with a few inches cut off and slicked back. It was time to shave. Alex pulled out his razor and a pair of scissors.

Alex pulled his medicine cabinet mirror around and angled his head so that he could get a clear view of the back. He pulled his scissors up and went about the work of becoming Victor Garducci. His hands almost trembled with the excitement building up inside him. Everything about this shit on protocol.

As he finished trimming the length of his hair down so that it was about the length of his ears, Alex wondered how much time he would have once he went under. He had a day or two, three tops, before his friend Ricky asked someone about Victor's reactivation.

Alex might be able to buy more time if he talked to Ricky, Ryan Slate, before he talked to his supervisors. He didn't want to get the guy in trouble though. He would just have to wait and see how the conversation went later that night. As for now though, Alex was going to begin the process of re-infiltrating his old crew. If he couldn't buy extra time, then every second undercover counted. And the clock was ticking.

With a shake of what was left of his brown mane, Alex took a look at himself in the mirror. It was interesting to him, half between Alex Vaughn, and half between Victor Garducci. He looked down at the razor sitting on the sink. He reached out and turned the hot water on and waited as the water began to warm as it streamed from the faucet.

In a few moments, Victor Garducci would be back. The son of a bitch that killed Jack was going to face a reckoning, and soon, very soon, Alex would be well on his way to arranging that meeting. What better place to start, then the old pool hall across from Inhaled Imports. Two birds, one stone.

*

It was seven minutes after seven when the phone rang. Alex jumped out of his skin at the sound. He fell asleep for a few minutes watching the news on his static filled television. The phone rang again. Remembering that Ricky Vincenzio was going to be calling him, Alex jumped up and ran to the phone. He took a deep breath, and then lifted it off of the receiver.

"Hello," Alex said, with the excitement edging his voice.

"Hey, Alex. It's Ryan Slate." Ryan seemed relaxed, and he used his real name. He was away from anyone related to his undercover assignment.

"Hey man, sorry 'bout earlier. It's sort of an emergency that I get this information out there. I am going to be making an appearance at the Inhaled Imports tonight." Alex was trying his best to fill Ryan in without telling him too much. The last thing he needed to do was make an unwilling accomplice out of his friend.

"Alex, what's going on? I mean this isn't exactly on par with procedure. I mean fuck man; I was right there in the damn bar."

Ryan's thick New York accent was permeating the conversation. He was a learned man and tried not to have any noticeable accent. It was his academic elitism that worked against his natural speech tendencies. However, when Ryan was bothered by something, the accent was back full force. Right now, Alex detected that Ryan didn't enjoy the possible implications that could have been caused by the impromptu call of Alex's. Something told Alex he should tell Ryan the truth. After all, he had gotten Ryan into this mess of his.

"Ryan, we've known each other for a long time. Through the years I haven't done much that we could call, well, crazy."

44

He was hoping to convince Ryan of his own sanity. He knew what he was going to say next would sound every bit of insane to his friend. He heard Ryan's reaffirming grunt on the other end of the line, so Vaughn continued.

"You know my friend Jack was killed last night. I think he got into some business that was over his head. The homicide guys are gonna do their best to figure out who killed Jack. I'm sure they are. But, Ryan, I want to find out first."

There was a moment of silence on the other end. Then Alex heard a slow breath of air exhale into the phone.

"Jesus Alex," Slate's voice was now that of a New York cab driver's. All semblance of hiding his accent was now gone with the man's obvious unease.

Alex started to explain himself. "Man, just listen to me for a second, hear me out." Alex was speaking fast now.

For some reason once he started talking, he couldn't stop. He needed someone in his corner. As brave as he felt, as brave as he wanted to be, going headlong into the mob was not an easy task and the mere prospect of it was leaving its mark on Alex's nerve. He poured everything out to his friend. He told him of Jack coming to him for help, Jack's death, the cigarette, and his decision to go undercover. When it was all over, Alex paused to catch his breath, paused hoping for some sort of response from Slate.

"Alex, I don't think so. This is too much, even for you".

Alex felt his heart sink. He had to convince Slate. "Ryan…"

"No. Find someone else. I'm serious." He had a sound as if he couldn't be won over and Alex panicked.

"Ryan, if you don't help me with this, I'm gonna tell people in the I.A. to take a closer look at you. We both know you haven't done everything on the up and up. No one undercover ever does." Alex hated saying it.

"You son of a..."

Alex cut him off. "Listen, I don't judge. I understand. We all have to do things. But I need you for this. I need your help."

The reply came after a few heartbeats.

"Okay asshole. I'll see what I can do. Just one thing though, why not just go and ask the guy at Inhaled Imports who buys Sobranie cigs?"

Ryan was pissed off, but he was also excited. Perhaps this was right up his alley.

"Well, 'cause Inhaled Imports is run by Old Joe Falzone's crew. Anyone that snoops around that place is sure to be made. I definitely do not need that kind of heat right now."

Alex let out a relieved and nervous laugh. He slumped against the wall in his kitchen. His legs felt weak. The severity of what he was about to attempt was catching up to him, and smacking him like a sledgehammer.

"Ah, and you knew I couldn't do it 'cause my assignment takes me as close as Joey Ciancetta lets me get. I'm still in the fringe." Ryan was right on the mark. "Okay man, I'll do what I can. I'll let it loose to a few mobsters at the bar, you know Jimmy Taps, that Garducci was due back any day. If they ask me how I know something like that, I'll chat 'em up about some cousin of yours that dated my friend's niece. And asshole, don't think this is a free one. You could always repay the favor to me by dropping a thing or two about how I'm a good guy, you know, with the crew. Might get me a little bit closer and I might forgive your threat."

Alex's relief was now complete. It seemed to him that he had enlisted a valuable ally.

"Alright, but if I do that, we will need to devise a way for Victor Garducci to leave town again in an amicable fashion. That way no one assumes I'm a rat and your cover remains intact."

Now that he was not alone, Vaughn's brain was working a mile a minute; things were coming clearer to him.

"I'll think of a way, you just drop me some help. Let's talk again tomorrow morning. For now though, I need to get going. Big date at Louie's. A blonde you wouldn't believe. She's a total knockout."

With that Ryan hung up the phone with a click. Alex, too, hung up the phone. He went into his bedroom. The room was sparse. A nightstand stood on either side of the bed. A walk in closet, the bedroom's lone redeeming feature, was to the bed's right.

Vaughn went into the closet and pulled out his Guido uniform. The uniform consisted of a black leather jacket, a slick, dark red button down, black slacks and black leather shoes. His shirt was open at the neck and his gold cross was hanging in the middle of the opening.

He took off his Saint Christopher medallion and slipped it into his shoe, right next to a worn and torn photograph of his wife, Charlotte. As he placed the photograph in his shoe, he thought back to his reasons for keeping it there. When he was lost, he seemed to find comfort in the familiar yet worn ridges of the photo. They took it a dozen years before at a fair and it was one of Vaughn's most cherished memories.

If only I could turn back the clock.

Alex looked at himself in the full-length mirror on the inside of his open closet door. Something was missing. He walked to the nightstand on the right of the bed and pulled open the drawer. Inside were a gold watch and several gold rings. He slipped them on. Satisfied, he walked back and stood in front of the mirror again.

The transformation was complete. Victor Garducci stared back at him from his closet. He no longer saw anything that remained of Alexander Vaughn. Even his eyes seemed to carry a different presence.

He then glanced to the side and saw the lone picture hanging over the nightstand to his left. He glanced at the smaller duplicate of the picture of his ex-wife and child that was also hanging alongside of his bathroom.

As he exited, he looked back once again at the picture of his wife and whispered to himself, "So this is why you left."

Alex turned around, and flicked off the light to his bedroom. He patted the Beretta under his left shoulder, and walked outside. Victor Garducci was back on the streets of Buffalo.

Chapter 7

With a subtle shake, he tossed the snow and water from atop his shoulders. Rontego slipped catlike up towards his apartment. As he got the top of the stairs that led to his apartment, he paused. At first glance, nothing was awry. The light gave off a promise of visibility, but nothing more. Rafael's eyes, however, had already adjusted to the gloom. Not many people were more adept at conducting business as usual in the shadows of the world than Rafael Rontego.

His door was closed, and the assassin inched another step forward. That's when he noticed it.

In front of his door, sparkling off of the light in the entryway was a puddle. Not much of a puddle, more like a streak of water that followed the noticeable outline of something longer than it was wide. Perhaps a boot print.

Rafael Rontego had not lived for years through some of Buffalo's most brutal Mafia wars by ignoring his instincts. In fact, it was that very instinct that helped him to survive, and at this moment, the sixth sense of the assassin screamed to be heard.

Silent as a whisper, Rafael took a dime out of his pocket. With a peculiar ease, and standing to the side of the door, he wedged the dime into the peek hole of his apartment door. He waited a few seconds for an internal response, from his room, for whatever awaited him to give itself away. Nothing happened for several long moments.

Rontego, still not satisfied, crossed to the other side of the door, careful to not show his feet underneath between the door and the floor boards. He then proceeded to place his left ear against the door to try and discern what, if anything was inside. He heard everything he waited for. A lone cough, a cough that, to the assassin, was the death toll to whatever awaited within.

As quiet as he slipped up the stairs, he descended.

Once outside in the whiteness that matched his descent upon Buffalo, he didn't hesitate.

Less than a dozen strides brought him around the corner where he pulled himself onto the dumpsters that were used to gather the surrounding residents' filth. From there, his nimble fingers found a crease in the brick frame of his building and he slipped up on to a six inch ledge that outlined the entire rectangular structure, its usual purpose was aesthetic. Tonight, however, that precipice served as foothold to the assassin.

A man who did not harness the perfect balance of Rontego might have fallen down to an uncomfortable cement impact on a day when the weather was perfect. But those men would not have survived the life of Rafael. With the ease of a hunting cat, the veteran hit man inched along the ledge until he brought himself to rest against the wall, right next to his window that overlooked the street below.

He looked around the indent that led to the glass of his window. The blinds were shut. Of course they would be shut. Whoever was inside would not want anything that went on to be viewed from the outside.

Rafael reached into his coat pocket while maintaining his grip with his free hand. Like a surgeon, he worked his black-hilt steel dagger, no more than six inches from hilt to tip, in between the frame and the window's locking mechanism. He waited.

For many minutes, Rafael, indiscernible from the streets below thanks to the blizzard conditions around him, waited perched on that ledge. With one hand on the wall and the other paused between frame and lock, he strained his ears. Then it came. The cough that Rafael waited for, came.

The flu, it's deadly.

Just as he heard the cough, Rafael popped the lock. It was quiet anyway; mixed with the cough it was almost inaudible. The assassin moved in front of the window to prevent as much of the breeze as he could from entering his apartment and giving away that the window was open. Silent as death, he slid it open.

Hoping that whoever was within had their eyes fixed to his front door, Rafael pushed back on the vertical blinds and slipped into the apartment. A slight rustle announced his arrival but he moved fast and crouched behind the lazy-boy chair to his left. He hid there for a moment so that he could gather himself and take stock of his surroundings.

From his vantage point he could see two men. With a start he realized one was leaning in *his* chair against the wall right next to the doorway. He was looking right at him. Rafael choked, but began reaching for his pistol. Halfway there, he paused. The man didn't move. His chin rested against his chest.

Asleep, Rontego thought to himself.

The napping man was dressed for business, Rafael could tell. He wore a long trench coat and black suit pants that bulged on one hip. The man had a piece.

Rafael glanced at the other man. He was leaning with his back against the wall in the assassin's kitchen. Similar attire and the unmistakable bulge on his right hip, he too was packing heat.

As Rafael was contemplating how he intended to get to either of his victims, a gust of wind swept into the room. He eased further behind the lazy-boy, cursing his bad luck. The man in the kitchen, however, felt the breeze. He walked over towards Rafael. The hit man readied himself for the inevitable confrontation. Every muscle in the killer tensed as the intruder neared his hiding place.

Just as Rontego felt that he would be discovered, the man walked past him, and stopped in front of the window. With a cough, the intruder reached up and pulled the window down. Rontego saw the man reach a hand towards his hip.

The gun.

His back was to Rafael Rontego. The assassin pulled his knife to his front and slipped, still crouching, behind the man. With one clean stroke he sliced.

The knife hit its mark. The intruder never felt it. The cut in his Achilles was clean, the nerves severed before they ever even registered the pain. All he knew was that he was falling.

He grasped upward to find a hold, and found nothing but air. He landed, but not hard. Something stopped him. A pair of arms broke his fall. He looked for the person that caught him. Instead, he saw the blood trailing from the back of his foot and his eye caught the glint of the knife's blade in the fist of whoever caught him.

He looked up as he was laid down behind the mattress in front of the window. He tried to shout, but a gloved hand clamped firmly over his mouth. He couldn't brace himself on his foot to push upward against the force of his assailant. He reached upward with both hands and tried to pry off the hand that kept him from screaming for help.

Rafael leaned over him. His hand was like an iron vice. His other hand came swiftly across the man's throat. At first, there was nothing. The man looked at the assassin, a question forming on his lips, and then realized his doom.

A red line followed the slash that the assassin left in the man's neckline. At first it looked like a scratch, but the pulse that came next showed the truth. Like the cut on his Achilles, it was clean. He tried to struggle. His hands lost their strength and rested powerless against Rontego's as it clasped on his mouth.

The blood was pouring too free now. With each beat of his heart, more blood oozed from the perfect line across his Adam's apple. With each beat of his heart he felt more of his life drain away. He died contemplating that simple irony.

Rontego looked over his shoulder as he held the man down as the last nervous impulses twitched through his legs and arms. When the movement subsided, Rontego eased upward, his dark silhouette outlined against the window frame.

His next victim was still asleep. He walked right in front of the man. His head tilted to the left as he contemplated the man in front of him. He paused as if undecided. Then, having made up his mind, Rontego leaned forward and placed a hand over the man's mouth while digging the point of his knife into the man's neck.

The man woke up, his eyes confused. As the sleep ran from him, his eyes opened wide and fright crept into them. He too realized his doom. Rontego leaned forward to within an inch of the man's ear.

"Listen carefully. I am going to ask you questions and you're gonna answer. All answers will be done with a simple shake of your head, yes or no. Unless you want to end up like your friend over there. Do you want to end up like him?" Rontego goaded his prisoner.

The man shook his head from side to side.

"Good," Rontego purred. "Now, is there anyone else with you?"

The man paused. Rafael pushed the point deeper against his throat and a trickle of blood slipped out and traveled down his neck. He shook his head up and down so fast it almost rolled off his shoulders.

"Well, I don't need you then, do I?" Rafael smiled at the man.

Nothing pleased him more than playing with his victim before ending him. The man began to protest, but again Rafael's hand muffled any sound.

"Now, that's not nice! I wasn't gonna hurt you. But alas, you broke the rules my dear friend. And around here, when you break the house rules...."

With that the hit man leaned forward and with one hand still pressed over the man's mouth, he pushed in with the other and plunged the knife deeper into the man's throat.

He smirked with satisfaction as he felt his blade slide against the top vertebrae of the victim's spinal column and as he retracted the blade, felt the pull as he snapped the final wavelengths that sent all commands to the brain's epicenter. This one didn't twitch. The life simply, drifted, away.

Both kills took no more than several minutes. There was one place the remaining intruder could be. His suspicions were confirmed when he heard the flush of his toilet.

So, the bastards found the secret entryway to his porcelain throne room. Not only did they find his bathroom, the fuckers were desecrating it. What kind of person would break into his place, and then, take it upon himself to *SHIT* in it?

Rontego felt the heat rise to his face.

Disrespect for disrespect.

He slipped into his closet and waited outside for the guy in the john to walk out. He rested his back against the wall to the side of the bathroom and melted into the shadows. He waited as he heard the man turn on the faucet to wash his hands. He waited as the man dried them. Then he waited as the man opened the door and walked past him. He walked past the assassin and paused in the entryway to the closet. There in front of him he saw both of his downed partners.

"Aw...Fuck," the words passed out of the man's mouth just a moment before the crush of something hard against the back of his skull throwing him into unconsciousness.

Rafael knew the man must have thought death had come for him. When he awoke, he would wish it had.

The assassin rolled the man over and bound his feet and wrists with plastic binds that would tighten but never release unless cut. He then scooped the man up and slung him over his shoulder. He wasn't that heavy. He probably weighed less than the assassin.

He plopped the man down on the bed and went over to the Lazy-Boy. He sat on the arm of his chair and glanced at the face of the man he just knocked out. The man had an angular chin and cheekbones that jutted out from the rest of his face, giving him a permanent expression that looked as if his jaw were perpetually clenched. Rontego noticed a disturbing scar that ran from his left eye downward to the middle of his cheek.

More disturbing than the scar however, was the fact that Rafael Rontego knew this man. This man was Sonne Pieri, the son of Sal Pieri. He was a small time crew member who was allowed to scrape together a living because Joey Pieri, his uncle, peacefully abdicated from the Buffalo Mafia's top spot. The only thing that happened to him was the scar left on his face, a scar to remind him of his place.

More disturbing to Rontego was that this guy had been allowed to operate with the exclusive supervision of one man. That one man was Joe Falzone, the underboss for Don Ciancetta.

*

His black slacks and his jacket blended into the night. The few distinguishable features that stood out on Victor Garducci were his necklace and other gold paraphernalia. They glinted off the street lamps, no matter how dim, as he walked with purpose towards Wizeguyz Billiards. This was the local meeting place of Joey Falzone and his crew.

The rumor about Victor Garducci was that he was

a master at fixing bets. The easiest for him to fix were fights.

The way it worked for the mobsters was that they gave their money to Victor, who in turn put the money on the guy who was supposed to lose. He then got the winning pick to toss the fight in whatever round that Victor placed his cash, and then Victor returned to the gangsters with exponential amounts of cash. A safe investment for them and Victor got to keep his percentage off the top of the take.

Victor pushed most of his take up to Joe Falzone through a man named Frankie DeRisio. He was a member in Sal Pieri's crew and Sal answered straight up to Falzone.

Victor's cash went to Frankie, he took his cut, then the money went to Sal, who took his cut, and from there it went up to Falzone.

Though the mobsters were greedy, they were sort of fair in their own right and told Falzone what a good earner this new guy Vic was. In reality, Victor got his gambling cash straight from the FBI who he was working in concert with. He would just say that he 'bought' whatever fighter happened to lose and from there everything worked itself out.

His associates trusted that he kept the information confidential until after the fight. Most believed he did things covertly to keep his system of earning confidential so as to impede others from infringing upon his turf. To them, it wouldn't be out of place, it would be logical protection of one's livelihood.

Now, as Victor neared the entrance to Wizeguyz, his heart was pounding and it took every bit of skill to keep the persona of Alex from surfacing while he was anywhere near the Mafia stomping grounds.

He reached out a hand to open the door. His hand resting on the pale green door, Victor felt himself tremble. With a deep breath, the mobster steadied himself.

A moment later he was through the doors and into the smoke-filled room in front of him. In the back was a wooden rectangular bar with a robust and grey-haired bartender who polished the same beer mug over and over. He wore an apron over some jeans and an old, faded, green T-shirt that had the place's logo stenciled on it.

Three pool tables in a row led outward from the bar towards the door. On the left of the pool tables were four booths and on the right were four freestanding tables. The chairs and booth benches had the same green colored cushions, worn with age.

Two men sat in the rear booth with their backs to the entrance. Two more men stood around the pool table. They were heated over whether or not the bet they made prior to the game was two dollars a ball or five.

"Fuck you Jimmy, I'm telling you I ain't gonna pay you no more than two a ball and that's that," said a small man no more than five feet seven inches tall.

He weighed maybe a hundred forty and had brown hair that fell over one side of his forehead in a nasty cowlick. The other half slicked back parallel with his cheek bones that seemed sunken along with his green eyes. He held the pool cue with his right hand and planted in the floor at his side. His feet were set apart and his bluster was almost laughable against the other fellow who Garducci recognized as Jimmy 'Jacks'.

He got his name from a haul in Vegas where he took the house for almost thirty grand with four jacks. He kept the cards and ever since that time in Vegas has carried them around in his back pocket for luck.

He was a big man. Jacks stood over six feet tall and two hundred pounds. His dark hair was cropped short and his eyes were brown and hard but not mean looking. He spent a few years in the pen and his muscles showed it as he flexed them, more from habit than from threat, at the smaller man's rant.

The smaller man was Tim Coughlin. He wasn't even a WOP, but the Italians kept him around because he helped bring them the Irish in the numbers racket, that and he was a scrapper. Garducci once witnessed the small fellow beat down two men that owed him twenty bucks for a late payment. Twenty bucks and he came away with two bruised fists and two hundred dollars richer.

"I'm telling you Tim, it was five dollars a ball, and if you...."

Victor decided now was as good a time as any. He walked further in and as the door slammed shut behind him he announced his arrival, demanding attention.

"Hey you two grease balls, you see Sal around here anywhere?"

"Holy Shit, if it ain't Vic back from New Mexico! We heard you was coming back. You better be debt free though, we don't want some filthy Mexican crew breathing down our necks for your spendthrift ass!"

Jimmy Jacks gave a warm smile and greeted Vic, but Garducci saw that Tim was annoyed. The conversation about who owed whom what was now at an end, and that meant one of them got away with three dollars a ball. Jacks took a quick look at Tim as he hurried toward Victor and smiled at him when he noticed that Tim wasn't talking economics anymore. He came forward and gave him a firm shake of the hand.

"How you doing Jimmy?" Garducci needed to make small talk, seem as calm as possible. Soon enough the questions would come.

"I'm alright, you know how it goes, winning some, losing some."

"Tim." Victor leaned over and clasped the man on the hand.

"Fuck Vic, you better talk to Sal when he gets back. He was happy you was coming home. Shit has been edgy here you know."

Tim looked troubled and Victor figured that he would hear an earful from Sal when he got back.

"Sal pissed I had to leave so quick?"

Garducci needed to know from what viewpoint to assess the situation in which he thrust himself.

"Nah," Jimmy interrupted as he rubbed a blue block of chalk along the tip of his cue. "Other things are about to happen. Some shit going on upstairs. It's between the higher ups and no one knows what crews are siding where. We know where mine and Sal's crews stand and we know where the Ciancetta's stand and they ain't on the same side of the aisle if you get my drift. We stand with Old Man Falzone. "

"Fuck Jimmy, quit talking so much. Vic, the other guys will fill you in over there. Sal should be back soon and then we will know what's what."

Tim shot a glance at Jimmy; he was more guarded then his counterpart. He always was the more intelligent of the two.

"Who's sitting over there?" Garducci didn't want to go into any situation without realizing what awaited him.

"Just Aldo and Muro," Tim said with a mischievous grin as he threw his cue on the table and walked through the restroom door on the right of the room.

Jimmy glanced at Victor with his lips pursed in a thin line across his face. The presence of those two men was not lost on Jimmy nor was it lost on Victor. Though Victor was not positive of the hierarchy, Alex Vaughn was. These two men were Falzone's left and right hands.

Aldo was ancient. He was a thin and bald man with a white goatee. His small stature hid the enormity of his true power. He was by all accounts a genius and had never been arrested in connection with any crime. He knew people who knew people and he could read pretty much any of them with a good degree of certainty. Aldo Marano was Falzone's brain.

If he was the brain, then Muro was the brawn of Falzone's enterprise. He was thick and smelled of cheap cologne. He always wore a suit and it made his already broad shoulders seem enormous. His gray hair was speckled with remnants of his primary black, and waved backwards in an unkempt slick. Muro Lucano had been arrested three times, all for murder or being involved in the conspiracy to commit murder. Each time the jury acquitted him. Many were surprised, but not Victor. It seems that everyone has his price.

Victor walked toward the rear booth. There was an ashtray on the table and it was filled with half-smoked butts. Also on the table were several empty shot glasses and the men were murmuring to themselves with apparent unease. The men must have been sitting there a while. As Victor Garducci approached the table, they didn't notice his arrival. With a clear of his throat, both men jumped and turned glares upon the interruption. When they noticed it was Victor, they glanced at each other then back at Vic.

"The boys told me you wanted to see me 'bout something." Victor felt his hand tremble and slipped it behind his back.

They sat there for a long moment, which to Garducci seemed like an eon. Aldo asked him to have a seat.

"Sit down my boy. It has been a while. Too long. Many things have happened since we saw you last. Your friend Sal is conducting business. He is overdue. Hopefully, he will be back soon."

Hopefully. That seemed like an odd choice of words. Aldo never used a word without a purpose to it.

"Hopefully, Mr. Marano? Why hopefully? He should be back soon shouldn't he?" Victor sensed some serious implications here.

"He gets to have all the fun this night," Muro said as he squished the end of another cigarette on to the glass of the tray in front of him.

"His business is dangerous, but we have confidence in him." Aldo said the words with a calm and matter-of-fact air, but his tone indicated that he was very worried that things were awry.

"I don't understand Mr. Marano. What's going on? Why have you asked to talk with me about all of this?"

Victor was confused. They were being very open with him all of a sudden. He didn't want them to tell him anything that could be considered 'too much' later.

"Well, Sal vouched for you. Now you must do a favor for him, for us." Aldo was eyeing him now, gauging his reactions.

"Anything Mr. Marano. What do you need?" Victor was worried. His cover wouldn't last all that long and he didn't have a lot of time to get back in the good graces of everybody one at a time.

"Real simple Vic. Sal was supposed to collect some money from a client of ours. We don't know if he made it there to collect since he is running so far behind."

Muro was talking to him but at the same time his eyes kept shifting to Aldo. Garducci's sixth sense was buzzing now and he felt like something was out of sorts. He couldn't put his finger on it.

Aldo looked at Victor and slid a folded piece of paper across the table to him.

"All we want you to do is check on this address. If you see Sal's car parked down the block from here, and you pass by the address, see if you notice anything out of the ordinary. Then come back to us and let us know what you see."

Victor Garducci grabbed the piece of paper and slipped it into his pocket.

"Sure thing. I'll get right on it."

With that, Victor Garducci stood up and started to

leave. As he exited the building, he looked back over his shoulder. He noticed that both men were watching him as he left and both Tim and Jimmy were pretending to play pool once again.

Victor walked out the doors and stood outside breathing in the crisp cool air around him. From under this overhang, the snow and hail danced in front of him. After contemplating the situation for a moment, Victor decided to do as the old men directed.

He figured that if something were indeed going on, at least his loyalty in this situation would endear him enough to get by on the next few days. All he needed was enough time to get over to Inhaled Imports and see who was in the habit of buying Sobranies.

He walked with a brisk gait into the freezing night toward the address now in his hand.

This is for you Jack, he thought. The chill of the night air crawled up his spine and he pulled his jacket in tight around him. Victor Garducci, aka Alex Vaughn, felt total and complete isolation amidst a sea of uncertainty.

Chapter 8

"Oh Sonne boy, wake up Sonne boy."

Rafael was standing over Sonne and his face was expressionless. Rontego moved his captive to a small metal foldout chair in the kitchen. There was tile in the kitchen; the blood would be easier to clean up later.

Sonne remembered what transpired before the blackness overtook him and now he was starring wide-eyed at the assassin, trying to mumble something. The duct tape that covered his mouth and stuck to the hairs of his mustache with cruel stubbornness would allow nothing but muffled incoherency.

Rafael Rontego noticed that he had Sonne's full attention. He walked over to his stereo, taking his time, and with a glance at his captive, turned the knob to 'on'. There was a brief moment of static that irritated the already frayed nerves of Sonne Pieri, as his eyes became even wider.

Rontego took no notice of his victim's concerns. He flipped through a small black booklet of compact discs. He settled on one with a slight scratch but that Rontego loved all the same.

With a clearing of his throat the assassin put in an album by The Animals. The album, entitled *The Animals Is Here* was Rontego's favorite for many reasons, but most of those reasons had to do with the number one track from 1964 called "House of the Rising Sun." He glanced at Sonne, still eyeing him like a hawk from above the tape that held his mouth silent. Rafael Rontego cranked up the volume one click at a time. The music was coming through the speakers with more clarity now.

Rafael walked towards Sonne as the hypnotic guitar work introduced the song. He lifted his foot and rested it on the knee of his victim. Reaching behind him he pulled his black-handled blade out and rested it against

Sonne's neck.

As the organs began to join the guitar work, Rafael pulled back a corner of the tape from Sonne's mouth and leaned next to his ear. The breath from the assassin as he spoke, so close to Sonne, sent a chill through his captive. Rontego noticed the goose bumps that found their way down his captive's neck.

"I'm gonna pull this tape off of your mouth now, Sonne, but I want you to understand a few things. One is, you are going to die. The second is, how many pieces you die in is up to you. I am gonna ask you questions. You answer them you get to keep your fingers, toes, nose and ears. If you so much as lie to me, I start taking them off one at a time. Do you understand me Sonne boy?"

Rontego's nose was now just a few inches from Sonne's face. The assassin leaned forward on his knee, his foot still resting on the captive's leg and his hand still dangling the knife beneath Sonne's chin. With his eyes shut tight and his breath now coming out in quick rushes Sonne shook his head in agreement.

As Rafael Rontego ripped the duct tape off of Sonne's mouth there was the noise of hair tearing out of skin, mingled with the lyrics blasting from the speakers:

There is a house in New Orleans/ They call the Rising Sun
And it's been the ruin of many a poor boy/ And God I know I'm one

"Shit Rontego, man, I'm just following orders...." Sonne began talking as soon as the tape was free from his mouth.

Rontego snapped his head forward and shut Sonne up before he could finish. Rontego's forehead blasted into his captive's nose and splattered it into a bloody mess across his face.

For a moment Sonne's head fell forward and Rontego thought he might pass out. A sharp sting across his left cheek brought him back to his senses and he looked at Rontego through his watering eyes.

Rafael noticed the tears in Sonne's eyes—a shattered nose will do that to a man. The blood from his nose was running down his face and into his mouth and down his neck onto his shirt, staining the white Armani a thick, almost purplish, crimson.

My mother was a tailor/She sewed my new blue jeans
My father was a gambling man/Down in New Orleans

Sonne, silenced except for a low moan and a slight gurgling of his own blood, looked up at Rontego with a questioning look in his eyes. Rontego almost felt sympathy for the man. In a flash, however, he remembered that this man came here to kill him.

Sonne broke into his home with the intention of murdering him. But why? That was what Rontego needed to find out. Who wanted him dead and why?

Rontego leaned forward, his dark eyes were steeled and his penetrating glance did nothing to assuage the many fears that were no doubt running through the imprisoned capo's mind. All the while, the song drained on in the background.

Now the only thing a gambler needs/Is a suitcase and a trunk
And the only time he's satisfied/Is when he's on a drunk

"Simple question Sonne, and don't make the mistake of feeding me excuses again, we aren't in a confessional. You spoke of orders, before you felt the need to taste your own blood. Whose orders?"

He was met by silence and the slow drip of blood, but Rontego continued.

"And before you answer, remember you have a father and a brother that I can repay for any of your foolishness once you're far from this world."

Rontego spoke, not in anger but with a coolness that promised the certainty of his words. He saw Sonne's eyes flash with the recognition of his truth. Rontego was considered a lot of things, but never a welcher. With a moment of hesitation, Sonne confirmed what Rontego suspected.

"Raf, you know my orders come only from Falzone."

Oh mother tell your children/Not to do what I have done
Spend your lives in sin and misery/ In the House of the Rising Sun

Pieri continued speaking even as the disc continued spinning the music Rafael chose for this special occasion.

"Man, just let me out of here. Think of it bro, together we can...."

He was cut off by the sudden impact of a solid backhand on his already tender cheek. This time, though, Sonne's cheek did not absorb the impact of the blow, but rather split into an unnatural seam perpendicular to the scar he already wore on that side of his face. The two marks created an eerie looking crucifix design for a moment before the blood caught up with the sudden rip and dripped over the cross, hiding it beneath the spreading liquid.

The hit, however, had the desired effect. Sonne resumed his silence and waited for the assassin's next question. Rafael noticed the control shift; there was no doubt whose show this was. He smiled.

"I know Old Falzone gave you the order, but did Don Ciancetta tell him to give it to you?"

Well I got one foot on the platform/The other foot on the train
I'm goin' back to New Orleans/ To wear that ball and chain

Sonne's bloody smile cracked out of the corner of his mouth and his eyes revealed a slight edge of superiority that flashed for a moment. The gleam in his eye was not lost on the assassin.

With a half-scoff Sonne spat at the assassin, "You stupid fuck, the old Ciancetta has no clue what's going on. We all know Falzone holds the real power with his union support. You think that old bastard lets Falzone have control over the unions out of the goodness of his heart? You were just the first target in a hostile takeover man, one of Ciancetta's bitches that were deemed 'in the way' and 'expendable'."

The arrogant and victorious tone that Sonne took with the assassin did not sit well with Rontego and Sonne found that out with another sharp rap to the left side of his face. Rontego then took a step back from Sonne and reached into his shoulder holster which held his pistol.

Well there's a house in New Orleans

Rafael Rontego reached into his left pocket and pulled out a thin metal tube with screw ridges protruding from the bottom of it: a silencer. Sonne's eyes began to widen even more, so that the whole of his face seemed unable to contain the enormous apertures.

They call the Rising Sun

The assassin screwed the silencer into the barrel of his pistol. His eyes snapped up and focused on those of Salvatore Junior—Sonne—Pieri.

And It's been the ruin of many a poor boy

Sonne opened his mouth as if to scream, his eyes never leaving the assassin's, sweat trickled down from his forehead and mixed with the blood still flowing unabated from the wounds in his cheek. His neck strained and every muscle in his face became taut as he tried to let out some sort of noise to voice the protest welling up inside of him. Rafael lifted his pistol and took aim.

"Seems Old Falzone deemed you...expendable," Rontego stated it as fact.

Sonne was now quite certain that this *was* fact.

And God I know I'm one

With a flash of the muzzle and a slight emanation of sound through the silencer, the bullet impacted the center of Sonne's forehead at a speed in excess of three thousand feet per second. The .22 caliber bullet penetrated the forward section of Sonne's skull but did not have enough force to drive through the back of it as the speed slowed down thanks to the initial entrance into the capo's cranium. The result was a ricochet effect that sent the bullet and pieces of skull ripping into the soft tissue of Pieri's brain.

If death had not consumed the man so fast, and if he could have registered each shred as the foreign material cut new paths into his brain matter, he might have described it as hundreds of migraine headaches happening in rapid succession, nanoseconds apart. As it was, death was as instant as death can be and the blinding flash of the muzzle was the last thing he ever knew.

His eyes remained wide open and his head snapped backward with the impact. Then, it eased forward with the force of gravity and his chin came to rest upon his chest as if he dozed. Rontego stood there for a moment and looked at the fresh kill. And as if frozen in time at the instant of death the song repeated over and over.

And God I know I'm one. And God I know I'm one. And God I know I'm one…

The damn thing was skipping. Rontego shook his head and broke from the eerie trance. With a grunt he walked over to the stereo and yanked the plug away from the wall and sent a shower of sparks into the air. Just like that, there was silence once more.

*

Victor Garducci walked silent with his thoughts into the cold Buffalo night. He glanced at the now crumpled piece of paper in his palm. The address was not so far away, and despite the blistering cold, Victor decided to walk the distance. He traveled two blocks, and then the two became four. As the snow began to saturate his clothing, Victor slowed as he came to within a block of the address on the paper.

1371 West Boat Shuttle Street was a decent place. Garducci frequented the place quite often for more pleasant business, a few months prior, when he was 'officially' undercover. He shared in a pie 'on the house'.

It didn't make sense though. As far as he knew, the place was controlled by Don Ciancetta himself. He would never have to make a payment to a capo like Sal. The funds always shifted up the chain of command.

The money chain. He would have to explore this more. Victor decided that the best thing to do, for the moment, would be to continue on and see what came of the inquiry into Sal's whereabouts. At the least it would gain him confidence with the crew and might allow for him to gain information on the Sobranie which littered Jack's death scene.

As he walked, Alex Vaughn thought of the times he spent with his dear friend, within the snowy confines of the Buffalo winter. They were both adamant Buffalo Bills fans and spent a large percentage of their income on season tickets. Year after year they were let down, but each year was followed with a 'this year is our year'.

They spent the crazy years of '91 to '94 together getting drunk in glorious AFC championships only to get drunk later in depression due to horrid letdown after horrid letdown in the Super Bowls. After the third loss in a row, Jack defined the character which he embodied and which appealed to Alex. Vaughn was depressed, thinking the ultimate glory would never come to fruition.

"Always second best man, the story of my life," Alex muttered over a stiff Kessler Whiskey.

Jack looked at him and a frown crossed his face, the look was etched into Alex's memory now.

"Second best eh? Well, I don't think it's that bad, to be honest," Jack said with a certain tone that made Alex look up from the drink he sipped.

"How so?"

Jack looked him dead in the eye and said, "Bro, these are our boys, and they have proven better than all but one team in the entire league. 'Least we were still able to go out, root for our guys, get drunk together and have a good time, one more night then the other guys out there. And best yet, we get to hang out together and get drunk one more time before the Monday morning grind."

Then he laughed. Not a fake laugh that you often

get in those stupid moments of depression. He laughed a full- hearted, schoolboy laugh, a laugh that made you feel better about any situation, no matter how dreary it was.

Jack was like that when Charlotte left. Even when she took Ella away. He made Alex laugh and made any darkness seem like a fleeting thing.

Now, though, the light that he brought to Alex's world was extinguished. Alex's brother had been taken from him. The clue to who did it was tucked away within Inhaled Imports. If this trip to Super Nova Pizza, to Sal's collection, helped shed any illumination on the shadowy enterprises that surrounded Jack's death, then that's where Alex was going to go.

As the snow fell down around him and settled on his shoulders, Alex walked to the vicinity of Sal's dark green Escalade. He was now close to wherever Sal was and he needed to make contact with him and bring him to the bosses at Wizeguys.

As he neared Sal's SUV, Victor Garducci smelled smoke. Not the smell of cigarette smoke, but rather the smell of burning paint and timber. Alex looked up and into the swirling winds he saw the unmistakable thick clouds of gaseous smoke. The smoke rose from the approximate location of Super Nova.

Before Victor could contemplate the ramifications of the situation, a small man ran into view. He stood about 5'7". He wore a pair of wrinkled and worn blue jeans and a thick brown turtleneck. His face was set in a sort of impenetrable scowl, but he was unemotional except for the breath coming out in rasps from what must have been a recent run. He had gray eyes that seemed to never blink and slick black hair that fell on one side in front of his right eye.

Salvatore Senior, Sal, was now in plain view of Victor. As Salvatore ran up to his Escalade, Victor Garducci ran up and yelled out to his old pal.

"Hey Sal-e! Wait up, man!"

Sal stopped with one hand on the door handle and looked up towards the voice. With a start he realized who it was calling his name.

"Holy Fuck! Vic! Hurry up and get in man."

Sal jumped in the SUV and reached across, unlocking the passenger side door. Victor jumped in, happy to be out of the cold. Sal didn't wait for Victor to get settled. Instead, he backed up out of his parallel parking spot and let the tires squeal as he punched the accelerator too early. After that, however, there was silence as Sal sped off, checking his rearview and side mirrors in turns. They rounded the block and headed up towards Wizeguyz Billiards, and Victor broke the paranoid quiet. He summoned the courage to ask his old captain, "Sal, what the hell is going on around here?"

Sal looked at him, but did not answer.

After another long pause he asked, "What do you mean? Falzone didn't send you up to get me?"

Garducci thought about all the possible answers he could give, truths and lies. He decided the truth might work a bit better in this situation.

"No, Marano and Lucano sent me, said you were late and might need a hand. They didn't tell me what you might need a hand with though. Shit, man, just tell me what the hell went down. I get back after a few months settling my debts and the next thing I know, before a 'Hi, how are ya', I'm sent off to find you and they don't even know what happened to you!"

Victor knew his face was red, and he could feel his heart rate jump. He hoped Sal would relate it to anger, that he didn't enjoy being so out of the loop.

It worked.

Sal gave him a look. Victor could see he wanted to assuage his old pal's fears, and was happy when Sal decided to fill him in.

"Well, best I can figure is they thought I wouldn't be able to handle the job, that or I had gotten caught or something. It wasn't so hard; it just took me longer because they didn't close up till late."

Victor looked at Sal. Sal glanced over from his watch on the road and flashed a wicked smile at his pal. Garducci was confused.

"What job? What did you do?"

Sal looked over again with an excited tremor edging his voice and said, "Burned Ciancetta's place to ashes, man. Old man Falzone is making his move on the top spot. Just between me and you though, he had it coming to him. We all run his illegitimate businesses and then that fat fuck decides to have an untouchable legitimate business? Who the fuck does he think he is, hording all the wealth himself? And let's be honest. We all know that a lot of illegitimate activity takes place in his so-called 'legit' pizzeria."

Sal was looking self-important by this point. Victor decided to take some of the wind out of his sails.

"Well whose bright idea was that? Ciancetta is just going to collect the insurance anyway."

Pieri Senior's head snapped around and almost with an accusatory tone stated as flat as if he were reading stock quotes from the Wall Street Journal, "Well, maybe so, but each week that place is outta commission, that shit-bag loses thousands. It's gonna take that bastard months to rebuild that place. Too bad though, I did like to eat some pizza there! Am I right bro? That was some good shit!"

With that, Sal began to laugh in an adrenaline-inspired frenzy.

Victor almost said, "What if he just runs his business through his other joint across town?" but decided against further pushing his friend's already tenuous mental and emotional threshold.

They drove along in silence after that, the only

noise the steady hum of the engine and the back and forth scrapping of the windshield wipers pushing snow off of the car. Sal would look over at him and after a second of contemplating (which Victor Garducci pretended to ignore) he would exclaim something along the lines of "Damn good to see you, bro" or "Glad you're back, man."

Victor would voice how agreeable it was indeed to be back and then glance out the window and watch as the buildings rolled on by into the snowy blackness beyond. Sal kept looking over, as if he were itching to say something, but then at the last moment decided to keep whatever it was to himself.

Although the drive was less than ten minutes, the tension that Victor felt made the ride seem like a grueling journey. Serious things were afoot here, and Victor was now smack dab in the middle of it. It seemed he'd thrust himself right in the middle of a damned mafia power struggle.

His plan was to get in using his undercover guise, and then get the information he needed and then disappear again. He was low level enough under normal circumstances that no one would miss him that much, especially with the disorganization of modern organized crime. Now though, every man would be accounted for. And retaliation would be rained down for the burning of Don Ciancetta's prize jewel, the Super Nova.

As far as Victor was concerned, he might be sitting next to a dead man. Another cause for concern was for Alex Vaughn's buddy Ryan Slate. He too would be enmeshed in this mafia war. Even worse, he would be connected with the Ciancettas. The two of them might find themselves on opposing sides of this mess.

Also, being a low level associate of Joey Ciancetta, Leo Junior's son would make him a prime target, if just to send a message to the Boss. Ryan Slate, also known as Ricky Vincenzio, might just be in line to be used as cannon fodder.

There is an old saying that you should never shoot the messenger. Well, the way things worked with wise guys was that the message was a bullet riddled corpse.

Joseph Falzone enjoyed a lot of power; he controlled the numbers and with the support of the Union he was a hard man to touch, but Ciancetta boasted the backing of the other organized families, the ones in New York City.

It would be interesting to see if they tried to snatch up some territory in the midst of this war. Perhaps they would let the Buffalo crews duke it out themselves. Wars were notorious for being sloppy and getting people pinched. They might just stay out of the mix.

Then again, mobsters were known for being greedy and getting pinched might just become an afterthought. Most of the other families would stay out of it but a select few would ask to get involved and they would be allowed to go to the highest bidder, or the faction that would be most able to line the pockets of the other families.

Of course, those select few mercenaries would be allowed to enter into the fray with the understanding that they were, in fact, not allowed to go; but only if anyone asked any questions. The plain fact of the matter was that the mercenaries would still be expected to kick some percentage of their earnings back upstairs to their superiors, permission or not. Permission mattered if and when you were caught, or whether or not you funneled the correct percentages upstairs.

The car stopped. They were not at the pool hall though.

"Where are we?" asked Garducci. He tried to mask his concern with a touch of annoyance.

Sal looked at him and said, "Man, you forget places quick. What happened, that sun and heat over in New Mexico melt your brain? We're at Frankie DeRisio's.

You think I was gonna make you sleep on the streets? Not a guy in old Sal's crew. Come on, we'll make this bastard give us some food."

For a second, Victor was hesitant, but then it dawned on him that he hadn't eaten that day.

"Yeah, but let's be quick about it, the bosses want to talk with you." Victor needed to look good so if he needed to ride Sal all night to get him over to Aldo and Muro then Victor was going to do it, right after a quick, late night snack.

Chapter 9

One thing was for sure, Rafael needed to get the bodies out of his house. Three bodies in one's home never looked good. It did not look good if most precincts, and the FBI, had a dossier on you as well, and then three bodies are found in your home.

Though these shits broke into his place, calling the police was out of the question. If they got involved it would be forever until Rontego could operate on a subsistence level just for fear of getting pinched. The local squad cars were bought off at any rate.

At first, the assassin was tempted to go over to Don Ciancetta and warn him of the dangers heading his way, and then ask for some help disposing of the bodies. But Rafael wasn't quite sure how he was going to play his cards regarding the issue of this mob war.

Despite all the implications, one thing was for sure; the bodies had to go and had to go soon. Three bodies couldn't very well be tossed in one trunk. Rafael grimaced as he considered the fat fuck that fell asleep during the botched assassination attempt on Rontego.

If he did them one at a time, it would take hours. As much as he hated it, Rafael was going to need to bring in help on this one.

He worked before with this guy from out of one of the local villages outside of Buffalo, Hamburg or Angola. They called him the Cleaner. The guy ran his business under the guise of a carpet cleaning operation he liked to call Busy Bumble Bees.

He was hard to book; he hated anyone calling him in unless it was a planned operation. He thought spur of the moment killings were best left to the gangland hits of the unorganized "niggers." The prick was a racist, but he did his job well.

His one worry was getting caught and if he thought

you were going to bring him down he would just hang up the phone on you. He even had a code for ordering hits, and you got the code if you were referred by a big boss or if he told it to you himself.

Lucky for Rontego, after he worked with him on the hit for Ciancetta, years back during Old Leo's rise to power, the Cleaner told him to call whenever he needed and gave him the code.

Rafael looked at the mess in his apartment. He checked himself over, no blood on his clothes. That was one good thing. Rafael put his coat back on and exited his apartment. On his way out, he dead bolted the lock. It wouldn't do to have any late night and unexpected visits from the landlady this evening.

Rontego walked down the stairs and into the late night air of Buffalo. The blast of cold wind hit him like an anvil as he exited the heat of his building. To call the Cleaner he needed to get to the payphone at the end of the block.

Rontego wouldn't let a phone line into his home. He saw too many wiser gangsters take twenty years in the pen for a careless word or two on the phone.

When Rafael got to the booth where the payphone was located, he entered it and pulled the door closed behind him, shutting out the snow, which continued to fall outside. He didn't know the Cleaner's number, but the great part was that he was listed in the yellow pages. Nothing like great service.

He flipped through the pages and found the ad he was looking for, "Busy Bumble Bees 'Our Prices Don't Sting'."

Bullshit, Rontego thought.

This was going to cost him a pretty penny. Maybe he would go to Don Ciancetta, make him reimburse him.

Rontego inserted two quarters and dialed the number placed in the ad. After one ring a voice answered,

"Busy Bumble Bees.   We're closed for the evening. Is this an emergency?"

The voice was that of the Cleaner. He had a nasal voice that you don't often forget.

Rafael replied, "Yeah, I spilt three gallons of grape juice all over my carpet. I need it cleaned as soon as possible."

There was a long silence and Rontego wondered if the man still provided that type of service.

Just before Rontego thought he must have forgotten part of the code the voice replied, "Ok, payment on arrival, who is this?"

This might work out after all.

"Rontego. Need an address?"

"No, I know where you live. I'll be there in twenty minutes."

With that the voice hung up. A few minutes later and Rontego was back in his apartment looking at the guys he dubbed the Three Stooges.

The assassin sat on his Lazy Boy and though there were bodies littered across the breadth of his home, he found that he was tired. Killing always took a lot out of him.

He dozed off for what seemed like a second when he heard a soft tapping on his door. With a start, he took a glance out the window. There along the street was the Busy Bumble Bee carpet cleaning van.

Rontego checked his watch; twenty-five minutes went by. This guy was pretty damn punctual. Rontego went to the door and looked out of the peephole. Damn, he forgot that he stuck a dime in the way. All he saw was blackness. He pulled his pistol out and held it in his right hand behind his back.

Just in case, he thought.

With his left hand, he glided the door open a crack. In the hallway was a slight man. He was in his early forties and had brown hair with just a touch of gray. He was about five foot five and was in decent shape; he couldn't weigh more than a hundred and forty pounds. He wore a pair of faded blue jeans and a black polo shirt that had a yellow logo of a bumblebee holding a broom. Under the shirt was a long undershirt that helped against the cold. He carried three large navy blue duffle bags; one that was quite full and the other two seemed to be empty. It was the Cleaner, but something was different. He used to have glasses.

Before Rontego could dwell on it, the man pushed himself into Rontego's apartment and surveyed the scene.

"Quite a massacre, unlucky for them," he stated.

Rafael Rontego fancied that he sounded like that to other people when talking about killing.

From the second he got there it was all business. He had a way of doing things and he expected Rontego to follow him with precision. Rontego didn't mind, though, it was better than the alternatives, none of which seemed very pleasant.

"Five thousand a head, total of fifteen grand. Here is what you do, take guy one over there and bring him to your bathtub, but first lay this plastic covering along the path you're going to take. We don't need any more blood getting on the carpet."

While he was talking he was handing Rafael a rolled up section of plastic and emptying the contents of the first duffle bag onto the living room floor. It was filled with saws, knives, clamps, things that looked like walnut crunchers, and picks. For the next three hours they were busy dismembering the bodies of the would-be assassins in the bath tub, one at a time.

At first, Rontego was told to "separate the limbs from the torso" by himself.

When Rontego looked at the Cleaner, he was told, "Ok, I'll do it if you think you can re-carpet the sections of your floor that got blood all over 'em. And must I remind you that you decided to let the blood out of those two in the living room like fresh hunted deer? Honestly, who slits a neck in their own home! The blood in here is ridiculous."

A little taken aback, Rontego went in to the bathroom and began the gruesome task of sawing through chewy tendons, tough muscle, and bone; and sifting through layers of fat in order to pull the limbs off of their rightful owners.

The assassin looked over his shoulder and saw the Cleaner busy ripping up the carpet and stacking the contaminated sections in a pile in the kitchen. Every so often he would take a measurement and then cut out another section of carpet.

After a while of both of them cutting—Rafael bodies, and the Cleaner carpet—the Cleaner went down to his truck. He was gone a moment when he came up toting a bundle of new carpet which he then cut into the measurements he jotted down before. The carpet didn't match exact, but it was close enough in the bad lighting.

After the first body was dismembered, head from torso, hands from forearm, shoulder from torso, feet from legs, and so on, Rafael needed to take a break and sat down on the closed lid of his toilet.

He smoked a quick cigarette and enjoyed each drag all the more, knowing it was an extra second away from the tub of blood to his left. He was looking down at his feet when he noticed a rustling sound coming from the living room. The Cleaner finished with the carpets and was now dragging the second body in from the living room along the plastic lining.

A few moments later and they were side by side on their knees, hacking and tearing, and sawing along in relative silence.

At one point Rontego asked, "Didn't you used to have glasses?"

The Cleaner replied in between breaths, "Laser eye surgery."

Rontego glanced over; the Cleaner sawed away, intent. "No shit? That stuff work very well?"

The Cleaner stopped sawing for a moment to wipe some sweat off of his forehead with his forearm.

"Yeah, worked real good, a lot of people get that done now."

The Cleaner was happy to have a distraction as well, but he continued on cutting into the flesh.

"No thanks," Rafael said. "No one is getting near my eyes with some damned laser. Want a smoke?"

"Don't smoke"

Rontego shrugged. He lit one for himself, glad to have something besides the stench of iron filling up his nostrils. With a cigarette hanging from his mouth, he lifted up a hammer and he shattered apart a knee cap. It helped to separate the ligaments so that he could finish tearing the leg off of Sonne Pieri.

Rontego looked up at the Cleaner and noticed that he wasn't paying attention to the work, just sawing and ripping, a clear method to the work. Rafael let the cleaner have most of the gold paraphernalia found on the bodies, but noticed that the family crest ring on Sonne's right hand was still there. He supposed that no one, not even the Cleaner, wanted to try and peddle that ring and be attached to the murder of Sonne.

A thought came over Rontego and he stole a careful glance at the Cleaner, making sure he was not paying attention. When he was satisfied that the coast was clear, Rafael tore the finger, ring and all, from the hand and wrapped it in a white handkerchief he used to dab the sweat from his forehead. With a subtle shift in his weight, the finger fell into his pocket. A glass of water later, and it was chilling on ice in his freezer, until such time as Rontego decided it might be useful.

For now though, the hacking and sawing of bodies commenced.

After that, there was very little conversation between them as they focused on finishing the task at hand. By the time they all three bodies were dismembered and stuffed in two of the plastic lined duffle bags, the floors, bathroom and tools bleached clean, and they were changed and showered, it was close to midnight.

Rontego stood in his living room wearing an all light blue jumpsuit, unzipped at the neck revealing a little gold chain that hung there.

"What are you gonna do with our friends there?" Wherever the Cleaner took the bodies, Rontego wanted to be sure that they wouldn't be found, ever.

"Don't worry. I'm gonna burn the bodies in my furnace, then after the fire dies down I'm gonna smash the bones with hammers until it becomes a fine dust. Then it's just a matter of sprinkling the powder over Lake Erie."

"And our clothes?" he asked.

"Burn them, too."

The Cleaner's face looked gaunt. Even he had a threshold for this type of work. He gathered up the bags and supplies.

As he headed to the door, he turned to look at Rafael and said, "Hey, tomorrow meet me for dinner. We'll discuss the disposal I'm doing. I have some things I want to go over with you, but I'm too beat right now. Good?"

Rafael nodded his approval and opened the door for the man carrying all three bags. He was stronger then he looked. Then again, maybe a bloodless body was a lot lighter than a normal one.

"Alright then. I know a great place to get some spaghetti and meatballs. Chef's Pasta Place. Be there at eight?"

Again Rafael nodded his approval.

"Wait right here," Rontego said.

Shutting the door, he slipped away and went to a compartment in the floorboard of his closet. A brown paper bag was inside, and inside that bag was the prettiest color Rafael Rontego knew.

Green cash.

He counted the money, left some in the bag and removed the rest, setting it back in the compartment. He rolled the bills into a tight ball and opened the door.

The Cleaner held out his hand, knowing full well what Rontego was up to. Rontego looked the cash into the Cleaner's hand.

"Half now, half at dinner".

Closing his fist around the green roll, the Cleaner tilted his head and left. Fatigue assaulted Rafael and he stumbled towards his mattress. He lay down on his bed, thinking that he could get some food in a bit. He lit a Sobranie, took a drag and then left the cigarette burning on the edge of his glass ashtray, next to the mattress.

Seconds later, though, sleep began to overtake him and he slipped into a dream. As he dreamt, the lit Sobranie cast an eerie gloom about his living room for a while, before it burned down to a low ember. Then it too was asleep as the last spark was distinguished by a brief gust of air. The smoke-induced gloom lingered for a while, then it dissipated and the room waited in stillness and quiet.

The rhythmic breathing of the assassin echoed in the otherwise silent room. Fast asleep; he swirled amongst dreams of slaughter houses and the ghosts of acquaintances past.

*

Frankie DeRisio rumbled with a heavyset frame and a wad of curled black hair precariously clumped on top of a very round and red, puffed face. It was on account of his reddish hue that people thought they called him Frankie Red. Though, if you asked him that, you better be ready to defend yourself from slow moving fists that would pulverize you if they connected.

Among his associates, when Frankie was around, the word was that he was called Frankie Red because he was fond of smoking Marlboro Reds.

"The only decent American nicotine," according to DeRisio's sworn testimony.

He was Alex Vaughn's initial contact and the man who vouched for Victor Garducci at the beginning of Alex's undercover operations.

They left his seedy apartment building several blocks from the vacant Bethlehem Steel properties and drove about fifteen minutes back toward Wizeguyz Billiards. Victor was hungry. Despite Sal's bragging on getting Frankie to feed them, he was ill-prepared for company and a bag of potato chips was all they took with them.

It was apparent to Victor, the way Sal was fidgeting, that he brought Frankie along for support. Frankie and Victor, as far as Sal was concerned, were his guys. And unless he got called into a meeting one on one, he was not going to go anywhere without 'his guys'.

Sal was driving his Escalade and Victor was in front passenger, courtesy of a well played "shotgun" call.

DeRisio shot back,"I'll show you a real shotgun, up close and personal like."

His voice was as thick as the lasagna he loved to eat and came out slow and purposeful. Though he didn't stutter, he made you take time in order to listen to his thoughts, which developed as slow as the words which formulated in his mouth.

Frankie was sitting in the back middle and reshuffling his weight as they drove along; making it very noticeable how there was not enough room for his stumpy legs. Though the truth of the matter was that, he had problems getting his considerable belly situated on his knees. As the occasional sighs slipped out in breaths of disgruntled air from DeRisio, and the steady hum of the SUV's heater added a constant background noise, Sal Pieri kept talking about the meeting with Aldo and Muro, and perhaps Falzone himself, waiting for him at Wizeguyz.

"Well, I'll bet the big guys over at Wizeguyz will be happy as pigs in shit now. They needed proof I was with them after what my Uncle did back when he and Crazy Joe fought that war and my Pop's got whacked...er died... when I was little kid. Kinda funny though that the proof these guys needed was that I would go against Leo Ciancetta. It's ok though; my move wasn't the only one going tonight. Muro Lucano was insistent on that fact. A few of Old Leo's gunners needed taking out in the first wave. 'Clean house right from the start, leave Ciancetta with no firepower.' That's what Muro said. Guess he learned something from the war with Uncle Joey and Ciancetta. They want to try and get the boss to hand over the reins, something about making it a matter of respect. They figure if they don't kill the boss to become boss, then if something similar happens to them, they wouldn't be the ones to get whacked."

Sal was rambling about how his father, of the same name, played it smart. In his eyes, his father was a genius, but his short tenure at the top, and quick fall to the grave, would beg to differ.

Though there were a few exceptions, most of the big bosses had a tendency to be egotistical braggarts that get the top spot through killing and talking big. Most of them merely threw enough smoke and mirrors to get them up top, not to sustain anything of significance. That made it all the more interesting to Alex.

Joe Falzone, by all accounts, was as smart and crafty as they came. He'd been the underboss or consigliore for the better part of fifteen years and survived numerous shifts in power. He accomplished this by staying away from the top spot. Why had he now decided to go for *capo di tutti capi*?

Sal's sudden, "Damn it man!" interrupted Garducci's thoughts. "They better know I'm with them now. I hate meetings though. I'm all fucking nerves, Vic."

Victor shifted in his seat and took a glance over at Sal. He was worse than he thought. Sweat was beading up on his forehead and his knuckles were white while they gripped the wheel. Victor studied the grip. Sal just torched the prized business of the most powerful underworld figure in the greater Buffalo-Ontario area.

"Don't worry Sal-e buddy, me and Frankie are going with you. Everything will be fine, won't it Frankie?"

Sal looked into the rearview mirror at Frankie.

"Yeah Sal, everything's going to be fine. The big guys asked you to do it. If you said no, you'd be dead anyway. Now, they know you're with 'em. Maybe they'll bring you up the chain with 'em for this. This, this ain't no small favor they asked of you. And when you move up, take me and Vic with ya, ya know? Make us all big guys."

The way that Frankie spoke made Victor beg for an eventual end to his droning, but he noticed an opposite effect on Sal. It seemed that Frankie's little speech calmed Sal down as he basked in the daydream of future power.

"Yeah, that's right. Instead of us all working for them, maybe one day you two bums will work just for me."

Sal was a little more relaxed now and he gave Victor a little punch on the arm and flashed him a smile.

"Still, it is good to see you. I'm glad the guys sent you to get me. Tonight is a big night for my whole family man. And on top of it all this shit with Falzone and Ciancetta."

With that they pulled up to the abandoned parking lot in front of Wizeguyz. They exited the SUV and with

Sal leading the way, Victor and Frankie went into the double doors of Wizeguyz Billiards.

When they entered the building, things were much they way they were when Victor left. Aldo and Muro were sitting in the rear left booth, the cigarettes piled up more and the smoke hanging above the pool hall stagnated. Jimmy Jacks and Tim Coughlin were no longer playing pool, but by the shot glasses stacked in front of them, and the way the heavy bartender was pouring out a line of fresh shots, it looked as if they nursed a healthy buzz. All of their backs were to the entrance, and the two old men were still very busy chatting amongst themselves.

The doors slammed shut behind them, causing Jimmy to almost fall off of his bar stool. Aldo and Muro strained around to catch a glimpse of who entered. They paused for a moment and then began discussing, in even more earnest, whatever it was they were talking about before. Sal didn't take notice of them and went straight up to the bar and ordered a round of drinks.

"Three Wild Turkey shots, one for each of us. Fuck it, make it five and give these two bums one, too."

He waved his hand at Jimmy and Tim who were too happy for the free booze to even regard being called bums. Victor stole a glance at the two elder Mafioso's sitting in the booth, Muro seemed to be agitated and it was confirmed when he stood up for a moment and slammed his fist on the table. But as fast as he got up, he sat back down, and with a sharp word from Aldo, they resumed with their conversation.

At one point Aldo Marano looked up and nodded at Victor, who nodded back and put his hand on Sal's shoulder. This seemed to shift the conversation a bit, but Victor didn't think much on it as Sal was proposing a toast of sorts, well a toast for Sal at any rate. Sal stood up a bit from the rest of them, making himself appear important.

He cleared his throat to ensure the effect of his

words as he eloquently began. "Here's to the breezes that blows through the treeses and lifts the girls' skirts above their kneeses and shows the spot that teases and pleases, and yes, spreads diseases, oh jeezes. Here's to the snatch, down the hatch."

Victor heard him make the same toast a dozen times. So had Jimmy and Tim, Victor heard it with them every single time. Sal didn't drink with anyone else, except his son.

Jimmy and Tim didn't care, though, they laughed as if they heard it for the first time. In fact, Victor was pretty sure they were laughing harder now. Perhaps it was the booze speaking, or perhaps it was the nature of Sal's work this evening that had huge promotional value written all over it. Victor looked at them hard for a moment and he thought that maybe, just maybe, there was some brown shit on the tips of their noses.

Victor shook his head; he was the only one still holding his shot. Sal looked at him and made a look towards his shot glass hand. Victor looked at it a little sheepish, then in one gulp swallowed the whiskey down, for a moment letting the last drop fall into his mouth. He must be getting tired. He felt irritable and his mind was wandering.

Sal couldn't help jabbing him for the delay and Garducci could hear him muttering something about "First New Mexico fries his brain then it makes him forget how to take a shot like a man. What the fuck?"

Then he heard something indiscernible and Sal was taking down a second shot. The liquor and being on his home turf, or at least his own little island of security, was doing wonders for Sal and he was starting to regain his cockiness.

He put an arm around Victor and his other around Frankie and whispered into their ears, "To the top boys, to the top."

As he whispered his dreams of glory into their ears, Aldo lifted a hand, and in a calm voice said, "Hey Salvatore, can you come over here for a moment? We have things which we would like to discuss with you."

With that Sal whispered one more time into his comrade's ears, "To the top."

He whirled around and walked over to his superiors with long strides. After a moment they sat down and started discussing what transpired. Victor noticed how tired he was as a yawn escaped his lips. It was time to get some sleep.

Victor Garducci lingered there for a moment, had another shot, and then stood up to leave. He waved to Aldo and Muro, letting them know he was leaving and then walked out of the double doors at the entrances. Those two were some tough old gangsters. That's why when he was a few blocks from home; it didn't surprise him to notice that a second sound of footsteps was shadowing his. And it surprised him less when he rounded a corner and stole a glance over his shoulder and noticed Tim Coughlin in the distance, minding his own business.

Garducci wasn't worried though, he was pretty sure Aldo just wanted to make sure that he wasn't running to Don Ciancetta with all that he learned that evening. It would be best to report to the billiards hall in the morning.

Victor walked on for a few moments then decided to take a left, where a right would bring him home. A few blocks later and he was getting a room at a local motel. It promised a rate of thirty-five bucks a night and free HBO. More to the point, it offered an immediate bed. He registered under the name John Smith and after a suspicious and yet indifferent glance from the clerk; he got a key to room 126.

At least I didn't have to walk up any stairs, he thought.

He entered the sparse room which contained a bed,

a nightstand with two drawers and a small bathroom. The T.V. was set on top of the nightstand across from the foot of the bed. The sheets on the bed looked like something out of the seventies, but that didn't bother the exhausted Victor Garducci. In the morning he would report to Wizeguyz, and then find his way over to Inhaled Imports.

It was there that my journey is sure to begin, he thought.

He began reminiscing taking shots with Sal at the bar. The last time he drank with anyone was with Jack at the Old Irish Pub outside of Angola. Sal's face began to morph into that of Jack's and the toast morphed into the soothing lyrics of Lynyrd Skynyrd as reality succumbed to dream. A few moments later, and he was asleep on the rough mattress that made it feel almost like home.

Chapter 10

The sun drifted in through the bend in the blinds covering his living room window and set upon the assassin's closed eyelids. He lay there for a minute, knowing that the sun had risen and was the reason for the warmth he felt even as winter continued on in Buffalo.

After a moment or two he blinked his eyes open and strained his neck to the left and heard a satisfied crack as his joints released the pressure that built up inside of them during the night. He was surprised that he fell asleep so deep and for a moment he worried about his carelessness. What if Falzone sent another hit squad after him?

As the assassin stood up and stretched and walked toward his fridge to drink some milk, he began to think with a clearer mind on the events which transpired the previous day. The thing that bothered him the most was the issue concerning the attempted hit on him. What if Ciancetta arranged the hit, to do away with someone with as much knowledge as himself? Knowledgeable personnel had a way of becoming an ill-affordable luxury, especially with the turn coats like Sammy 'The Bull' Gravano in the Gotti crew, or the Henry Hills that were running rampant all over La Costa Nostra.

Perhaps the wary Don decided to do away with Rontego. Perhaps Sonne Pieri was lying all along. He knew he was a dead man, perhaps he wanted Rontego to fly off the handle and make a mistake.

However, Falzone was smart. For years he succeeded in manipulating the politics while staying out of the limelight. He even helped clean the crews of informants who worked to link his guys to undercover police and FBI units, most of them anyway. He served Ciancetta in a fair and faithful manner and used his clout in the unions as a rare bargaining chip. And if a war was indeed going on, then what if Sonne was trying to stir shit up by having Rontego think it was Falzone, when all along it was Ciancetta? All he had to go on was the word of a dead man that he bound in his kitchen, not even a dozen feet from several of his dead friends.

Rafael was contemplating what his next move would be when it came to him. He hadn't even taken a moment to look at the matchbook Don Ciancetta gave him at their last meeting.

A few strides took him to the kitchen counter where his wallet was resting. He slammed the milk carton down on the counter and some of it splashed out on to the counter top. With his left hand the assassin scooped out the matchbook from the side pocket of his wallet and flipped the little white cardboard flap up. On the inside was written a name in cursive script: *Muro Lucano*.

As Rafael Rontego read the name he stepped backwards and leaned on the counter. Sonne was not as smart as Rontego assumed. Neither was Joseph Falzone. Ciancetta wanted a hit done on the muscle of Falzone's crew. That meant war. Either Ciancetta had a leak, and Falzone was moving to eliminate Ciancetta's muscle, in other words Rafael Rontego and maybe another couple of the Don's hitters, or the old don heard about Falzone's hostile takeover and was acting to eliminate the threat.

Either way, the assassin had to kill Muro, a mob veteran, and that would be no easy task.

He lifted his hand to his head and rested his forefinger on his pursed lips. He had no clue how he was going to get close enough to the tough gunner of Falzone's. Even if he could get to him, the implications here were tremendous. War was going down, and it was never a profitable enterprise, always ego on ego. Well, for Rontego it was profitable but the risks were exponential as well. And Muro, he was a guy that Rontego always respected, even considered a kind of mentor.

Then with a sudden realization, he decided, *Fuck Muro*.

That bastard knew about the hit on Rontego, and he would get what was coming to him. It would have to be planned to perfection. Muro would die, that was for sure. For now, though, he needed to report to Ciancetta and let him know about what transpired. The lines were drawn, and Rontego was curious to find out what he could discern about what other events occurred last night while he was busy. He also needed to remember that he had to meet with the Cleaner for dinner that night at Chef's and garner what information he could from him.

The next few minutes were busy with the assassin taking an Italian shower, which consisted of cologne being squirted over his clothes and a fresh application of deodorant. He slipped on his second favorite Armani, black with grey pinstripes and a dark blue shirt. He strapped his guns to his sides and tossed on his jacket and felt hat.

Suits were the few extravagant items he purchased, as he saved most of his money in secret hiding spots around his apartment and in other safe houses he set up.

He walked over to the door and noticed the broken string across the doorway; the bastards broke his early warning system last night. He retied another one and stepped over the breakaway thread. He shut the door and descended the spiral staircase of his apartment.

As he came outside, he was pleased to note that the snow subsided for the time being and with a clear blue sky overhead, it was a bit warmer. He saw his breath come out in wisps of white smoke, but at least some of the bite had been taken from the chill.

The snow pushed up against the side of the street by the snowplow was stained black by the filth and grime of a city, and the sidewalks were bare except for a sprinkling of salt that most businesses placed in front of their shops out of courtesy. Rontego supposed that business wouldn't be as well off if the customers were breaking their legs as they attempted to purchase their goods. Here and there though, there were patches of fresher snow that melted with the newfound warmth of the exposed sun and glistened with a certain purity which contrasted with its more noticeable surroundings.

Rafael paused there for a moment just outside the entryway to his building and pulled out a fresh cigarette. He shielded the flame of his lighter as a gust of wind swept by him and lit the tip of his Sobranie. The flame licked at the tip and then, catching to the black paper, it leapt a bit higher, then simmered back down and, with a slow burn, it traveled up the cigarette as Rontego took a drag and inhaled the sweet nicotine.

He stopped at the newsstand to his left and grabbed up a copy of the Buffalo News. He didn't read it; it was more a matter of habit. With another puff of white smoke, he kicked his heel around and started on the walk towards Rumors and Ciancetta.

The day was nice and the walk seemed to go by in a matter of minutes. He passed Shea's Theater and didn't even notice what was showing. In truth, it was closer to a half hour later. Rontego knew it because he already smoked through two cigarettes. He walked past the bum that was always begging in front of the night club. He tossed him a five dollar bill without taking notice and was about to push open the club's doors when he paused.

He walked around to the corner of the building and peered around the side. There were quite a few more cars in the parking lot than usual. The place buzzed inside.

Only one way to find out why.

He walked through the double doors, and without pausing for his eyes to adjust to the gloom, he darted towards the door of Don Ciancetta. When he got halfway there, his eyes came into focus and he noticed that the place was indeed in frenzy. The back office was open and five guys were sitting there talking and smoking cigarettes. Two guys from the bar to the left were coming towards him, fidgeting at the bulges in their hips. Another, larger man was at the door of the Don's office, obstructing any entrance into the boss' room. The two men coming towards him were not sure who he was and were still advancing on him in order to ascertain his business.

Rontego snapped his head around to face them. He cast a narrow glare on them and patted the gun at his hip with an ease that shook any confidence they might have. His black stare made them feel quite sure that their weapons were mere toys and they looked at the man in front of the Don's door as if asking for direction.

The glance was not lost on the assassin and he snapped his head back around, not sure what to expect from the guardian at the door. Perhaps Ciancetta ordered the hit after all. A moment later though, his fears were brushed away as the guardian raised his hand and waved the now ridiculous looking men away.

The man pushed the door open and let Rontego inside, where the Don was busy discussing things with Leonard Ciancetta Junior and a capo that he recognized as Christian 'The Pope' Biela. The guy was half WOP and half Polish, talk about a disorder waiting to happen. Despite the odds stacked against him in his heritage, the guy was damn smart. He was Don Ciancetta's consigliore and a lawyer when he was being 'legit'.

It must be bad times for sure if this guy was being called in. He sported dark hair, but more of brown than black. He worked out and wore his suit well, not loose like so many of the gangsters did. He carried himself like a professional, as did Rontego, and there was a certain sense about him that Rontego respected.

He wasn't sure if it was in a mutual respect for the devious demands required of them both, or if it was just the no-nonsense attitude that they shared. He spoke in a definite structure and a handshake that a businessman would have. He spoke with a slight southern touch to his voice, but not that of a redneck. He was here now, and that meant that the Don was worried.

*

The knocking on the door of room 126 came again and louder this time. It woke Victor up from a sound sleep. He rolled over, still groggy, and looked at the clock on the television set. It was six minutes after five AM. Wearing just a wife beater and a pair of boxers, the undercover officer approached the peephole of his squalid motel room door. He grabbed his old friend, the nine-millimeter Beretta still inside of its holster, by the grip and curved his index finger along the double action trigger. It looked goofy but the leather wouldn't stop a bullet if he needed to squeeze off a few rounds of lead. He looked through the peephole.

With a start, two things grabbed his immediate attention. One was that Sal Pieri was glancing back at him and hammering on the door. The second, his hair was wet and matted to his forehead. He unlocked the door, twisting the deadbolt around. The moment the door was open, Sal came in. It was raining outside, he tracked a puddle indoors and got Victor wet when he shook his hair from side to side tossing the water from his frame.

Sal shook with agitation. He began pacing around the room while Victor closed the door behind him. Garducci turned around and ran a hand through his hair. He was unsure of what to say. Sal stopped his pacing and sat down on the bed. He looked up at Victor and his expression cut deep frown lines into his brow and cheeks. Something was eating at this man. Victor decided to wait and still he clutched the Beretta in his hand, standing there in his boxers. Sal dropped his head to his hands and he remained that way for some time. He stayed like that for so long that Victor began to think that maybe Sal dozed off to sleep.

After all, he noticed with a twinge of annoyance, it was quarter after five in the morning. He waited another moment and then began to shake Sal to try and wake him. The whole thing was surreal and the drowsiness was beginning to get the better of him. Then he noticed Sal's slumped shoulder's moving up and down in slight spasmodic shudders. The man wasn't asleep at all, in fact, he was crying.

Victor couldn't help but feel awkward. Here he was in a motel room with a grown man who was crying on his bed, while he himself was standing around in his boxers trying to make sense of it all.

What the hell is going on, he thought. Victor's patience wore through and he shook Sal firm on the arm.

"Hey Sal, what's going on?" He asked it as gentle as he could but he knew that the tone of his voice did not conceal his aggravation.

Sal didn't notice for a long moment. Then he looked up at Victor, and with all the anguish that a human can endure, cried out, "He's dead, Victor. They got him. If he isn't dead he will be. They didn't come back Vic. They'll never come back!"

As soon as the statement passed his lips he renewed his open sob. Garducci winced at the spectacle. He needed to keep Sal talking; he wasn't sure how much more of this crying he could take.

"Who's dead, Sal? What are you talking about?"

Sal looked up and attempted to control himself.

"Oh God Vic, it's a big mess. Tonight was supposed to be huge, bro. Me and Sonne, we were gonna make these big moves for Falzone against Don Ciancetta. We had this whole idea of restoring credibility to our family name after Sal, my father got... ousted. And you know how my uncle Joe was removed from the top spot and made to retire by Don Ciancetta. Well, this opportunity came up and, man, we couldn't resist. All I had to do was that thing with Super Nova pizza and Sonne...."

Here he began to tear up again and fought down his emotions to continue. With considerable effort he went on.

"And Sonne, he had to get rid of this guy that Falzone says was Ciancetta's muscle. You gotta understand man; this was our chance to get back IN. No more of this scraping together a living on the scraps from Ciancetta's leftovers. So we took it. But now, Sonne hasn't come back. I thought well, maybe he is just hung up or something you know? So I sat there with those two Sicilians, Aldo and Muro, and waited. 'Bout an hour ago they decided that he was either gone or he jumped town to stay clear of the mess. But Vic, he's my boy. I know he didn't jump town. He had his two guys with him and they were planning the job these past two nights. So I walk on over to the fuck's place who it was they were supposed to deal with and I saw the light still on at his place. I thought that maybe they got the drop on him and were still conducting business inside. But I stood across the street watching for a bit longer then I noticed this man drive off in a carpet cleaning truck. Vic, this is when my heart sank. I recognized that truck, but more important, I knew the guy driving it. He's the Cleaner. And I know now that I'll never see my boy again. Even if I were dead Vic, I know the curse of hell is on me and the flames of that curse will keep us apart even in death."

At this Sal began crying again but it was brief and Victor could tell that he was cursing himself for crying in front of another man, and cursing himself for his lot in life and cursing himself for not being the one on the more dangerous assignment.

Victor didn't know what to say. He was already resigned to his mission of vengeance. It seemed that the entire world would one day be embroiled in vengeance upon vengeance, but Victor Garducci didn't give a damn. He just wanted to taste his share of it before his time came.

He asked Sal, "So, what you want to do now Sal?"

Sal looked at him, vacant, for a moment then asked, "What?"

Victor repeated himself, "So what you want to do now Sal?"

"Just put on some clothes. We're heading on over to the pool hall soon. We're supposed to meet up early, but I can't fucking sleep, not knowing that the curse of whatever God there may be is on me. Let's go eat. I'm not much hungry but I bet you could do with some coffee or something. When I don't sleep, you don't sleep."

He was standing up now and his face looked resigned to some decision he came to in the privacy of his own thoughts. Victor recognized that look. He saw that look everyday he looked in the mirror since Jack's death. Vengeance was the order of the day.

In a few moments, Alex wore his slacks and a white T-shirt that Sal had in his trunk. He tucked his Beretta into the small of his back. Over the top of it all he slung his leather jacket. The two walked out of the motel. They stood there for a moment and Victor popped up the collar on his jacket to keep out the bite of the rain and cold.

Sal lit a cigarette that became a soggy mess. It took him a few tries to light it, his hands were shaking so bad he almost lit the middle of the tobacco roll. There was a flash of light in the morning gloom.

"What the fuck was that?" Victor asked Sal.

"What? What are you talking 'bout Vic?"

Victor glanced around, "You didn't see that light?"

"Fuck Vic, it was just some lightning."

With that he got into his car and leaned over unlocking the door for Victor.

As Victor stood outside he took one more glance around then muttered to himself, "Yeah but lightning is usually followed by thunder."

He got in the car, and Sal drove them back towards the pool hall. He stopped for a moment and got two coffees for them at a Wilson Farms drug store. As the two of them entered Wizeguyz, Alex Vaughn was beginning to hate the place. Here he was, searching for his friend's killer but he hadn't seen much of anything except the inside of this two-bit joint.

The haze in the hall bit at his nostrils and his already weary eyes felt the burn as the smoke turned his eyes a bloodshot red. The doors of Wizeguyz swung shut behind them and a table full of punks who were playing cards stood up and started walking toward the duo. They muttered curses and fanned out.

A sharp word from Aldo in the back stopped the youngsters in their tracks and they sat down again to finish their game. One of the kids, who grew a black mustache and wore a black beanie, never took his eyes off the two of them as he attempted to posture himself as a hardass. Maybe that was why he wore a thick gold chain around his thin neck. Compensating.

"Man, I'd love to break his face in two," Sal said.

"You know it," Victor said to appease his comrade.

Aldo Marano shuffled his way up to Sal. "Things are getting a little hectic. We still haven't heard from Sonne. We need to talk to you in the back." He glanced over at Garducci and with a wave of his hand dismissed him. "Vic, go sit down and get some coffee for God's sake. You look terrible." He didn't even notice the coffee already in his hand.

"Yeah, sure thing. Where are Jimmy Jacks and Tom?"

"What's with all the questions? They're in the back." Aldo looked over at the teeny boppers playing cards and snapped, "Hey Mikey, go and get Jimmy and the Irishman out of the back."

The thug with a staring problem put his cards down and walked past Sal as if he had something to prove. He brushed past giving a slight bump to the street veteran. Sal dropped his left hand towards his coat pocket as an angry cloud sifted through his already strung out gaze. Aldo touched Sal's arm, snapping him out of it, and led him towards the back of the billiards hall.

Tom Coughlin came strutting out of the kitchen followed by Lil' Mikey and Jimmy, who wore a confused look on his face as always. Tom walked straight over to Victor.

"Hey Vic. Me and Jimmy are gonna go and run a few errands. Sorry but we will catch up with you when we get back."

"Why don't we bring Victor with us?" Jimmy asked.

"Jesus Christ you fucking bastard, if you didn't have the luck I'm supposed to have, I'd knock your head off." Then, as if catching himself he muttered, "Besides Victor wouldn't want to run our boring errands. Let's get going."

"Well, maybe next time Victor," Tom said.

"Yeah, maybe next time Vic. Come on Tom, let's get out of here." Jimmy gave Garducci a smile that said he didn't care about all of Tom's threats or his desire for secrecy.

Tom Coughlin led Jimmy out the doors. Just before the doors closed, Victor saw Jimmy kick at Tom's heels and send him stumbling forward. The large wooden doors shut behind them but Victor Garducci could still hear Coughlin yelling at Jimmy as his larger counterpart laughed while they wandered out of ear shot.

Victor Garducci found himself standing alone in the bar. Tweedle Dee and Tweedle Dum left, the punks were playing cards, and Sal was busy in the back.

He glanced around, and then jumped at the opportunity. He walked out the doors, pulling his collar up around his neck. With a brisk gait, he crossed the street and grabbed the brass handle of a tiny shop situated in-between two large buildings. Victor Garducci stepped inside letting the door swing shut behind him. As the door slammed, a sign suctioned onto the dirty door window clanged against the glass.

Just before Garducci slipped inside he saw Tom Coughlin's lime green sedan inching along the road with Jimmy in the passenger seat picking at his teeth with a gnarled fingernail. Tom squinted at Victor as he drifted past. With his customary grunt, Tom pushed the gas and let his tires squeal in protest as he sped around the corner.

The door swung behind Victor slamming a sign suctioned on the window as it closed. It read, "Inhaled Imports. Open for Business."

Chapter 11

Rontego shifted in his chair as he sat facing the Don and his consigliore, The Pope. He always hated interrogations; they reminded him of talking to cops. Don Ciancetta was rattling on about how pissed he was at Falzone for making this move against him by trying to eliminate Rontego. The wily old man succeeded against several of the Don's other, less fortunate hitters.

Rafael wasn't listening much. The Don was known for going on these tirades and the assassin didn't care much for all the drama.

Tell me who to hit, tell me where, and tell me who is winning so I know whose side to pick, he thought as a thin grin escaped his lips.

He started playing with the decorative buttons that lined the leather chair in which he was reclining. He couldn't help but notice his chair's lower stature than the Don's. Just like Ciancetta to convince people of the power of his position through illusion, through perception manipulation. In reality, for all the power that those like the Don appeared to wield, that very power was the illusion that was perched as precarious as a house of cards.

Rontego saw several bosses, all as untouchable as the Don, go down in a hail of gunfire, or by the smashing of a judge's gavel.

Rafael Rontego snapped to attention as Don Ciancetta slammed his fist on his desk as he was emphasizing some point or another. It sent a case of chocolates across the room and squished the chocolates against the wall. Red cherry dripped down the wall as the crumpled chocolates revealed their insides.

"So you were able to whack all three," Christian asked.

He was still in a bit of disbelief over the whole thing. The Pope stifled back a cough and his face went red from the buildup behind his eyes. Their release was through a bit of moisture that leaked out of them, as they strained to remain inside his skull.

"Yeah. And one was the lil' Pieri kid."

"Are you sure it was Sonne?" The Don's voice was on edge and he got so loud when he was frazzled Rontego wanted to tell the bastard to quiet the fuck down. "'Cause a few of Falzone's crew look a lot like that snot-nosed punk."

"You better be sure Rafael."

Even though The Pope was now getting on his case, Rontego didn't mind the double team. The Pope was an information glutton and he didn't make a move without knowing all his facts.

Rafael was tired of the inquisition though. He stood up and paused a moment, letting his hand slide into his coat pocket. He fumbled around inside the crease until his hand touched what it was looking for. It was cold. Icy cold. And the frozen conditions outside only helped it in that regard. Rontego pulled it out of his pocket and threw it on the Don's desk.

The sudden motion made The Pope leap up from his seat and caused the Don to freeze like a deer in the headlights. A checkered handkerchief lay bundled up in front of Ciancetta. The Don unraveled the cloth and let his gaze linger for a moment as his consigliore came over to see the item. After a moment, Rontego held his hand out. With a little laugh, Ciancetta returned it to the assassin who slipped it back into his pocket.

"Jesus Christ." Christian sat down, contemplating what he'd just seen.

"Don't blaspheme, Chris. I'm Rafael Rontego and don't you, either of you, forget it."

The Don and Christian glanced at each other. Rafael was satisfied to see that this time The Pope's cough rang out in a mucus-filled hack. In more peaceful times, the Don might have the balls to admonish Rafael's tone. But with a moment of wisdom, the old man decided to let this one pass.

"So what will you do now?" Ciancetta asked as he folded his hands on the desk and leaned forward. Back to business.

"Since they want war, what do you think of Rafael delivering a little message to our friends over at Wizeguyz?"

It was a decent suggestion, but still Rafael hated how The Pope put other people in a position where *they* were the ones who would have to pray.

"What do you have in mind?" purred the assassin.

*

The doors to Rumors flew open and Rontego stepped out onto the street. He grabbed the crease of his fedora and placed it onto his head. The assassin took a deep breath and felt the cool air enter his lungs. He let the breath hang for a moment as his body warmed it up, and then let it trail out in a wisp of smoke.

His hand reached inside of his Armani and he pulled out the creased *Buffalo News*. As he stood there, a curious moment overtook him and he unfolded the front page. There was a headline there which caught his attention though it didn't startle the hit man. "Search Ongoing for Cop Killer," it read.

He scanned the page again and saw nothing about gangland warfare. That is always a good sign. As for the dead cop, well no one would ever solve that one. After all, who cared about a dirty dead cop? Tough luck kid, next time pick your friends better.

"Too bad there won't be a next time," he muttered.

The assassin tossed the paper in the trash as he walked down the street. He hoped there would be a next time for him. What the Don and The Pope wanted him to do was nothing short of suicide for most men.

"But I'm Rafael Rontego, remember that," he said aloud as he quickened his pace.

I am Rafael Rontego, he thought again, and that thought comforted him.

Chapter 12

The clerk looked up from his magazine and for a moment, Victor felt as if he was unmasked. Alex Vaughn crept from the recesses of Victor Garducci as his sixth sense became heightened and more aware of the situation in which he immersed himself. His pulse was racing so fast that he could hear his own heartbeat throbbing in his ears, he could feel it pulsating along his neck and his temples were knocking from the inside out in perfect rhythm.

His hand remained steady. He fought the instinct to turn around and walk out.

People buy cigarettes every day, he thought to himself.

After a calming breath and a mental count to three, Victor Garducci shook the cold off of his shoulders and started walking the aisles of the little smoke shop. Bongs and pipes of blown glass lined one wall while their loose tobacco counterparts hung on shelves behind the clerk's counter up front.

This place was a lung cancer breeding ground. He walked along the aisle pretending to admire the craftsmanship of the various glassware, but in reality Victor was buying time. He tried so hard just to get to Inhaled Imports that he never came up with a plan for once he was inside.

It was not as simple as asking who smokes Sobranie cigarettes. This clerk, so close to the mafia den, had to be on the payroll of the shadier elements across the street. It would be different if Alex Vaughn could come in and strut around like he owned the place. It was amazing what a badge could do to get people talking.

But he was Victor now and as such, the rules were different.

Quit stalling, he told himself. *You know what to*

do, do what you always do and wing it.

Victor walked up to the counter and pulled his folded twenties out of his pocket.

"Whatcha want?" The kid never looked up from his magazine. He couldn't have seemed more disinterested if he tried. Victor admonished himself for getting so worked up. He slid a bill across the counter towards the clerk who was still reading his tabloid.

"I'll take a pack of Sobranies."

Garducci eyed the kid. He was waiting for any type of reaction, any hint that what he said registered on some level or another.

The clerk, eyes still glued to the article he was engrossed in, reached up and pulled down a black pack of cigarettes. The design on front was delicate and emblazoned in a regal gold set against the blackness. The clerk handed him the box and started counting his change.

At least he had to put the magazine down to handle the money, Garducci noted with a bit of satisfaction. This didn't seem like it was going to be as easy as he thought. Victor didn't know what he expected, but the kid wasn't going to just offer up who in the town smoked the cigarettes.

Victor scoured his brain for a way to break the ice, to get something, anything, out of this silent clerk. Who did he think he was anyway? Didn't anyone these days know about customer service with a smile? Damn kids. He didn't know much but he did know that he would never let his daughter date a slacker like this. If she did she would have a lot of questions to answer...

Focus!, he told himself.

What would Jack do in a situation like this? Alex Vaughn thought back to when Jack made a stunning breakthrough in a case when he interrogated the lone witness in a murder his first year as a detective. What was it he said he did? Damn, if he could just remember.

Then, in an instant, it hit him. Jack's smiling face while Alex pleaded with him for the secret to garnering the precious information.

"You know what it is Alex? I just kept him talking. People love to hear themselves talk. So whatever you do, get them talking and keep them talking."

"I'm surprised you had these. I haven't been able to find 'em anywhere." The clerk handed Victor the change. Victor laid the cigarettes on the magazine and started folding his extra bills while the clerk eyed him up.

"Yeah, not too many people have them."

It wasn't what he said as much as how he said it. The slight roll of the eyes. The heavy sigh afterwards, as if having to talk to Victor was a huge burden to have to shoulder.

The clerk was a little irritated at having to interact with Victor. If Victor wasn't trying to keep a low profile he would drag that clerk over the counter and put a boot on his throat. Instead though, Garducci remained calm and acted as though he were unfazed.

"I don't know why, they are great cigarettes."

Garducci creased another bill. He needed to get this kid interested. If he needed to irritate him to death, he would.

Victor put his money in his pocket. As the kid went to grab the paper though, Victor pulled it towards himself and pretended to be reading it, as if he were interested in the four armed woman from Vermont who breast fed all six of her children at the same time.

And that's when it happened. The kid got irritated and gave Alex Vaughn the golden opening he looked for.

"Maybe because there are like two of you in the city that actually smoke the damned things. I don't even know why we stock them."

He was trying to piss Victor off. But Garducci was too excited inside to let it faze him.

110

"Oh yeah, who else? I bet he has great taste. I'd love to shake his hand."

Victor laughed it off as if it was a joke but he was hoping the kid would keep talking. He was not disappointed.

"I seriously doubt that, dude. The guy is creepy. Even the guys across the street steer clear of him. They say he is 'badder than LeRoy Brown'."

Victor laughed again. "No one is that bad. Who are we talking about? I want to stay out of his way."

The clerk shrugged his shoulders. "Hell if I know, man. But he goes over to Wizeguyz a lot and no one ever fucks with him."

Victor decided he obtained as much information as he could out of the clerk. With a nod of his head, Garducci walked out. The cool air swirled about him but he didn't notice.

Although the visit at Inhaled Imports yielded little of real substance, he did affirm the fact that if he found the guy that smoked Sobranies, he was well on his way to finding Jack's killer. That left few to choose from and if this guy was as tough as the clerk seemed to think he was, then the hunt would be quick.

Victor looked down at the black pack of cigarettes in his palm. He didn't even smoke. Garducci stashed the cigarettes inside his coat pocket and pulled his arms around his chest as the biting cold sneaked in underneath his collar. A shiver found its way along his neck and sent a chill along his back. Midday was ending and the weather was starting to take a turn for the worse.

*

Rafael Rontego was walking pretty damn fast. He knew that if he stopped to think about what he was doing he just might bail on the situation. It wasn't that he didn't think about the best way of accomplishing this new task, it was just that the scenario for success was a little different than the professional jobs the assassin was used to.

Things were getting a little too messy for Rontego. The Pope said that Rafael wouldn't be killed.

"No one kills a messenger, Rafael. Why? 'Cause sooner or later everyone needs to send a message. Deliver ours."

Rontego knew that although he was a valuable commodity to Ciancetta's crew, he was still just that—a commodity. He was a pawn in a very real, very high stakes game of chess. Well, maybe not a pawn, but no better than a knight.

Still, he would rather that be the case than to be the king. Every piece on the board wants a chance to take out the king.

So the Don and Christian wanted a message to be sent, so be it. Rafael felt into his pocket as he ran through the crosswalk just in time to dodge a little minivan in a big hurry. Seemed like everyone was in a rush today. The van careened around the corner missing another pedestrian by mere feet, and then disappeared out of sight.

Rafael Rontego dismissed the van as he felt the cool item in his pocket. Rafael smiled. He was getting close now. It was time to stop for a minute and make sure he was prepared. He darted into an alley and began a check of his inventory.

He leaned against the brick wall of the alley. Heart racing. Out of breath. He unbuttoned the shoulder holsters containing his silenced pistols. Access would need to be easy.

It was cold out, but he was hot. The sweat on his neck embellished the cold around him, but told of the warmth coming from his nervous system's response. His palms, dry. His gaze, unflinching. The grayness of his eyes matched the weather that was coming in from across the

Canadian border.

Rontego faced the wall and switched the safety off of his pistols. He paused a moment, looking down on the twin set of dice engraved onto the butt of his pistols. Rontego was never one to believe in fate. He believed in carving your own destiny, it mattered not that he had to carve his into the souls of other men. God and fate seemed to often intertwine themselves into Rafael's line of work.

Well, maybe it wasn't the line of work so much as it was Rontego. The social values in which he was surrounded, coupled with the likelihood of, at the very best, an indifferent God, led to Rafael's choice in decoration of his equalizers. He had been dealt snake eyes from birth.

But Fate? Fortune? Or was it calculated risk? Fortune was never achieved without risk. Fate—the whole concept was the one of the three which could be tossed to the wayside and still allow the other two to flourish.

Click. Just like that, and Rontego was ready.

He slipped around the corner of the alley and walked towards his target. As he crossed the street off the busy midday traffic, he looked neither left nor right. His focus was his target. He walked straight towards those ugly green doors. He walked quick and his face was stoic, for once he entered Wizeguyz, the die will have been cast and fate would take over. What a rush. The gamble of a lifetime.

Chapter 13

Victor Garducci paused for a moment outside of Inhaled Imports to collect his thoughts. He already deduced a few things about his prey over the course of the last couple days. He leaned against the wall of Inhaled Imports.

First of all, he knew that whoever Jack's killer was, he was quick on the draw. Jack hadn't even pulled his gun against his assailant in a situation where he knew there was imminent danger. Thus he was on high alert, and still never had time to react.

The murderer, whoever he was, also enjoyed a reputation among the goodfellas on the street of being a hard ass. Yet, for some reason the clerk right across the street didn't seem to know his name. That meant either the clerk was oblivious, or the guy was smart enough to keep a low profile. A heavy handed gangster without the braggart ego was a hard thing to find these days.

Victor snapped his head up as he saw an old white minivan squeal around the corner and speed about half a block past Wizeguyz and into a parallel parking spot.

Idiots.

It seemed people were always in a rush to get nowhere.

Perhaps it was a gangster in the old school tradition. Then again, it could be a foreigner. That would explain the peculiar choice of Russian brand cigarettes.

Was the mafia employing Russian hit men to kill cops in Buffalo? No, that didn't seem right. The Italians were proud of their blood lines. There is no way they would have a Russian latching on to one of their outfits.

Besides, the Russians and the Italians had bad blood of their own. It was pretty much common knowledge among the organized crime units that the brief Russian exploration into Buffalo was snuffed out in the early 80's. They had to settle for the less glamorous situation across the border.

However, there were some recent footholds as of late established by the Russians as near as Rochester, just a quick car ride down I-90. There was no way the two sides would be cooperating. Not in the risky endeavor of cop killing. Besides, Jack would have said something if he was in a situation that crossed Mafia bloodlines.

Alex Vaughn knew he was missing something. He was close, but not close enough. He knew that this wasn't a situation that would require a lot in the way of detective skills. Like most infiltration operations, the key would be to remain undiscovered for as long as possible. The hard part was always gaining acceptance.

Alex glanced down the block towards the van. It looked familiar somehow. His mind already scattered, he dismissed the van.

Stay with it Alex, this is a mission of vengeance in the name of justice, he thought.

He liked how that sounded. Justifiable vengeance.

He refocused on the evidence he gathered so far. He was already *in* with the organization, but as much as patience was required, he didn't have the time to play the waiting game. Unless something happened soon, something big, he would be forced to push things, an act that got undercover cops killed. With half a dozen operatives such as Jack being on the wrong side of dirt-covered coffins, this was no time to get revealed before he could accomplish his task.

He pushed his back against the wall, giving himself enough of a push to stand upright. The van was sitting there with the engine still on and he wanted to get a better look at what the inhabitants might be doing.

He shivered again. His hands were getting cold, and the chill of the wind kept biting at his neck. Alex hunched his shoulders and snapped his collar up to shield himself from the harsh Buffalo winds riding the freeze of the Niagara River right through the city streets and across his exposed neck.

He walked steadily, looking at the ground as he contemplated what unfolded and the many different ways the situation might continue to develop. He kicked a rock that'd been thrown up onto the sidewalk by passing cars as he ambled by the building at the end of the block.

Shit.

The light at the crosswalk was about to switch from the 'walk' sign to that always annoying hand indicating 'stop'.

Vaughn picked up his pace so that he could get to the other block parallel to Wizeguyz. As he darted towards the crosswalk, another pedestrian was heading perpendicular to him. Alex never even saw him. The stranger clipped him and with a grunt, kept walking. He was in a hurry, too.

Alex stood there a moment to catch his balance. He glanced over at the pedestrian, but he was already halfway across the street. For some reason, the brass set of balls on this guy bothered him. It couldn't go without some sort of notice.

"Nice going asshole." The guy stopped walking as the sound of Alex's voice carried over to him. "Next time watch where you're walking!"

The guy paused, his back still to Alex. He hesitated as if he wanted to say something, and then continued on his way across the street.

Figures, Alex thought.

Seemed like everyone was in a hurry these days. Vaughn walked across the street and was about five paces from the minivan parked across from Wizeguyz. That was when he noticed the path of the stranger who knocked into him just a few moments earlier. The man was heading towards Wizeguyz.

Curious now, Alex slowed down to a stop and leaned against the side of the minivan. He peered around the back of it and watched as the man stood for a moment in front of Wizeguyz.

Who was this guy? Was he one of Falzone's crew? Was he a player in the war that was going on?

Alex hoped that if he *was* a player, he wouldn't remember the guy's face who yelled at him from across the street. That could present some real problems later.

Alex squinted. He wanted to get a look at the man's face. The hat on his head obscured his view though as the man was looking down at his pocket.

What is this guy fumbling with, Alex wondered.

The man was still standing there. He was motionless now.

Alex started to creep between the rear of the minivan and the adjacent car parked behind it.

If I can get a better look, I might be able to place this guy, Vaughn mused as he crouched between the automobiles.

The man lifted his head up and started to turn around.

Here we go buddy. Just a little bit more…. Alex begged the man to show himself.

All at once the van doors in the rear opened up. The front one blocked Alex's view of Wizeguyz and the rear one cut off Alex's escape.

Vaughn peered into the van and what he saw startled him. There were four masked men, two of which reached out to grab Alex. There was one way out. Vaughn grabbed the hood of the car behind the van and leaped from his crouched position as hard as his legs could catapult him.

It was too late.

The dual sets of hands from his kidnappers held him just firm enough that his momentum carried him forward, instead of up, blasting his head into the hood of the car rather than up and over. The pain was quick, but it was searing.

He stood up. His forehead felt warm as he faced his enemies. Vaughn reached for his pistol, but his arms didn't move. He stumbled forward towards the waiting arms of the masked men who helped his descent into the van. Alex knew this feeling. His peripheral vision dimmed and blackness threatened to overtake him. He was laying on his back now. He looked up as several of the masked men leaned over him.

"Damn it," one of them said. "I hope no one saw us."

Alex fought against the blackout and for a moment the blackness lifted. Then, all at once, it came back with a vengeance.

"C'mon let's get out of here," another of the masked enemies yelled.

Vaughn tried to lift his head up to push away the impending oblivion. It was a bad idea. The blood rushing to his wound coupled with his distraught equilibrium sent the blackness spiraling as it overtook him. For the first time in a while he wished he were home. He thought of his daughter as the unknown and the oblivion overtook him.

*

Rontego heard the words despite the swirling wind echo in his ears. He didn't like it. He stopped dead in his tracks when his mind interpreted what was said.

"Nice going, asshole."

Who the hell would speak to him that way in this town? In his town? Everybody this side of Route 5 and in all five major families knew the reputation of Rafael Rontego.

Nice going, asshole.

It raked on his every last nerve. He stopped but he didn't turn around. A civilian would talk to him like that. No time to deal with civilians, though, he was in the middle of a war zone.

The guy said something else, but Rontego continued walking. He was lucky he couldn't make it out in the wind. He was also lucky that Rafael had a mission on his mind.

The assassin walked across the street. It was almost the time of reckoning and he needed to clear his head. Why couldn't he get it out of his head what that guy said to him? Maybe it was something in his tone that crawled under his skin. He didn't sound like a civilian to the hardened street warrior. He shook his head. Let it go. Do what is needed and get out.

Rafael eased up in front of the doors of Wizeguyz. Putrid green. He disliked the place. He disliked even more the little punks that worked for Falzone. The place seemed to attract the younger gang-minded kids. The macho punks who had no clue about the old school values upon which "this thing of ours" was created.

Old Joe Falzone deemed it necessary to recruit the youth in order to sustain his numbers. Besides a wrangling for power, this was a big thing that separated Ciancetta from his underboss in times past.

Ciancetta liked the old traditions. He recruited from overseas. More than half a dozen of his best spoke more Italian than English. Outside of Muro, Aldo and that weasel fuck Sal; none of Falzone's crew grew up immersed in the old ways.

Perhaps that was what Falzone liked, seeing as how these punks were anxious to prove themselves. They would use a gun to do it, too. Though that concept didn't rub Rafael the wrong way, he did prefer controlled chaos. The last thing he wanted to have happen was some punk, for no rhyme or reason, lodging lead in his spine because he felt the trophy kill would be too much to pass up.

Rontego took a deep breath. It centered him. He had to survive the now in order to worry about the future. But damn if his nerves didn't seem to be showing up today. Maybe he was tired.

Rontego pushed his hands into his pocket and let his fingers search around for the familiar feel of stiff cardboard. There they were. He was going to need this in the moments that were sure to follow. The assassin started to pull out the packed Sobranie cigarettes when he felt the odd sensation overcome him that he was being watched. He paused for a moment.

He snapped his head around. He scanned the sidewalk peering beneath the rim of his fedora. No one was there. He scanned the cars parked along the side of the road. Nothing. He looked back at the door.

Enough stalling, he told himself.

With a flourish, the hit man popped a sturdy Sobranie between his lips and struck a match. Smoke enveloped him and spread into his lungs, calming his nerves. The moment of truth was upon him.

Looking at the ground he pulled the door open and slipped inside. Once inside the assassin pulled out his twin set of silenced pistols and looked into the smoke-filled room he'd seen many times before.

Chapter 14

He was lying on the left side of his face and it was numb. The lack of feeling was in stark contrast to the warmth spreading across his right eye, along the jaw line and toward his neck. Alex opened his eyes and let out a moan. He discovered the source of the warmth on his face as a blinding light striking his still slumbering eyes. Sunlight poured through a set of blinds in a direct path to his cornea, penetrating deep into his pupils as they adjusted to the illumination.

Though blinded, he could hear seagull's faint cries in the distance. Louder, but still quiet, he heard the sound of waves coming to a crash on a beach.

Vaughn rolled over, away from the thin trail of beaming light. His vision cleared and he took note of his surroundings. He sat up.

The room was small and felt like home. He was on a red cloth couch; the upholstery had a bad flower pattern that did nothing to fit in with the rest of the room. Wood flooring trailed out from underneath the ugly, yet familiar, couch. A recliner was to his left and an ottoman sat as sentry nearby. The leather was ruffled.

Alex placed his hand on the seat. It was still warm. Someone sat here moments before. He followed the dark wooden flooring until it came to rest at a modern kitchen. Marble tiles lined up against one another across the breadth of the room until they disappeared at the foot of a carpeted staircase. The countertop cut along the back of the kitchen following the wall in a half rectangle. It too was made of marble. Above the sink, there was a window which was opened upward.

Alex walked to the window and rested his hands on cool countertop. He peered outside. The sun was just beginning to descend on the horizon and its rays sent a multitude of colors streaking across wisps of clouds. The brilliance of the sky was reflected and magnified by the sea below as light shimmered, brightened, and disappeared in cohesion with the rolling waves. When there was a lull in the cycle of waves, Alex couldn't tell where the shining sea ended and the white sand of the beach began.

It was a thing of beauty that Vaughn knew could never last. The perfect alignment of sun, weather, waves and cooling breeze occurred for ten minutes a day several times a year.

Alex opened up the sliding door next to the kitchen and stepped out onto the wooden deck, its warmth absorbed into Alex's toes. A breeze stretched comforting fingers against his face. As he breathed in the salty sea air, he realized he knew this place. He couldn't quite place it but he knew he'd been here before.

He heard a quiet shuffling behind him. Alex knew that he had nothing to fear here. He turned around and saw what he expected to see. Charlotte came through the doorway and onto the deck. She was wearing a pair of black suede pants that hugged her waist and came about three-quarters of the way down her leg before they loosened and flew with the breeze sweeping onto the deck. Her belly button was showing beneath a tiny white tank top that didn't try to hide her natural curves and her dark auburn hair fell against her tan shoulders with a gentle elegance. Her soft features were accentuated by her full lips that pulled taut when she smiled. Her brown eyes danced and her bare feet completed the beautiful, relaxed look.

Charlotte, his wife.

She walked up next to him and gazed at the scene playing off of the sea, taking it all in.

Despite the strokes of God's paintbrush laid out before him, Alex's gaze was immediately drawn down to that which she carried. He parted the pink cotton blanket and saw her laying there.

Precious Ella.

Her eyes were closed, squeezing out the bright light allowed in by this intruder. Vaughn didn't care; he wanted to gaze on her. Her soft cheeks reflected the pink of the blanket and her nose crunched up in dismay as his baby girl thought about crying.

Alex put his finger against her tiny palm. Her tiny fingers clenched shut on his index finger barely able to grasp this smallest part of the giant.

Her giant, Alex reminded himself.

Charlotte smiled as she looked over at father and daughter. But as she watched him marvel, her smile faded and her eyes slowed, and then all together stopped their dance.

"You're going to miss so much," she said in a whisper.

Alex took the bite of the remark square on his heart but he dared not show the breadth of the damage caused by her words.

Instead, he fumbled out a reply, half true, half in token response, "I wish I weren't going."

Charlotte's eyes lit up at the opportunity of the statement. "Then don't go," she said. "You don't have to go, just tell them your situation has changed. Look, you have a baby daughter now!"

As if to emphasize the point she held Ella up in her arms and made a bouncing motion that tore at every string of Alex's heart.

So, just for the night, just to make Charlotte smile, he lied.

"Ok, love. I'll stay."

He looked deep into her eyes. She searched his face, hesitant to accept his words. The clouds descended into darkness behind her. Alex's heart began to race. The darkness consumed them both and a sudden flash of lightning illuminated Charlotte and Ella's silhouettes.

"I'm so glad you're staying Alex," she whispered. His name echoed in the darkness. "Alex."

Alex.

"Wake up Alex!"

Alex tried to open his eyes. He was lying on the left side of his face and it was numb. The lack of feeling was in stark contrast to the warmth spreading across his right eye, along the jaw line and toward his neck. Alex opened his eyes and let out a moan. He discovered the source of the warmth on his face as his hand wiped across his forehead revealing the all too familiar sight of his own blood.

*

There was a moment where everything in the Universe paused. Rafael took everything in. Twin pistols at the ready he scanned the room, taking advantage of Father Time's courtesy. Several tough-looking kids were playing a game of cards near the center of the room.

Probably fresh meat, Rafael thought.

Past the kids, in the back of the room, sitting at a booth were the patrons Rafael came to see. Aldo, frail and old as ever, was sitting across from the ox of a man that Rafael once called 'mentor.' Muro locked eyes with Rafael for a moment.

Rontego never flinched; instead he drew a slow steady breath through his Sobranie. The black paper flared and came to a crackling burn that told the assassin Time was again on track. He reached into his pocket as he drew in the smoke and pulled the pawn from his pocket. In one swift motion he threw it in the air to Muro. Muro looked like he was going to let it hit him square in the face, when he snapped a hand up and caught the pawn in his fist.

Pandemonium.

Three of the youngsters at the table stood up,

pushing back from the wooden slab. The fourth one, wearing a black beanie and sporting an ill-advised mustache, sat still. His eyes widened like saucers and he started to bend to his side. Rontego didn't have time to worry about reacting to what these kids might do.

Instead, he took two steps towards the group and then sidestepped into a spin, his coat twirled behind him. It caught two bullets from the quickest of the kids.

Rafael's eyes centered on the gangbanger closest to him. This one liked to eat. Twice the size of the assassin, he was fumbling for his gun, lodged in his waist band.

Kids, scoffed Rontego.

When were they going to learn that packing heat wasn't for fashion? Guns weren't accessories like their bling.

Rontego took two more steps toward the large youth and the juvenile gave up on his search for his weapon. He raised his fists and stepped toward the assassin. The goal was easy to discern. He hoped to squash Rontego's head with his meaty fists.

Not today, however.

Rafael took a pivot step into his adversary and raised the side of his pistol straight into the teeth of his charging assailant. A cloud of blood and teeth puffed into the air and the youth's fist forgot to find its target. His hands went to his face and covered what was left of his maw.

Eat this, fatty, Rontego quipped to himself.

A whistling sound sped past Rontego's ear and was followed a split second later by the bang of the pistol that sent the bullet close to Rafael's head. On instinct, the assassin crouched behind the writhing form of the large youth hunched over in pain. He needed some cover so he grabbed the largest thing in his area.

Coming out of his crouch, Rafael Rontego swung

his pistol upwards against the exposed face of his young sparring partner, lifting him upright with a scream. Rontego slid behind his injured enemy and brought one of his pistols to rest against the young man's head while bringing his other cannon to bear in the direction of the youth who shot up his nice coat.

When things are moving fast, one had only to slow the situation down, thought Rafael Rontego.

He took stock of the situation. Aldo was still sitting in the booth smoking a cigarette, but Muro was gone and the swinging doors of the kitchen advertised his escape route of choice.

There were more pressing issues though.

Besides the kid hiding behind the facial hair who had not left his chair, the other youngsters were on the move. They each drew their pistols and were moving out, one on either side of Rontego, away from the table at the center of the room. They were trying to flank the assassin.

Only one thing to do.

Rontego maneuvered his hefty and whimpering shelter toward the youth on the left exposing himself to the youth on his right. But with his right pistol placed against the back of the head of his cover, he leveled his other pistol at his unsure and inexperienced adversary to his right. The bullet shattered his knee.

The youth hit the deck like fly on a car window, his weapon falling from his grasp and sliding across the slick bar room floor. Simultaneously, the assassin kicked into the back of the fat youth's legs, dropping him to the floor and leaving his own body exposed.

The enemy on the assassin's left was quicker than the other youth. Several bullets left his gun, none of which found their mark.

The steady assassin took his time, took aim, and took off the youth's right shoulder blade, sending blood and pieces of clavicle against the wall behind the young man.

The man wailed as his fingers lost their strength and dropped his gun. He groaned as his legs failed him and dropped him to the floor, incapacitated. Rontego took a second to take out both of Falzone's soldiers.

He saw a movement out of the corner of his left eye.

The hairy bastard at the table, he realized.

Rontego swirled around pulling both pistols parallel to each other in front of his chest.

The youth discovering puberty had a butterfly knife with the blade pinched between his fingers, arm cocked back to throw. Rontego pulled the hammer of his pistols back generating the unmistakable warning click. The agonizing groans of the wounded continued behind him. The boy pulled up. When a rattlesnake hisses, you take notice.

"You a hero, boy?" Rontego hissed. "Please, be a hero."

The youth hesitated for a moment and then slammed his knife into the table in front of him. Arms up, he backed away.

Apparently, facial hair doesn't make a man, thought the assassin.

Rontego walked to the motionless Aldo. He hadn't moved except for the increasing ash of his cigarette. "Hello Rafael," the taut and weathered lips cracked. "Took you longer than I thought."

Chapter 15

Alex Vaughn was in a dimly lit room. A bed, a nightstand, a dresser, bad carpeting; a hotel room. It was nondescript, but Alex knew this place. It was a safe house used by the undercover units. Vaughn spent many nights here during that first year of narcotics duty.

He sat on the edge of the bed trying to shake the cobwebs out of his consciousness. Ryan Slate came out of the bathroom area and handed Alex a bag of ice.

"Sorry to startle you Alex, but the masks were necessary. None of us feel like getting made."

Alex pressed the ice to his throbbing head. He was still confused as to what was going on, but all things considered, he was happy it was his side who grabbed him out of the street. But why had they pulled him? Ricky Vincenzio or Ryan Slate rather, promised not to let it leak.

"Who are those guys," he asked, motioning to the other three men huddled and talking in whispers on the far side of the room.

One of the men, seeing that Alex was asking about them, walked over and extended a hand. Alex accepted the handshake. This was all way too confusing.

"They call me Elliot here."

"Nice to meet you Elliot."

Vaughn studied Elliot, his long sideburns and disheveled dark hair looked familiar to Alex. He knew he had seen this man before, but where, he couldn't tell. It wouldn't be uncommon in a city as large as Buffalo to come across another officer and not be acquainted. That was even more probable if they were in different divisions.

"Actually, Alex, Elliot isn't my real name. None of us here use our real names."

Alex's radar was going off. What was he into here?

"Well, I don't talk to people who know my name

but won't give me theirs." Alex stood up to leave but Slate grabbed his arm.

"Alex, there is a reason, just hear Elliot out."

Vaughn sat back down on the edge of the bed, as Elliot gave Ryan a glance and took a deep breath.

"First, let me introduce you to the other two. Granted, these are their operating names. This one is J.P. 'Hambone.'"

The larger of the two men, a real brute of a man with an obvious dislike of shaving tossed a wave Alex's way but remained where he was, posted up near the blinds with a view of the parking lot. This was a guy on edge. Judging by his corded frame and scarred left eye he was also a real bruiser. Alex recalled having met this guy several times throughout his career. He wasn't a bad sort, at least as far as Alex could tell. He used his sidearm before, and that was a bonus in the type of operation that Vaughn currently was undertaking.

"And this squirrely bastard is 'Hi- Def'; we call him that because he runs all the surveillance for our little unit. You see we're all badges in here."

Hi-Def was as skinny as Hambone was large. Although he was small, he was not nerdy looking. He was not decked out in glasses and he looked wirier than he did wimpy. There was a tuft of unkempt blonde hair perched atop his head. His ears came out in a prominent fashion. Even if they were not larger than average, juxtaposed as they were against his beady eyes, they loomed large.

He was also carrying various high end electronics. He wore a wireless earpiece for his cell phone and had a computer opened up on the hotel table. Various windows were open and music was humming from the speakers. It looked like something was uploading or downloading at the same time.

Alex leaned forward to get a better look out of curiosity, but Hi-Def locked the screen when he noticed

Vaughn trying to sneak a peek.

"Then why all the secrecy with names, and why am I not in cuffs? You guys gotta know I was not authorized to reestablish my cover."

Alex's curiosity was piqued at this development. It was also nice to deflect Hi-Def's slight glare with a new line of thought.

"Jack had more friends than just you," Hambone made a noise from the window.

Elliot pursed his lips in a half grimace, a bit of his pain at the mention of Jack's name flashed through.

"We all want to find whoever took Jack out. "

Alex looked around the room at these new friends of his. Some things were not adding up. Ricky Slate was fidgeting in the corner, and seemed lost in his own thoughts.

He was able to discern the need for fake names, after all, no one knew who the rat was that was getting cops killed. But some things needed immediate answering.

"Ok, if we are all here to get the guy that took down my best friend, why the hell did you grab me off the street? If anyone saw that, then I might as well walk away or shoot myself right now because going back under might be seriously fucked."

At that point, Hi-Def came over and pulled out a tiny digital recorder. "Because if we didn't keep an eye on you through this then you might have walked right into this mess," he said.

He could hear chairs in a room sliding around, followed by a shriek of pain and then the unmistakable retort of gunfire blasting out of the speakers. A voice whispered through the ensuing silence.

"You a hero, boy? Please, be a hero." A few moments later, footsteps were followed by another voice, older. "Hello Rafael. Took you longer than I thought."

Then there was static and finally silence again.

"Who is Rafael?" Alex had not heard of him.

"A ghost," Elliot interjected. "Everybody knows *of* him, but nobody knows *him*. We were closing in on getting a visual of him thanks to some work Ricky has done infiltrating Ciancetta's crew. Ricky, why don't you fill Alex in?"

Elliot sat down and began fidgeting with a small Zippo lighter. He would flick it, igniting a small flame and extinguish it with a flick of his wrist causing the lid to clamp shut around the heat.

Ricky shook off whatever was bothering him and flashed a mischievous grin. He started in on the conversation, as if on cue, with the eager hand waves that fit in with his Long Island accent.

"I don't know if it was something you said to your guys, Alex or if it's this war going on, but either way Joey Ciancetta has been opening up to me lately. He isn't that bad of a guy either, he just gets swept up into what his pops does. Anyway, we are over at his Dad's place, Rumors, and we're shooting a little pool. I can kick his ass at pool, but I always let him win. Fucking makes me sick to do that, I don't know why. Whatever. So he says to me that things are getting nuts. Apparently this war is heating up. He tells me this and that and says something about how a lot of hitters for Don Ciancetta are getting their tongues handed to them, and are disappearing on boating trips and showing up in meat lockers, if you catch my drift. Jesus, one guy all they found was an ear!"

Alex brought a hand up to his ear as Ricky went on.

"But there is this one old school gangster who is still kicking. He not only avoided a hit on him, but took out not one, not two, but three of the hitters in his own apartment. This guy is none other than our guy."

"Rafael," Alex interrupted.

Hambone let out a low whistle. "Every time I hear

it, I still don't believe it."

Ricky tossed them both a look and then continued. "So, anyway, this guy has been sent, solo, to go and deliver a message right into the den of Joe Falzone's crew at Wizeguyz. Once I heard that, I got on the horn with Elliot here, and we got the team together. Only thing was, we were too late and we saw you right outside of that place. That's when Elliot decided to make a move to grab you out of there. We didn't know how to get to you without exposing ourselves and then fortunately, you walked right over to us."

"That was because I thought I recognized the van, I just couldn't place it."

Alex was still a little unclear about why the van looked so familiar. It must be like every other surveillance van he has ever seen, unmarked and ugly.

Hi-Def hit a button on his computer, open again on the crude synthetic wood table the hotel provided. Another button later and the computer began to slide a photograph out of a side compartment. He handed a grainy photograph to Alex Vaughn.

"This is the one photograph anyone has been able to get of this guy."

Alex studied the color picture. It was grainy and the face was obscured by a fedora.

Useless, he thought. "Christ, you might have well shot it in black and white. How is it that this day and age we can't take a real picture of a known gangster?" Alex looked up from the photograph; he noticed a slight hint of offence creeping up on Hi-Def. "I mean, at least we have this one, but what's the story?"

"The problem is that this guy just crept up onto our radar. Frankly, it is a bit of an embarrassment. All of the 'family trees' constructed of these guys, and this guy never came up. Not once. That means two things. One, he is smart and two, he is smart. This guy has been right under our noses for over two decades."

Elliot was in awe and frustrated at the same time. It always seemed like guys in this line of work were torn between admiring the fantasy and clinging to their morality.

"What does any of this have to do with who killed Jack," Alex wondered out loud.

Elliot did that thing where he pressed his lips together again.

"Nothing. Maybe everything. From what Ricky told us, this guy Rafael is *known* by everyone. They call him "The Ghost" or "Il Fantasma" in Italian."

"So why are you telling me all of this?"

Vaughn was not against being part of a helping hand to this unit but he did not want to be bound to them either. After all, he was out for blood. He wanted to find the guy that killed Jack, and strike him down with the hand of justice. As he thought, he patted his pistol tucked in the small of his back.

"Listen, we all know your motivation to catch these guys is great. We just want to direct that energy to not only catch the guy that took Jack from us, but also to get deeper into the Ciancetta family. With Ricky in with Joey Ciancetta, and you in with the Falzone crew, we can break this thing wide open."

Elliot was getting excited as he spoke. No doubt promotions and medals were jumping around in that cranium of his.

"I won't wear a wire, if that is what you're asking."

Alex was no fool. Wires got people killed.

"Not asking that, just want you to keep those eyes open, let us know what you know. Anything big comes your way, toss us a line. You can get to me through a secure line at the department. I will authorize them to put you through to me."

"What is in this for me?" The idea of being a 'Johnny-on-the-Spot' did not sit well with Alex.

"For one, you won't be acting without authority."

They had him there. Alex nodded his head in agreement. It would be nice to be on the good guy's side again, on the official record anyway.

"Also, you get some help as far as actually investigating this case. You have just been running around and frankly, you're too deep in to get out and do real detective work. Things you think of but can't get to, call into Hi-Def and Hambone. They will be on standby to do some of the investigative aspects regarding Jack's death."

At first Alex was offended at the notion that he hadn't done enough investigating. But as he thought about it, he realized that Elliot was close to the mark. It took him days just to get to Inhaled Imports. Alex agreed to the terms. In fact, he liked them. He had his own 'Johnny-on-the-Spot', two of them. A nice turn of events.

"Good then." Elliot extended his hand which Alex Vaughn shook in mutual accord. "I have to get going, but stay a few minutes and get the numbers for the secure line from Hi-Def. I think this will work out nicely."

Hambone took a peek out of the blinds, and then motioned to Elliot it was clear to leave. Without hesitating, Elliot walked out of the room. Once he was gone, Hambone dead bolted the door and looked at Alex. "So, how do you propose we get the guy that killed my boy?"

Vaughn flashed an arrogant smile and sat down to get acquainted with his new crew.

*

Rafael Rontego stood in front of Aldo Marano; both of them looked at each other unblinking. The only sign of life between them was the slow burn of Aldo's cigarette and Rafael's Sobranie.

The assassin mused for a moment about this relic of a man. He was always old, as far back as Rontego could remember. The odd thing was he never aged. The white goatee he wore was in stark contrast to his brown and weathered face. He didn't seem like much. A single punch to his face seemed like it would disintegrate him, sending him back to the dust from whence he came.

Rontego was scared of no man, so it must have been respect that stayed his hand. Respect or common sense. The connections that Aldo Marano had were strong and deep. The moment passed, and Rontego broke the silence.

"Surprised to see me, *Uomo Anziano* Aldo?"

The assassin let loose a thin line of smoke as he talked. He waited for Aldo to speak.

The old man was in no hurry as he took a prolonged drag on his cigarette. When he spoke, it came out slow and with purpose.

"No, I think not, my old friend. To be surprised I would have been forced to underestimate you. I fully know what you are capable of doing. Tell me why you are here."

Rafael scoffed at the statement, "Do you not know? No, I think you do."

Aldo slammed his fists down onto the table with a force that belied is age. "So then, are you here to kill me?" he yelled. Anger rimmed his eyes and he stood up halfway, leaning over the table toward Rafael Rontego.

As he stood up, Rontego shifted his feet to blade the target, years of experience coming together. His pistol stood between the two of them, dice looking up at the assassin as the barrel tilted downward forty-five degrees between the two men.

"I am but a frail, old man. What good is it to you to see my death?"

Rontego, unfazed by the outburst, put his cigarette

out on the table in front of Aldo. "Frail in body, Marano. In body only. If I could unlock your brain from that ancient head of yours, you would already be dead. If I was here to kill you, I would not have spared them," Rafael motioned towards the youths behind him. "Nor would I have taken my time here with you any more than a hunter would take his time with a cornered fox."

"So you are not here to kill me. I am lucky then. Perhaps not as lucky as Sonne Pieri? Why are you here Angelo Della Morte?"

Aldo eased back down. He waved off the teen that was lurking in the background. Each of them was okay to let the matter between them and Rontego pass, as the uninjured one tended to his wounded compatriots.

Rafael almost smiled at the nickname "Angel of Death." As bad as it sounded, it was a sign of respect. Rontego took great pride in being able to strike fear into his enemies, but Aldo, just like Muro, was not always so. Aldo coined the phrase "Angelo Della Morte", in regards to Rafael after he did a hit for the old man at the beginning of his career. There was history here, but Aldo and Muro chose their side in this civil war.

"Listen careful Aldo. Don Ciancetta wants to have a sit down with Mr. Falzone. There has already been a lot of bloodshed. Something needs to be hammered out."

The assassin knew that it was useless to suggest a meeting between the two factions this late in the game. He had his orders though and he assumed that the advice of The Pope must be at play somewhere in all of this. Rontego felt that the pride of Ciancetta would never have allowed for the thought of anything but total annihilation of the enemy to enter his mind.

Aldo Marano must have had a similar thought, as he laughed. The old man's eyes twinkled in amusement at the statement. "Why does he think we would want to work out a deal with him? There is no ability to go back on what has happened, and we would not want to, Rafael. Or have you not noticed that we are winning this little war that Don Ciancetta perpetuates. Go back to your little boss and tell him that if he wants peace, all he has to do is step down. I am sure Falzone would allow Leo to retire peacefully." Aldo's voice was sarcastic and he developed an air of superiority that disturbed Rafael Rontego. He had the look of a man claiming checkmate.

Time to take him down a notch, Rontego thought.

Chapter 16

Marcus leaned over his wounded friend. Tony was bleeding from his shoulder and Marcus couldn't get it to stop. He glanced behind him and saw Aldo Marano talking, deep in conversation with the bastard who just shredded his buddy's shoulder. There was blood everywhere.

It wasn't that Marcus was scared of this guy, he told himself. Someone needed to make sure the wounded were tended to.

Fuck, Marcus thought.

Tony was shivering and looked pale. The blood was pooling around him now.

"Marcus, remember…remember when we were in ninth grade and we were in Ms. Salidina's class?" Tony was moving his legs from side to side and his lips were looking blue.

"Yeah Tony, I remember."

Marcus just wanted to keep him talking. If he was talking, he was alive. What he didn't know was that a fragment of bone separated itself from the torn clavicle and shot through Tony's lung. Each breath he took was drowning him. The question was whether he would bleed to death or drown first.

"Man, she was hot. I should have asked her out. I should of, I should of…."

Tony's voice trailed off into a gasp and his legs stopped moving. Marcus looked at his hands. There was blood all over them. A rage built upside of him and he looked back at the two men talking and then at the floor. He saw what he was looking for, a better weapon than his tiny blade.

There was Tony's pistol.

Marcus' face twisted onto the steel visage of resolve. He scooped up the pistol, saw his target, and began to sneak up on the man who murdered his friend. Marcus made a name for himself as of late anyway. Being a gun for Aldo and Muro had been life-altering.

*

Rontego dropped his back hand into the pocket of his coat.

"You would be wise to consider such a kind offer from the Don, lest you wind up like other adversaries of his."

As Rontego spoke he threw the contents of his pocket onto the table in front of Aldo. It was a waded handkerchief.

Aldo glanced at the cold stare of Rafael Rontego and then down at the handkerchief. His old hand reached forward and unfolded the unexpected package. As Aldo unwrapped it and the contents came into view, his face turned a shade of ashen grey and he paused.

There in his hand was the finger of Sonne Pieri. The family crest was still on the finger which turned pale with no blood to give it its normal color.

It took Aldo a moment to center himself. The air of superiority shifted to Rafael and he relished the moment. His grey eyes danced with the inner fire of victory. It was not every day that a mental victory could be claimed over Aldo Marano.

Then, just as fast as he was taken aback, Aldo regained his composure. Rafael could see the wheel turning in the old man's head. Aldo seemed to settle on some thought or another and then his lips curled upward into a knowing smile. A small laugh cracked forth from his weathered lips.

"Oh Rafael, you serve a small master and his victories are even smaller. So, you flaunt that you have killed a young man in our organization. Let me ask you,

Rafael Rontego, Angelo Della Morte," his voice was now dripping with sarcasm and Rontego did not like the nickname very much at all, "where do you suppose Don Ciancetta's other soldiers are? Why is it that you seem to be doing all the work alone? Do you suppose it is because you are the best? My dear Rontego, you are very good at what you do. So why is it that your boss would so misallocate his resources? Why are you here in this dangerous situation instead of some goat ripe for slaughter? Perhaps you are the only one left. Perhaps you know too much and your death would not be so greatly missed?"

Rontego gripped his pistol as the old man rambled. He wanted nothing more than to put a bullet in his brain and end his reign of mental domination. The assassin looked down at the finger sitting next to Aldo's glass of water. As he listened, he saw a slight flicker of movement in the glass. It seemed that one of the youths gathered up some nerve after all, during Aldo Marano's motivational speech.

Let him come.

The kid sporting the facial hair seemed to have grown a set of balls. He was stealthy. If Rafael had not seen him in the glass, the kid might have gotten the drop on him. It is amazing what someone's back to you can inspire.

"If only Muro and I collected trophies this week, we might be able to compare fingers with the great Rafael Rontego."

Aldo's eyes shifted to Rafael's left as he spoke and that was all the indication the assassin needed to turn and get the drop on his would-be ambusher.

The youth carried a pistol in his clenched hands. It was leveled at the back of Rontego's head. Rontego didn't hesitate as he whirled around. The youth did, however, as he did not expect Rafael to be aware of his intent. Marcus' eyes widened as he realized the miscalculation.

The skilled assassin swung his left hand around as

he spun, knocking Marcus' weapon from his grasp. Without slowing down his motion, Rontego's right hand followed through and up, smashing the butt of his pistol against the left side of Marcus' head.

Usually a hit like that would knock an opponent out at once. Instead, the youth seemed to roll with the hit, crashing sideways into a dive. It was Rafael Rontego's turn to register surprise as the youth flicked his switchblade out. It wasn't that this youth was still awake, though that was surprising enough, but the quickness with which he snapped his blade out and to the ready that troubled the assassin. This kid had some ability.

Chapter 17

Marcus shook the stars from his head and flipped his blade open. He was recovered now from the surprise of his failed ambush. More important, he was motivated by absolute anger at the death of his friend. He was going to taste the blood of this killer if it was the last thing he did.

Marcus sidestepped the barrel of the murderer's gun and caught the killer's arm between his body and his own arm. Marcus lifted his free arm up and smashed an elbow into the neck of his adversary. He was satisfied as he heard a gasp escape the man and was even happier when he heard his opponent's pistol drop to the floor.

Marcus released the man's weaponless arm and brought his blade towards the killer's throat. Perhaps this wouldn't be the last thing he did after all.

*

The assassin felt the full force of the blow on his neck and a gush of air escaped his throat. Through the pain, he realized that in these close quarters, his gun would be useless. Rafael dropped his piece to the floor.

Just as Rontego intended, the youth released his arm and went for his opportunity at the assassin's neck. Just in time, the assassin caught the blade-wielding hand at the forearm. This kid was strong. The blade inched closer to Rafael's neck as he backed against a pillar standing alone next to Aldo's booth.

The youngster brought his second hand up and pressed it against the tangled arms, using the leverage to gain an even greater strength advantage on the assassin. He wanted the kill.

It was the youth's ambition that was his undoing. He forgot about Rafael Rontego's free hand, which pulled a small blade of his own. At the last second, Rontego rolled to the side, sending his young opponent's head smashing into the pole behind the assassin.

Simultaneously, he slashed with his knife across the young man's chest and sidestepped the collision. He crashed to the floor, bleeding from a long diagonal gash stretching from his right shoulder down past the left side of his belly. The knockout blow to the forehead was a blessing in disguise. If he'd been awake, that gash would be the most searing pain he experienced in his short life. Rontego knew it.

Not short enough, thought the assassin as he walked toward his fallen victim.

He lifted his blade to finish the deed when he felt it. There was blood trickling from his neck.

Little bastard got closer than I thought, he mused.

The blood was trailing down his neck in a thin line and Rafael felt his knees getting weaker. Aldo was eyeing Rafael's gun on the floor at his feet. He went for the pistol but Rafael halted the old man in his tracks as he brought his second pistol to bear.

The assassin stumbled forward and scooped the hand cannon off of the floor, holstering it. His companion pistol still trained at Aldo, he offered a few parting words.

"Think long and hard about having a sit down. You think you know what I am capable of, but you have no idea old man."

With that, Rafael Rontego, still bleeding, walked through the back kitchen into the alley outside. His legs were getting weak as blood was still flowing unabated from his neck. He knew he was on borrowed time if he did not get some pressure on his wounded throat.

Moving fast, the assassin pulled out a set of keys. There was a safe house nearby.

Damn the daylight, he thought.

The last thing he needed was to get pinched. He lifted his collar up, hiding the bloody wound as best he could.   Then, without further delay, he half ran, half stumbled down the road.

Just a couple more blocks, feet don't fail me now. Rontego heard the remote sound of an ambulance down the road. The two blocks seemed like an eternity but he forced himself onward. The will to survive sustained him and he slammed into the door to the apartment building he used often as a hiding spot.

He unlocked the door and starting pulling himself up the three flights of stairs to his room. Blood was dripping down his pant leg now and leaving a speckled trail behind him. Then, as Rafael reached the fourth floor, he fell down, his legs abandoning him.

Rontego took his jacket off and pulled his shirt over his head.   Pressing the shirt against his wound, he forced himself to stand.   Stumbling forward, he fell towards his room and unlocked it. As the hit man fell inside, he tied the shirt around his neck. It was hard to breathe but at least it was tight. Rontego fell to the ground and rolled over on to his back. Mustering his last bit of strength, he kicked the door shut behind him and drifted into the familiar oblivion.

Chapter 18

Alex Vaughn shut the door to the hotel room behind him. The snow let up a bit and the sun was peeking through for a brief moment, making the day feel a bit warmer. The snow on the ground though, and the occasional gust of wind reminded Alex that it was still winter.

Vaughn thought about what just transpired in the hotel room behind him as he walked towards Wizeguyz. It was good to know that he had some allies. Alex had not realized it but he was feeling very much alone in all of this.

The plan for now was to go back to the pool hall and see what transpired. Alex asked Hi-Def why the recording went to static. There must have been some useful information missed due to the untimely end of the device. But Hi-Def told Alex that they did not even have a bug in the pool hall. They used a long distance microphone and once the van was out of range they lost the ability to eavesdrop on the conversation.

Hi-Def gave Alex the phone codes to the secure lines for each of the men in the unit along with a nifty radio transmitter that looked like a button on the sleeve of his jacket. He would be able to transmit to Hi-Def's laptop and he would get a notice on his Blackberry in real time as the message came in.

They also worked out a plan where Hambone and Hi-Def would be on the tail of either Alex or Ricky at various times. It would provide at least a measure of security for Alex who, up until now, had no backup. Ricky was going to go back to Joey Ciancetta's house and go to a wise guy party that night and see what he could discern.

All in all, Alex liked Hi-Def and Hambone. The two of them seemed genuine in their concern about getting some semblance of revenge for Jack and it didn't hurt that they were all still legitimately on the job.

Alex Vaughn noticed a telephone booth on his right as his thoughts rambled on and a sudden urge came over him. He stepped into the booth and pulled some coins from his pocket. Vaughn dialed the familiar number and waited as the phone rang. As it rang, he thought of Jack. On the day of Alex's wedding, Jack took Alex aside.

"Alex, how do you feel about Charlotte?" His face *was serious.*

"What do you mean?" Alex was startled by the *question.*

"Right now, right this second, what does she mean to you? Alex, it's not rocket science."

Alex composed himself. Thinking about it for half a moment, he knew exactly how he felt.

"I think she is my world. I can't remember a time before her and I don't think I want to think of a time without her."

"Good." Jack liked the answer. *"Now, no matter what happens in life, no matter what things get in the way, try and bottle how you feel right now, right this second. When something goes wrong, release the feeling you have bottled up and let it remind you of what she means to you."*

Jack flashed Alex a smile and walked to the mirror to fix his tie. He left Alex behind.

The phone rang one more time and then the voicemail picked up. It was Charlotte's voice. She waited a few months before removing Alex's name from the recording.

Alex thought about what Jack said, and he memorized what he wanted to say to Charlotte. He wanted to say how she meant the world to him, how he missed Ella, how he missed home. Alex was just about to reveal his feelings onto the therapeutic recording when Charlotte's tiny voice broke into the voicemail.

"Hello?"

Alex hung there for a second, petrified.

"Hello?" she asked again. "Alex, is it you?"

Alex froze and then did the only thing he could do. He hung up.

What if she had forgotten how she felt about me at that moment, he wondered.

He tried to shake his thoughts loose as he continued on his way towards Wizeguyz, but they kept creeping back to memories of his life before he became so immersed in the job that lost him everything. The life when he had a wife, a child, a best friend.

It wasn't even particular instances. It was flashes of bits of time. The thoughts came as a smile from Charlotte. They came as a laugh from Ella. The thoughts came as a general memory of things he may have done a thousand times or seen a thousand times but it was all summarized in one flash of memory. Jack in a booth drinking a beer. That memory summarized the dozens of bars they confided in. It summarized the hundreds of beers they shared. Alex shook his head as the memories assailed his consciousness.

"If only I could forget everything," he thought out loud.

A lady with a shopping cart walked past as he spoke. She cast a wary look at him as she pushed her pop cans along the sidewalk past Alex.

He pulled his jacket closer around him; he didn't notice her at all. The reminiscing wouldn't let him be. Though the sun shone on, the cold continued. The breeze bit at him and tore at his skin as the faded memories gained traction and became solid visions. The flashes came quicker now and became a full-fledged action movie in his mind.

He was alone in his thoughts and the visions whisked him away, far beyond the troubles and worries of that frigid Buffalo avenue.

He was alone. He was in *their* bed, but he was alone. He didn't know where she was. When he lay like this, she was under the crook of his arm. He would breathe on the back of her neck as her scent would come up to meet his nostrils. It was intoxicating at this hour in a way that always comforted him into a sound sleep. She was his magic elixir for all that ailed him after the hours, sometimes forty eight or more in a row on the streets.

Alex felt a dread that would not let sleep overtake him. He knew this feeling. It was a gentle ripping in his chest. It happened when they fought.

The adjoining bathroom was slightly ajar and Alex knew that she was in there. Her hand came through the doorway, and the rest of Charlotte followed. Even in her ferocity, she was beautiful. Alex couldn't remember why they were fighting, but he knew the outcome. The déjà vu would not release him. Alex knew that he had to try though. He sat up on the edge of the bed. His back was to her.

"Baby, will you come here please," he pleaded.

He heard her heavy sigh, but he also heard the soft padding of her feet coming to him across the carpet. Maybe there was hope.

"I know all of this is hard. But it's just you and me, love."

She was in front of him now. He put his hands around her hips and pulled her in. Placing his head against her belly, he glanced at her tear-streaked reflection in the mirror above the headboard.

"Alex, it isn't, though. It won't be ever again. Don't you see?"

Alex felt the lump in his own throat grow, but he would never let her see that.

"I know love, I know. But I mean right now. Can't you see that I love you? I always will. That has to count for something, right?"

148

Charlotte nodded her head in agreement, but the tears started squeezing out again.

"I just, I can't, Alex. Sometime, you have to start living for someone other than yourself. I can't stay here with Ella. You aren't any better than an absentee father."

"Don't do this Charlotte. I love her, I love you."

Alex saw this all happen before. He needed to keep trying though. There had to be a way to stop it before it happened.

If only I could just get her to stay the night.

She turned to leave. Alex grabbed her hand, tears were rimming his eyes. Frustration would no longer let him contain the raw emotion.

"Slow down baby. Please don't sell me out yet. Don't give up on me. Please, just don't give up on us. Come here, lie down for a while."

Charlotte looked into his eyes. Some part of her found the love that her own frustration was blocking. She crawled into the bed and lay her head down on the pillow facing away from Alex. Alex rolled to meet her and wrapped his arm over her slender form.

Soft tears fell down her face and rolled onto the pillow.

"I can't accept we're going nowhere."

Her words struck him right in the chest. Alex held her tight. He just wanted to be closer to her, to remember how they used to be. He kissed her cheek and wiped at the tears traveling along her tiny nose.

"I have to go Alex."

"Please, just one last time, let me hold you," he whispered.

After a moment's hesitation the soft reply, "Ok."

Alex got even closer and held on for all that she meant to him. She closed her eyes as he watched her. After several minutes, she fell asleep. Perhaps there was hope. The morning would lend a clearer mind to these situations.

Alex kissed her cheek. He fell asleep.

He awoke. Alex must have rolled away from her in his sleep. In a panic, he rolled back toward Charlotte. Before he even saw the empty space where she had lain, he knew the truth.

She was gone.

*

Alex stumbled forward, closing in on Wizeguyz. He was alone. His thoughts came back to the present and he reached the conclusion that perhaps he was destined to wander down the lonely road.

He was so stupid then, with Charlotte, so careless with what he had. What hit Alex hard was that he felt no wiser than the fool he was before. As he thought about these things, he realized that he reached his destination.

In front of him was Wizeguyz, and it was a bustle of activity. There was a heavyset, banged up youth standing outside of the pool hall. The fat kid looked dejected and by his bloody lip, the reason wasn't hard to discern. Tom Coughlin's car was pulled up diagonal to the front of the building. Half of the car was in the street while the rest was pulled up onto the sidewalk. Muro Lucano was walking towards the place with Sal Pieri and Frankie DeRisio in tow. Sal looked disturbed when he came up to the pool hall but as he saw Alex Vaughn, or Victor Garducci rather, he looked relieved.

Victor met him in front of the doors to Wizeguyz as Muro brushed against him on his way inside; the fat youth and Frankie were close behind. Garducci was about to follow Muro in as well when Sal grabbed his arm and motioned for him to stay outside with him. Victor stopped and looked at him. Walking a few feet away from the door and any ears that might be prying, Sal started to speak with the look of a man who carried the weight of the world on his shoulders.

"So, shit is really hitting the fan now," he started.

"What do you mean?" Victor's curiosity was piqued.

"Well, Muro and Aldo just had me ditch a couple revolvers at one of our pawn shops down the road."

There were at least half a dozen pawn shops nearby, but if the weapons were used in any of the recent hits, then Victor was sure some of his partners would like to know where that evidence was being stored. Victor decided it was worth trying to pry the location out of Sal.

"Which one?"

"Which one, what," Sal asked, eyeing him.

Victor pressed him, "Which pawn shop?"

Sal stood up a little bit straighter. "You ask a lot of questions, you know that Vic? Especially for someone who was conveniently gone, according to big man Muro, when the shit went down."

Crap. He was starting to feel on the hot seat. There were three ways to proceed; he could let it go and get nothing out of this, he could keep trying to prod him and maybe arouse Sal's suspicion even further, or he could act slighted that Sal was getting suspicious and not including him. He decided on the last option.

"What the fuck Sal? That's bullshit. Last I saw fucking Muro was coming back to the place, too. Then, I ask you a fucking legitimate question and you come at me like that. At *me* like that! Fuck, Sal. You know what, look out for yourself next time 'cause I sure as hell am not putting myself out there for your sake anymore."

Victor turned around to go inside. Sal grabbed his arm again and pulled him back.

Sal was looking stern now. "First of all, don't you ever talk to me like that again. I'm a capo in this thing of ours. I can't have you talking to me like that. Definitely don't talk about Muro like that. That guy will have your head. Now that's *me* looking out for *you*."

"Well, how do you want me to act when you basically call me a rat like that?"

Victor kept his eyes away from Sal. Feigning anger and hurt, Victor hardened his eyes.

"Nobody's calling you a rat, Vic. I was just saying these are dangerous times. Somebody can't be too careful. Listen, I'm just on edge. I lost my boy today. My boy, Vic. I don't want to lose you, too. Now tell me what you were worrying 'bout poor old Sal for."

"Well, for one thing, what pawn shop was it, 'cause what if it's one controlled by Ciancetta's crew? You don't think they would be interested in something like that?" Victor knew Sal wasn't that stupid but he wanted the name of that shop.

Sal gave a little chuckle. "Vic, you don't think I survived this long by being a fool do you? *Amvet Thrift* is with us. "

Bingo. But he had to give him one more to keep him off of the scent.

"Ok Sal, but what about this. Why are Aldo and Muro having you hide guns? They could have any one of those punks inside get that job done. I hope you used a fake name. And I hope to God that place doesn't have any cameras."

Victor looked at Sal taking in the thought. He looked troubled for a half second, and then brushed the idea off.

"Well, first of all I used a fake name. Like I said, your pal Sal is no fool." He flashed Victor a smile and continued. "Plus, that just isn't how it works. They wouldn't do that. What the hell do they need a patsy for? All the cops that ask questions around here end up on the front page, if you know what I mean. Now, we're going inside. I heard it's a bit of a mess in there right now so just try and keep your cool. Stay close to me."

Without another word Sal went inside. Victor followed him but his mind ran record laps in his skull. What did Sal mean all the cops that ask questions end up on the front page? What did he know? Did he know something about Jack? Perhaps he knew something about some of the other officers who were murdered. Was he giving Victor an underhanded threat just in case?

As nightfall started to descend on the city, nothing could have prepared Alex for what he was about to see. He pushed through Wizeguyz' double doors.

Chapter 19

Rafael Rontego snapped his eyes open. He knew that something was awry. He was no longer on the floor, but was reclining on the bed inside the safe house. Had he stumbled onto the bed in his delirium?

As far as Rontego could figure, there was a good chance that he should be dead. His neck hurt and he could barely turn his head to look at the shades. The slight upward crack in the blinds let Rafael discern that sometime passed as nightfall descended on the city.

Rafael lay there, quite still, barely daring to breathe. The events from earlier began to unfold in a blur of recollection. The slash across his neck. Rafael Rontego's hand crept up to his neck and traced the three-inch long wound. It was closed and he could feel the unmistakable ridges from the stitches that pulled his skin back together.

With a groan, the assassin rolled over and sat up in the bed. He heard a noise in the adjacent room of the seedy dwelling, but he wasn't too alarmed. Whoever took the time to stitch his neck probably did not want him dead. Nevertheless, the wary hit man glanced to his right on the nightstand where his twin pistols were resting. He grabbed one from its holster and slid it under the covers and onto his lap.

Against the dim lighting, the silhouette of his unknown savior came out of the adjacent room. When he took a step closer, bloody dishrag in hand, the assassin took in a deep breath and cocked his head in a slight tilt.

"Truly, you are full of surprises," the assassin stated.

The Cleaner took another step closer and his eyes shifted to the solitary pistol on the nightstand. "I don't think you'll need that, but if it makes you feel better, by all means."

There was a pause as the two men regarded each other. There was a definite tension in the air, but it was borne more out of uncertainty than it was any particular animosity.

The assassin decided to keep it simple and asked, "How and why?"

It was The Cleaner's turn to tilt his head as he studied the assassin. He took yet another step forward and sat down on the edge of the bed.

"The answers to those questions are very simple. The 'why' is a little more so than the 'how'. I don't like being stood up for dinner. Which, by the way, would be right about now."

The assassin allowed a wry grin to escape his lips. It was true enough; they were supposed to meet for some spaghetti at Chef's Pasta Place.

"And the how?"

"Raf, you have persuasive friends. Let me tell you something, The Pope is no stupid man. He didn't send you into Falzone's place of business without having you followed. That Pollock bastard is watching you as well as watching out *for* you." The Cleaner looked the assassin dead in his eye. "You need to be careful. I'm not saying that just because these punks are burning the city down around themselves. People like me, you, The Pope, we're a dying breed. Hell, even old man Falzone and Aldo and Muro are getting swept up in the changing tide." The Cleaner stood up then and tossed the bloody rag into another one of his customary duffle bags. "You can only swim against the tides of change for so long, Rafael."

The assassin stood up and holstered his pistols as he slung the shoulder holsters around his frame.

"So, what now?"

"Now, you take me back to your place and get me the rest of my money, you still owe me half. I'm not betting you will be around to pay me in the future. Once you collect your stuff, we're also going to torch that place of yours."

"Torch it?" Rafael did not like the sound of that at all. Mostly because he was so damn tired.

"Yeah, you have been on a killing spree lately, in case you didn't notice. Oh, and Falzone and his guys know where you live; or did you forget that too?" The Cleaner took up his duffle bag and motioned for the door. "C'mon, let's go. Let's also hope that no one is there waiting for you as we speak."

With a nod, the assassin let the Cleaner lead him out of the safe house and out into the continuing bite of the Lake Erie winds. The Cleaner took a quick glance left and right and then melted away into the shadows along the alley. Pulling his fedora low around his eyes, and snapping his stained collar up around his neck to break the swirling winds, the assassin too entered into the comfort of the shadows, leaving nothing but the whisper of his passing in his wake.

*

Alex Vaughn, or Victor Garducci, looked at the carnage that was Wizeguyz Billiards. Tables and chairs were strewn about the place; blood was splattered on the floor and walls. Bullet holes were speckled about the interior and some younger thugs were running all over the place. Aldo Marano was in a heated discussion with Muro. Sal saw the animated conversation and went over to see what he could learn.

One thing caught the undercover agent's attention despite all the distractions in the room. Over where Muro and Aldo usually sat, immersed amongst the pile of yellow cigarette butts, there was one unmistakable black cigarette with a gold foil filter.

Garducci felt his pulse quicken as he approached the table. His hands trembling, he scooped up the cigarette butt. There was no mistaking it, this was a match.

He glanced over in Sal's direction as the conversation took a dramatic turn. Aldo was showing Sal a napkin, the contents of which were sending Sal into a frenzy. With a shout, he grabbed the object out of Aldo's hand and marched towards Victor Garducci. Victor held out the cigarette in his hand as Sal came up.

Sal slapped the cigarette out of Victor's hand and yelled, "That fuck Rafael Rontego smokes those faggot Russian cigarettes." With that, Sal threw the napkin on the table, allowing a finger to roll across the slab.

"That's my boy's finger." Sal stated it so devoid of emotion that Victor caught himself staring at the emotional gangster. "Frankie," he called out to his friend across the room. "Get the car." He tossed Frankie his car keys and the man hurried off.

Victor eyed Sal, waiting for him to speak. The man did not disappoint as he again stated, "Tonight, we avenge my son."

Garducci nodded his head and walked past Sal. He needed to tell someone about what was going down. This was about to be some serious shit. Every time he thought he might be able to find a clean way to disengage, this kept on getting messier. Now though, he had a name. Rafael Rontego. It had to be him. Garducci walked into the bathroom in a daze.

The undercover agent looked under the stalls to make sure he was alone. Establishing that he was, he pinched the sides of the transmitter button on his jacket sleeve. He spoke into the device.

"Suspect's name is Rafael Rontego. Find his residence ASAP. Prepare for fireworks."

Hopefully Hi-Def would receive the call and put the guys into motion. Alex took a deep breath. The moment for revenge was near. How odd was it that his unlikely allies would include both cops and cold-blooded gangsters?

Alex splashed his face with some water from the sink. As he toweled off he heard the door swing open and Sal entered the bathroom.

"You ready Vic?"

Alex Vaughn looked at himself one last time in the mirror as he patted his face. "Yeah, I'm ready."

With a wave, Sal led the way and Victor Garducci followed to the car idling in wait outside.

They rode in silence. A slight crack in the window allowed a small bit of cool air to whistle into the car. Frankie DeRisio turned the windshield wipers on pushing off flecks of snow as they steeled their resolve for the mission ahead. The street lights drifted on past one another into the darkness for about fifteen minutes until Sal spoke.

"Pull over here," he said. "We're about a block away."

Frankie did as he was bade, and pulled the car over under a light post on the corner of the block. Diagonal and across the street was a low rise building.

"That's where the fuck lives. I waited out here all night for my boy to come out. I should have had the courage to go in then. We'll say I was suffering from a bit of shock. But tonight, we'll finish what I should have before." Sal pursed his lips together and walked around the back of the car popping the trunk open.

Frankie came up beside Sal, and looking into the trunk, let out a low whistle. "That's what I'm talking about, serious firepower."

Garducci walked around the car and looked inside. There was a compact sub machine gun of the Israeli variety, an Uzi. Sal grabbed this and tucked his arm inside the folds of his overcoat. There was also a sawed-off shotgun, which Frankie scooped up and tucked along the inseam of his trench coat.

Seeing that there were no more heavy artillery pieces to be had, Sal looked at Victor and shrugged. "Since you don't have the big guns, stay a couple steps behind us and pull up the rear."

With a nod, Victor fell into step behind Sal and Frankie as they made their way across the street. As they hustled across the road, Victor took a quick glance down it and noticed a familiar white van parallel parked about a block away. He patted his Beretta tucked in its shoulder holster.

The trio paused for a second outside of the building's doors which lead into a small entry way with a dimly lit stairwell. They paused, as Sal took a deep breath, and then entered through the front door. They entered, as the back doors swung shut in the rear of the building. They entered as another car carrying a large solid block of a man parked at the rear of the residence.

Chapter 20

Rafael Rontego pried yet another floorboard loose and grabbed a stack of hundreds rubber banded together from amongst the rat poison that shielded his money from the rodents. He tossed it into a duffle bag that was fast becoming full of cash. He then moved on to the last place he had money stowed away.

As he walked to the closet, he looked at the Cleaner who was still peering out the window on the roadway below. The guy was all business. Rafael respected that about the man.

With a grunt, the assassin took his crowbar and pulled a panel off of the inside of his closet. Taking a flashlight he peered into the darkness inside the wall and saw the familiar green of his money, dusty but undisturbed.

"Hey Raf, I think we have company. A white van just pulled into a parking spot down the road and is just sitting there. Might be time to leave. You almost done?"

The Cleaner, not waiting to hear from Rafael, walked past him and into the bathroom. He took Rafael's metal trash bin and started shredding up paper and cloth from an old shirt, placing the material into the bin.

Rafael shook his head and tossed the rest of his money into the bag, zipping it closed.

As he continued filling the bin with material and dousing it with accelerant, the Cleaner continued, "Rafael, I was serious when I told you that you can't swim against the current forever. Times are changing. You need to think about getting away from here for a while. What do you have there? Two hundred, three hundred thousand dollars? You can lay low for a long time with that."

Rafael shot him a glance as he became aware of the fact that his life savings was very exposed at the moment.

Catching on, the Cleaner continued, "Relax tough

guy, you think I need your chump change? I'm getting out of here myself. I have a nice little nest egg and I don't plan on dying before I get to use it."

Rafael was startled to hear that admission from the Cleaner. He'd been around for as long as Rontego could remember. Maybe the Cleaner had a point. After all, he survived almost as many wars as Rafael. Perhaps things were getting too dicey.

As odd as it was, Rafael never thought much about retirement. He couldn't go on killing for money forever. It would be nice to get away from the life, maybe.

The Cleaner lit the material in the trash bin on fire as he flicked a match into the accelerant and walked out of the bathroom. Rafael made his way to the kitchen and placed his hand on the gas dial.

"Where will you go then?" he asked.

The Cleaner paused for a moment. "Me? I have a cabin up in Canada. I might just stock it with some food, and spend a year fishing."

"What should I do, if not this?" Rafael looked at the Cleaner, hoping for an answer.

"Fuck, I don't know Rafael, haven't you ever been happy? You know, doing something else? I don't know. I'll tell you what. If you want to leave and can't think of anything better to do, come here." The Cleaner handed Rafael a post card with an address in Canada on it. "Hell, it can get lonely fishing by yourself for a whole damned year anyway. But I will tell you one thing. When we walk out the back doors of this building, I am not looking back. From your apartment, straight to Canada. I won't look back no matter what."

With a nod, Rafael flicked the gas switch to 'on' and the two of them left the apartment. As they descended the stairs, Rontego thought more about the offer. It seemed like it might be a good idea. Rafael the fisherman? The assassin chuckled as they reached the back door. He couldn't believe he was even contemplating it.

The two men paused for a second, bracing to meet the cold Niagara air that was sure to blast them on the other side of the door. Rafael looked at the small man in front of him.

"Hey Cleaner."

The slight man turned toward the assassin.

"Are we friends?"

The Cleaner let a smile creep up on his lips. "Friends? You know men like you and I don't have friends."

The Cleaner grabbed the door handle as Rafael started to contemplate why that truest of statements disappointed him so much.

"But then again," the Cleaner continued, "if we weren't, than why would I let you know where to find me?"

With that, the amazing man slung his duffle bag over his shoulder and started walking down the road. Rafael stood there for a minute and smiled. He too opened the door and slung his duffle bag over his shoulder. That is when the smile disappeared from his lips.

As the door closed behind him, Rafael saw a large form, topped with a fedora, fall in step a dozen feet behind the Cleaner. He appeared as if from nowhere, materializing from the shadows, gun held out at a forty-five degree angle from his body.

Rafael knew who it was.

He grabbed a pistol from its holster and fell into step behind the figure, moving as quick as a cat to close the gap between himself and the Cleaner's would-be pursuer.

It seemed like an eternity. The large silhouette gained a step on the Cleaner for every two steps Rafael closed between himself and his sudden target.

At the corner, at the end of the block, the oblivious Cleaner paused to check for traffic. His heart racing,

Rafael thought he would be too late as the form raised his pistol and leveled it the back of the Cleaner's head.

In full sprint now, Rafael closed the gap, his own pistol raised and at the ready. The sudden rush of motion, however, alerted the dark form and it whirled around just in time. Just in time to catch a solitary bullet from Rafael Rontego in the side of the head. A solitary shot sent a cloud of bloody smoke onto the icy sidewalk. The form crumpled to the ground.

True to his word, the Cleaner, startled, straightened up, but didn't look back. He just kept walking across the street as Rafael watched him depart.

Rontego stooped over the motionless form, and rolled the man over. He avoided looking at Muro's face while he riffled through the pockets of his jacket. After a moment, he found what he was looking for. He pulled the small wooden pawn out, and slipped it into his own pocket. He stood up, stepped over the body at his feet, and took a left across the street at a ninety-degree angle from the Cleaner and continued walking as well. He holstered his weapon inside the folds of his coat and pulled a Sobranie cigarette from a pack.

As he paused to light it, he mumbled, "Goodbye Muro, my old friend."

*

The three gangsters padded along the corridor. Their footsteps were measured and careful in the insufficient light generated by the low wattage bulb suspended above the narrow staircase. Their shadows elongated below them, casting an eerie shadow along the wooden banister and cascading onto the floor below.

Victor Garducci could hear his heartbeat pulsating in his neck and working its way up to his temples. Sal Pieri and Frankie DeRisio inched along ahead of him, a full five steps up front. Victor was weighed down by the thoughts assaulting his senses as they crept along towards the door at the second level. How far was he willing to go to satiate his vengeance? So far, he was able to straddle the line. If the time came would he be willing to break all of the laws he swore to defend? How far was too far in the quest of bloody fulfillment?

Sal looked down and back at him, an evil grin spread across his face and his eyes danced with a wild fire. As Sal crested the top of the stairwell, there was a sudden 'pop' in the distance. It sounded like a car backfired, but it did not matter to the three men so on edge.

As one, they crouched in a defensive posture and sucked in their breath. Frankie's finger slipped to the trigger of his shotgun and the barrel rose to ward off the noise.

They waited for what seemed like an eternity, but hearing no further sounds, they inched along again. Sal reached the door first. He crept low in front of the door, regarding the lock. His hand went to the door and he turned the knob. The door knob didn't turn far though, it was locked.

Frankie gave a snort and Victor couldn't tell whether he scoffed in irritation, or in bemusement. Sal's hand slid down the door and came to rest on an almost invisible string tied taut about six inches off of the ground above the doors cracked and eroded weather strip.

"Booby trap," Frankie said, the alarm crept into his voice and he took a step backward down the stairs.

Sal shook his head, negating the concept. His voice etched with the stress and excitement of the moment, he wheezed declaring his own theory.

"Warning wire."

To emphasize his point, he flipped out a small three inch blade and cut the string in front of the door.

Both Victor and Frankie crept downward another

step. Their concern drew a scowl from Sal who motioned for the two to come back up. As much as he wanted his revenge, Victor admitted to himself that he was nervous. If this guy was better than Jack, he was unsure how well he might fare against such an adversary, even with his band of unlikely allies.

Sal took a lock pick from a chain around his neck and began fumbling with it in search of the right tool. This brought another grunt from Frankie, who lifted his shotgun again and jerked it in the direction of the dead bolt.

Another grin from Sal declared the capo's approval and it was his turn to take a step back from the door. His submachine gun came around and pointed at the front of the door. Victor decided now was as good of a time as any to bring his own firearm to bear and held the Beretta out in front of him at eye height, but due to his positioning on the stairwell, he was not aiming much higher than Sal and Frankie's waists.

Another pause ensued while the trio took a steadying breath, then with a nod from his leader; Frankie leveled his shotgun at the door lock and blasted a hole through the door about a foot in diameter.

The force of the blast shoved Frankie's arms upward and sent pieces of wood and metal flying into the apartment. With a kick, Sal flung the door ajar, and took half a dozen running strides into the room. Frankie took a step inside and brought his shotgun around the door, first left, then right.

Sal, frantic, looked around the empty apartment. He looked for any sign of his target in the immediate room. Not seeing Rafael Rontego in the living room, he began to creep towards the bedroom, to the right of the apartment's entrance. Still maintaining the illusion of stealth despite the noisy entry, Sal crouched as he walked, when a low hiss came from Frankie.

"You smell that?" Frankie's forehead was

scrunched up and he was sniffing the air.

"I don't smell nothing," Sal said.

Victor watched the two men and paused where he was, inside of the door frame, his back to the hallway. Sal pushed open a door on the side of the room, and a small billow of smoke escaped the previously shuttered room behind.

"Holy shit!" Sal coughed as he took a few steps backward away from the haze.

Frankie shifted his weight and glanced at Victor, perplexed. Sal looked at the two of them as if he were about to say something when an explosion rocked the room and a large fireball shot forward from the blaze in the room.

The flame seemed to jerk forward, encompassing Sal Pieri and catching his clothing on fire. The window behind him exploded outward, showering the street with glass and flaming material from the interior of the apartment.

Sal let out a shriek of surprise that soon became one of excruciating pain. At the same instance, the force of the initial blast sent Frankie DeRisio airborne over Victor and launched Victor off his feet and backward.

For a moment, the entire world slowed down and Victor could see all of this play out before him. As Frankie's airborne body flew over him, he could see that the blast ripped the skin from the man's face and singed the edge of the wounds.

Then everything sped up in double time as if time had to catch up with itself and Victor flew into the wall behind him. Frankie tumbled down on top of him and their bodies crashed together on the floor. For a moment, everything went black as Victor Garducci struggled to maintain consciousness.

A gash along his forehead burned with an odd sting and wetness which Victor understood to be his own blood falling down his face. He could barely breathe. His breath crashed out from his lungs as he collided with the wall and the weight of Frankie's smoldering body on top of him impeded his lungs even further.

Victor pushed Frankie off of him and rolled over onto his side. His jacket was on fire in several places and he rolled around on the floor extinguishing the flames relying purely on instinct.

What the hell happened?

Sal continued screaming inside the apartment and an unbelievable stench assaulted Victor's nostrils. The stench of burning flesh was something Victor was unaccustomed to. Unable to stand, he began crawling forward; his thought was to get to Sal and to do something, anything to help the tortured man.

Sal, too, was crawling and thrashing on the ground and his hair was burned, leaving scorched scalp and blistering skin as the unrelenting flames licked around his body in its pursuit to consume him as fuel.

Sal's lidless eyes flicked toward Garducci and his lipless mouth shrieked the most awful thing Victor heard in his life, "Shoot me! Shoot me! Shoot me!"

Thrashing and begging for mercy, Sal's voice came out in harsh screams, gaining pace with the urgency of his pain.

Victor pulled his gun from the scorched doorway, and pointed it at Sal's charred and screaming face.

Sal, unable to find the strength to move, fell forward despite the obvious pain of falling on burned limbs. He flopped to his stomach. His strength was leaving him or the sinews of the limbs that would support his weight burned and melted through, Victor could not discern which.

Pleading with his last breaths, he whispered, "Shoot me."

Victor, his face set with the determination of going

forward with an impossible situation, closed his eyes.

One last shriek blasted forth, and then there echoed the solitary pop of a well aimed bullet.

It flew straight and true, merciful; it found its way into the trapped and tortured brain of Sal Pieri, releasing his soul to whatever awaited it on the other side. Victor, knowing that if an afterlife existed, hoped that whatever God existed gave Sal Pieri, the last of the Pieri line, some credit for time already served in the fires of hell.

Chapter 21

Rafael Rontego kept his eyes straight ahead and continued walking, his pace fast and purposeful, for several blocks before ducking into an alley with a distant view of his apartment building. Once more showing off his agility, he leapt atop a dumpster and then scaled a ladder leading to the low building's roof. Stepping onto the gravel rooftop, the assassin lit yet another Sobranie. The nicotine comforted his nerves.

Nerves.

Rafael could not remember the last time he felt anything in his chosen line of work. Rontego took a deep drag off the familiar brand just as an explosion rocked the building and flames leapt out of his window.

He took another long drag and watched the myriad of orange speckles alight in the sky as scattered debris succumbed to the intensity of the heat that launched it into the night air.

He expected the explosion. His keen ears picked up the sound of screaming in the distance, or maybe it was a siren, Rontego couldn't be sure. He wasn't sure, until he heard a solitary pop rattle across the distance followed by abrupt silence. Other than the roar of the flames which were already dying lower as the gas vapor receded, the evening seemed serene.

The assassin stood there looking across the way at the burning building he once called home, a lone dark silhouette against the flickering orange backdrop amidst the midnight sky. He glanced at the cigarette in his hand, and saw for just a moment, a peculiar tremble, subdued. A lot happened to him in the half dozen hours or so since he followed orders and lay waste to Wizeguyz Billiards.

Orders.

Rafael glanced at his bag resting next to him on the rooftop. The culmination of a life of work. Rontego shook his head.

Muro.

He couldn't believe how easy he dropped his old mentor. Was Muro trying to kill the Cleaner? Rafael couldn't be sure. More likely, there was a follow up hit on Rontego for his actions at Wizeguyz earlier that day. That would explain the death scream that echoed from his burning apartment. Muro must have come in support of that operation and, in the darkness; he could have easily mistaken the Cleaner for Rontego. He would not have a reason to suspect another escapee darting out from the rear entrance of Rafael's building.

Rontego smiled. Luck did indeed seem to be on his side.

Luck.

That was what was bothering the assassin. The thought struck him. The usually unflappable killer came to rely on superior skill and smarter planning. Everything was so messy lately. Too much seemed to be beyond the professional's control.

Try as he might, he also was unable to get Aldo's haunting words from echoing out of the deepest recesses of his brain. Why *had* Don Ciancetta and The Pope decided he was expendable? Why put him in the position of sending a message in a situation well beyond messages?

The sheer volume of unknowns assaulted the assassin. Then there was the circumstances surrounding Muro. The man had, at one time, been as close to a friend as Rontego ever knew. Until recently. Was it unavoidable circumstances that lead to the final showdown that ended with a bullet bringing down a legend among gangsters?

The word 'unavoidable' stuck at the front of Rafael's mind. Until tonight, Muro stood as a solitary example that one could live the life of a killer, and survive the streets. Muro stood up as an example of how to navigate the dangers of the underworld. For years he seemed beyond the fray, but in the span of an unplanned ten seconds, he was gone.

Rafael took the last drag on his Sobranie and the distant wail of sirens rose up from the streets below. In a moment of clarity, the questions came to Rontego.

Do you want to rely on luck any longer? The answer came from Rafael's lips in whisper.

"No."

Do you want to take orders forever? Rafael spoke the word aloud.

"No."

Do you want to end up like Muro, face down on a city sidewalk with your brains splayed across Walden Avenue?

With a growl, Rontego answered again, "No!"

The assassin flicked his cigarette to the ground and crushed the gold foil against the gravel with the heel of his boot. Snaking around, Rafael Rontego spun toward the ladder and grabbed the side rail hugging the ledge of the building. With the ease of movement customary to the assassin, he grabbed the side of the ladder and flung himself over the lip of the building, entering a smooth slide down the ladder until he landed in the alley below. Rafael Rontego pushed his fedora into place against his head and with another twirl, snapping his jacket behind him, took off down the alley and into the night.

He knew now, that which must be done.

*

Water began to fall from the ceilings. The emergency sprinklers triggered due to the inferno that ate at the building. The fire was already starting to simmer down as the last of the gaseous fumes dissipated out of the reach of the multiple smaller fires that ignited.

Alex Vaughn slouched against the wall in the

hallway and looked at what was left the apartment. Smoke drifted out of the shattered window in a thick stream and more smoke trailed in thinner columns to meet with the retreating clouds of ash. Blood was flowing down the side of Alex's face and his eyes felt bloodshot and dry. The sting from the fumes and the remnants of the blaze bit at his eyes, water rimmed his lids as the body fought to cleanse him of the pollutants.

The smell of the place was assaulting the agent's nostrils, but he hadn't the strength to stand and leave. Still clutching his firearm, but resting the Berretta against the floor beams, Alex looked at the eerie scene. In front of him and face down, smoldering and quite unmoving, was Sal Pieri. To his left, Frankie DeRisio was lying in a heap and was unmoving. From the odd angle of his head, Vaughn assumed it was the neck that betrayed the large man to his end. Still, Alex, without looking at DeRisio, slid his left hand over and onto Frankie's neck.

There was no pulse. Still staring straight ahead, Alex felt his eyes grow wetter.

It must be all the damned smoke.

Alex Vaughn felt what might have been more than cleansing tears well up in his eyes as he sat there surrounded by the carnage. Thoughts began to spring up in his head. Why was he here? Was any of this worth it? So Rafael Rontego, whoever that was, killed Jack. But why? At that moment, Alex Vaughn felt weak. He missed his Charlotte.

I'd give anything to be home.

Sirens became audible in the distance. It was over. His body wouldn't let him leave, or maybe it was the will that was lacking. A piece of Alex was happy.

He tried. He failed. The plethora of laws, moral and ethical as well as legal, that he broke and disregarded, made Alex sick. He didn't like who he became over the last few days. He witnessed more death in the last forty-eight hours than in an entire career.

Dull footsteps pounded up the stairs and Alex's head fell forward to meet his chest. They were right on top of him, but still he did not open his eyes.

"Jesus Christ", the voice was thick and familiar but it seemed like it was muffled and coming from a great distance. "Grab him up. I'll check on those two."

Alex felt someone grab his arm and yank him to his feet. He let himself be led toward the stairs and looked at his crutch as they struggled downward. Hi-Def was supporting him and muttering over and over about how he couldn't believe it. Alex barely heard him though as they walked toward the exit.

A quick pop from up above drew Hi-Def's attention for a moment and Vaughn almost hit the floor as the support faltered for a moment. Hi-Def recovered, however and caught Alex in time to lead him out of the apartment and towards the waiting van. Elliot was driving it and had the motor started.

As the duo struggled towards the van, Hambone came running out of the building and grabbed Alex's other arm. The three of them made it to the van just as a pair of fire trucks came screaming along the avenue. Hi-Def and Hambone laid Alex Vaughn along the back of the van's interior and then hopped into the double doors as Elliot, hardly waiting for the doors to close, hit the gas and drove in the opposite direction. The van rounded the corner moments before the emergency vehicles descended on the building.

Alex closed his eyes and lay back as Hi-Def pressed a cloth against Alex's forehead. There was a general commotion around Alex and Elliot was yelling about something. Hi-Def was just listening but Hambone was yelling back as the van sped further from the scene.

Vaughn tried to close his eyes to shut them out, but all he saw was the screaming, burning vision of Sal Pieri.

Caught in between a place of semi-consciousness and cognizant-shock, Alex just let the van take him where it would.

Chapter 22

Rontego ran down the alley. The wind whipping across his face found its way into his chest quicker than his lungs could heat up the air to a serviceable temperature for bodily absorption. He made his way toward downtown. He traveled west, parallel along Walden Avenue and turned south down Mulberry Street.

The thought occurred to him as he traveled, that maybe this wasn't the best course of action. Maybe he was being hasty. Each time he entertained that thought though, the sting in his neck reminded him of the pure and simple fact that you can't remain ahead forever.

When the situation is beyond your control, leave the situation.

Muro told him that. The body count was getting higher. The way things were going, it was destined to climb still further. Not to mention the police. They were idiots, and the ones that weren't were paid off. Even this cluster-fuck in the navy blues, touting toy shields and popguns, wouldn't and couldn't, stand by forever.

In the end, sooner rather than later, the good people of Buffalo were going to reach a boiling point. It was ever the outrage of the civilians that spurred the boys in blue to action.

Rontego zigged and zagged along several side streets, all the while making his way towards the epicenter of downtown Buffalo. Rafael exited an alley and pulled up along Delaware Avenue.

He pulled up and slowed his gait as he neared the Del Avant building. It was a modern testament to the architectural prowess of man. The assassin took his fedora off and a cluster of his normally slicked back, dark hair fell forward over his eye. With a brush of his fingers, Rafael shoved the hair back into place and rested his fedora on top of his head at its customary tilt. His grey eyes gazed up at the vast expanse of steel and glass that raised fifteen stories before him.

This was where Buffalo's ruling class lived. The top three floors of this building were reserved to cater to the top one percent of Buffalo's wealth. Rontego walked past the entrance to the building where a well-versed doorman was serving in a dual capacity as public relations official and guardian. At this hour, Rontego was pretty sure he couldn't get in without an invitation. Besides, front doors were for suckers.

Rafael made his way along the back of the building to a service ramp for incoming truck deliveries. Thin plastic strands fell in front of the garage-type opening shielding the interior from public view. Rafael inched forward and crept from shadow to shadow. As he inched forward, Rontego took care to avoid the several cameras hanging over the lip of the first story ledge by hugging the wall way and rounding into the garage opening, barely disturbing the plastic covering as he whispered past.

He came into a large shipping and semi storage warehouse under the belly of the Del Avant. His eyes adjusted to the brightness inside the warehouse and, with a grin reflective of his fortune, Rontego glanced side to side, realizing he was alone. The assassin took his fedora off and tucked it under his arm. Rafael picked up a box and carried it toward the service elevator on the far right of the warehouse. Rows of trailers that hitched to trucks were lying at regular intervals throughout the front of the warehouse. The assassin couldn't tell if they were fresh deliveries, or waiting to go out.

Coming around the last such trailer, the killer made a beeline towards the elevator. The assassin began juggling the box and reaching for the arrow indicating up.

All of a sudden, the assassin heard footsteps rushing towards him. Almost dropping the box, Rafael Rontego whirled around just in time to see the cause as a large black man with a set of worker's overalls came upon him. A gloved hand reached past Rafael and pushed the up button.

"Let me get that for you," the man said.

Rontego, his heart racing, nodded his 'appreciation'.

The elevator doors opened almost at once, and it wasn't soon enough for Rafael. Thinking himself in the clear, he let out a slow breath. The man climbed into the elevator with the assassin.

Thinking he recognized the source of Rafael's sigh, the man muttered, "I feel ya. Long day. What floor?"

Rafael, unable to think, stared at this 'X' factor.

"Hey, what floor?" A sincere confusion came over the man's face.

Coming back to form, the assassin cleared his throat. "Fifteenth."

With a nod the man hit the button for the fifteenth floor. To Rafael's relief, he also hit floor five. It seemed like an eternity as the elevator rose up two flights and stopped to pick up another passenger. Rontego didn't even make eye contact with this one. Again he was relieved when no other button was selected.

When they got to the fifth floor, Rontego reminded himself to seem normal. The two men exited.

"Have a good evening," he stated.

They nodded as the doors shut behind them. Rafael rode the elevator up the remaining ten flights in peace and came out into a side corridor in the fifteenth floor.

He put the box down and headed on his way. There were four suites on this level. Rontego knew the one he needed to get to and started off in that direction. It was a straight walk of about a hundred yards. Then, there was a final turn up ahead that would bring him to the door.

This one wouldn't be unguarded. Rafael eased his head around the corner, he saw the door. Next to the large oak door was an empty chair. The plush, thick grey carpeting trailed down the hallway and in the distance, maybe another thirty feet, Rafael saw the reason for the empty chair.

A small man, with a bulge coming off of his hip revealing the heat he was stacked with, turned his back and to talk to a cute little lady with a cleaning cart.

Rafael steeled his gaze and pulled out a small lock pick from the inside fold of his jacket pocket. Heart beating, he scurried forward; he was doing his best to remain innocuous to the peripheral vision of the lovely lady distracting his chief obstacle.

Sidling up to the door, he slipped his lock pick in the deadbolt key hole, crouching to align his ear with the lock. These were always the easiest to Rafael Rontego. With a click, the bolt lifted.

With a great deal of caution, and a fair amount of apprehension, Rafael looked in the distance and saw the two potential lovers deep in conversation. Readjusting his lock pick, and stooping even further, aligning his eye with the hole, Rontego began sliding and shifting the three piece set. In a moment, the entry device was calibrated, and Rafael felt the grooves give way to another satisfying click.

The assassin turned the door knob. With one final glance down the hallway, Rafael disappeared into the private residence of Chris 'The Pope' Biela. The door shut behind him and he leaned against it in relief.

*

After a few minutes, the yelling died down and the foursome rode on in silence. Hi-Def leaned over Alex Vaughn and was trying to say something, but whatever it was, Alex couldn't understand. His voice was still muted, and Alex figured the blast temporarily blew out his eardrums.

Vaughn was pretty sure he could hear just fine if the damned constant humming in his ear would just go away. Hi-Def asked another question, as evidenced by the quizzical look etched on his face.

Alex tried to sit up and said, "I can't hear you, it's the humming."

He thought he said it normal enough, but he must not have been able to control his volume very well, as both Hambone and Elliot turned to regard him.

They shared a glance and Hi-Def turned Alex to face him and yelled, loud enough for Alex to hear, "It will go away soon, it's from the explosion!"

Vaughn leaned backward against the side of the van and closed his eyes.

No shit, he thought to himself.

As the van bumped along the Buffalo streets, the tall downtown buildings morphed into the low level buildings that defined much of the older part of the city. There were not many pedestrians out at this hour and the few that were out were up to no good.

There was a lady selling her feminine wares on the corner of one street, her skirt hiked up and a pair of leather boots indicated her intent. The van came around another corner, slowing down as rundown housing lined the street on either side. The houses in this part of town were in varying degrees of disrepair. Paint peeled from the sides of buildings and overgrown lawns threatened to swallow the sidewalks.

If Alex didn't know better, he would have thought several homes had late night garage sales, judging by the amount of personal effects littering the lawns and driveways.

As the vehicle drove onward, Alex noticed that his ears began to crackle as if someone was folding a piece of paper near his ear, but with each crackle his hearing began to return to normal. The van bounded down the uneven pavement until it got to a seedy looking home with a detached two car garage. The white paint was peeling on the sides of this house and it looked like it was a two story home. Its colonial style build was dilapidated, but Alex could see that once, maybe fifty years ago, this house was quite nice.

The two-car garage set back behind the house was equally as old, but looked like it'd painted of late. It was not your traditional, modern garage however, as the twin doors that opened outward were more akin to a barn type doorway than the mechanized garage doors that lifted to allow entry.

As they approached, the van slowed down and Hambone exited in order to pull open one of the garage doors. Alex noticed that he unlocked and removed a padlock in order to lift an iron hatch to allow for entry. When the latch was raised and the door swung open, Hambone disappeared into the side of the garage that remained shut.

The van pulled under the structure and Elliot, Hi-Def and Alex piled out. As they exited the rear of the garage, Alex noticed Hambone securing a tarp over what appeared to be another vehicle.

"Come on, I have something to show you." Elliot waved for Alex to follow and made his way towards the house's back door.

It was a yellow door with scuff marks along the bottom where a kick plate should have been installed. But it swung open with no trouble, and Hi-Def and Hambone fell into line behind the two men as they entered the building. They entered through a kitchen that was neglected as was evidenced by the Chinese takeout and pizza boxes that littered the counters. They proceeded through the kitchen and into what might have functioned as a living room, but was set up as a de-facto headquarters for this unit.

The blinds were pulled shut in an obvious attempt to keep prying eyes at bay. There was a card table with dual laptops on it, connected by a series of wires which is where Hi-Def made his home. He plunked down behind his screens and began tapping on the keys.

Ninety degrees from him were a pair of corkboards placed on top of easels and several known Mafioso's' black and white mug shots graced them in an effort to outline the two warring factions. Under each 'family tree' several members were listed as deceased. Notable among the Falzone crew were Sal Pieri and two of his men. All three had a large red X crossing over their faces.

Elliot wasted no time as they came in, and he picked up a red marker laying on the edge of the easel. He crossed an X through both Sonne Pieri and Frank DeRisio. Alex noticed that of the dueling factions, Joe Falzone's crew seemed to be taking the brunt of the damage. Most of Falzone's losses were being accrued at the officer level. Don Ciancetta lost only a handful of hitters, low level thugs for the most part.

A small desk was cattycorner to the easels but was not burdened by much in the way of paperwork. The place was set up for a quick exit. One thing caught Alex's eye as he plunked down on an uncomfortable plastic chair, the kind you would get for a few bucks at a discount shop. He noticed that there was a chart of monetary shipments that were made at varying times to varying mobsters on both sides of the war.

Most streams, at a glance, seemed to flow independent of one another, each to their perspective sides of the family. It seemed that Don Ciancetta and his crew made quite a large amount more than the other faction, but that could be expected as he was the boss. Beyond the monetary flow of several thousands of dollars here or there, one large payment leapt off the page, causing Vaughn to leap out of his seat almost as soon as he sat down.

He thought to go over towards the easel to study the outline in more detail, but Elliot came forward and flipped the easel around revealing a chalkboard with the name "Jack" scratched across it in chalk. There was the date of his murder, just several days earlier and a list of facts that were uncovered as of today. There was a photograph of the 9mm bullet that pierced Jack's lungs along with its dimensions before and after the bullet flattened during its destructive course. The Sobranie cigarette was listed along with both locations the brand was sold.

It caused Vaughn to do a double take when he noticed a picture of himself, but then again, why wouldn't they have documentation of him in action. There was the useless photograph that Hi-Def showed Alex earlier that they believed was Rafael Rontego.

Rafael Rontego.

They had been so close. He was long gone by now. He could have been in another state. If they knew what the fucker looked like, they might be able to put an APB out for him and head him off. If they knew what he looked like.

Alex took another look at the red X's that crossed the faces of men he spoke with just hours earlier. He felt his face pull up into a grimace as both the thought and the ache of his head wound assaulted him. He put a hand to his forehead tracing the outline of the cut. It was not as large as he thought; the amount of blood misled him.

Alex could imagine how he looked at that second. Coming back to the moment, he brushed his long brown hair backward away from the wound. A few strands stuck at first, but the momentum of Vaughn's hand tore them away, reopening the wound a little. Alex noticed that Elliot was giving him a serious look; his lips were pursed together again. He walked over to the picture of Alex and drew an X across his face. Vaughn, flabbergast, just about choked.

"What the hell does that mean?"

Elliot stood a bit straighter. "Alex, what happened tonight was damn near a disaster. We can't have you getting killed."

Vaughn felt heated rage well up inside of him, threatening to boil over. "My work's not done yet," he said.

Still, Elliot stood toe to toe with Alex, resolute. "Alex, think about it. Victor Garducci has already accomplished what he set out to do. It was you that called in who the killer is. Rafael Rontego killed Jack. That is a huge place to start. There is no need for you to be undercover and risking yourself. What purpose would it serve?"

Alex placed a hand on the easel and looked at the red X over his face. How large it loomed to him at that moment. He had, in fact, almost lost his life.

Vaughn felt the presence of someone else coming up to him and it was confirmed when a maul of a hand rested on his shoulder. Alex gave a slight turn to see that the size thirteen shoes staring up at him were Hambone's. His voice seemed thick even if he was, in some small measure, trying to soften it and seem friendly.

"You did a hell of a job up there, man. I mean, I haven't seen anyone survive a blast like that. You got Angels sitting on your shoulder."

There was a pause as Alex digested the brute's words. It seemed that Elliot thought that was his cue. "Besides, think for a moment about the position you were in. What would you have done if you saw Rafael Rontego up there? Would you have pulled the trigger yourself? Would you have let Sal or Frankie pull the trigger? Or were you gonna pull out your badge and arrest them all?"

Alex stood up and turned around. "I don't know what I would have done."

Elliot pursed his lips again. God, how Alex hated it every time he did that. He glanced at Hi-Def, who shrugged.

Elliot continued on. "Face facts man, that explosion was the best thing that ever happened to you. That was a no win situation up there."

Best thing that ever happened to him. Alex winced as the image of Sal Pieri resting on the floor, still smoldering and with Alex's bullet embedded in his brain, flashed across his consciousness. Alex shook his head in affirmation of his resignation. Hi-Def, reading the body language began pounding on his keyboard.

"Ok then, Victor Garducci died in the blast. That makes four."

As he spoke the words he spun the computer around to face the three men.

A case file on Victor Garducci flashed on the left side of the screen "DECEASED." On the right was a list of newspaper agencies that were at the same time emailed officer notations on finding multiple dead bodies on the scene. Listed were Sal Pieri, age 46, Frankie DeRisio, age 43, Victor Garducci, 28 and Muro Lucano, age 58.

"Muro?" Elliot and Alex questioned at the same time.

"Yep. Officers on the scene found a body near the back entrance. Seems a winner is starting to emerge in this war. Muro is a huge loss to Falzone."

Hambone let out a low whistle. It seemed whistling was his thing.

"Two guesses as to who got the drop on Muro."

Elliot clenched his face and you could tell he was thinking hard. His lips began to purse together again and Alex watched it hoping to God he wouldn't do it again.

"For God sakes Elliot, it was a joke. You know it

has to be Rontego."

Elliot let out a laugh and it interrupted his puckering. "It's not that, I was just wondering how Slate was doing. We haven't heard from him in a bit. I am sure he is fine."

Alex nodded his head, but made a mental note to make a call to his friend the second he was away from these rodeo clowns. Alex looked at Hi-Def. "So, Victor is dead?."

Hi-def leaned back. "Victor is dead."

His mind made up, Alex Vaughn pulled out his pistol and replaced the bullet he lost in Sal's brain matter. With the resounding click of his magazine, he walked towards the door.

"Where are you going?" Elliot asked.

"I'm doing what I should have done to begin with. I'm going to Jack's house to see what I can find."

Elliot strode towards the door and into Alex's path. "You think we haven't been there? You think the rest of the Buffalo P.D. hasn't been there? They found nothing. We found nothing."

"Yeah, well, you people don't know Jack like I did."

Elliot saw that he was not going to win this battle. Backing down, he crunched his lips together, "At least bring Hi-Def with you. Besides, how are you gonna get there?"

Elliot tossed the keys to Hi-Def. "Keep an eye on our cowboy here."

Hi-Def walked out the door Alex was holding open for him. As he strode past, Alex heard him mutter, "More like he is gonna keep an eye on me."

Alex let a small smile creep out and pulled his tattered leather jacket in tight around him. His smile crept out and the cold crept in.

Hambone's voice echoed back to him as the door

shut behind "*you got Angels sitting in your shoulder.*"

Maybe he did. Alex decided to let the Angels guide him. He let a puff of heated air escape into the dark night. He had some detective work to do.

Chapter 23

Rafael Rontego sat in a leather chair, his foot resting on his opposite knee in the spacious living room of Christian 'The Pope' Biela. This condo was the lap of luxury. A window lined the outer curve of the floor and created a one hundred and eighty degree arch of glass that provided a spectacular view of the city.

The night lights danced up the fifteen stories and reflected inward, casting a pale light across the polished dark tiles. Mahogany furniture filled in the voluminous dwelling and a large glass bar resided a dozen feet from the grandiose entryway.

The assassin took the liberty of pouring himself a scotch and was sipping it. His pistol rested on the arm of his chair, within easy reach. Oddly, the killer was relaxed and enjoying the moment of solitude. A strange calm overtook Rafael Rontego since he decided on a specific course of action. The hardest part of doing something was the indecision that often preceded it.

A few moments passed, and his thoughts were so focused inward that the assassin almost didn't hear the rattle of the lock as a key lifted the deadbolt. His eyes, already well adjusted to the gloom, noticed that The Pope arrived, though that infernal cough would have announced it even if Rafael wore a blindfold.

The Pope glided into the room. He was wearing his well-pressed suit, blue with thin pinstripes, which was a little ruffled from a long day of work. His briefcase was in one hand and with his free hand he searched the wall looking for a light switch.

Having found it, he flipped the switch inside the entryway expecting illumination. The bulb was out. The assassin maximized his advantage of darkness by unscrewing the bulb from the socket, just enough to prevent a connection.

Chris Biela walked toward the bar and pulled a cord on a tiny lamp. Still facing the bar, with his back to the assassin, the consigliore placed the briefcase atop the bar and began to pour a drink. As he poured the tonic, he flicked his briefcase open, still oblivious to the assassin waiting behind. He stirred his tonic with one hand and rummaged through his briefcase with the other. After a few moments, the consigliore spun around with a tiny derringer in one hand and smooth vodka in the other.

Rafael Rontego didn't flinch. He just took another sip of his scotch, his pistol pointed at The Pope and resting on the arm of the leather chair.

"I guess I won't need this," The Pope remarked with an annoyed smirk. He lowered his miniature pistol.

"What makes you so certain," Rontego asked. He took another sip of the scotch. It was a fine drink.

"You and I both know that if you wanted to kill me I would have never known you were here." The Pope looked the assassin in the eye and took a sip of his tonic. "So that begs the question, what does bring you here?"

"Two things," Rafael said as he took his hand off his pistol and went into his jacket pocket. He pulled a matchbook out and flicked it toward Don Ciancetta's right hand man. The Pope snagged it out of the air and flipped it over. "Muro is dead," the assassin stated. Christian Biela walked into the living room and sat in another chair across from Rontego.

"That explains much." The Pope seemed to be lost in thought for a moment but then he continued, "We received an offer a couple of days ago, for a sit down tomorrow with our friends Joe Falzone and Aldo Marano." He let out a low wheeze that grew into a steady cough. He brought his sleeve up and caught a bit of spittle before it flew out into the stratosphere of the room.

"It shouldn't be related." Rontego kept a straight face trying to hide how disgusted he was with the man's physical imperfection. "I killed him just a few hours ago."

"But it is." The Pope took another sip on his drink and looked again at Rontego. "If they killed you last night, or me tonight, or the Don's son Joey, or Don Ciancetta himself, they would hold all the cards come tomorrow evening."

"But they just came after me," Rontego said, hoping to learn more from The Pope.

"This means, more than likely, we are all open targets. Or we were until Muro was killed." The Pope retreated within himself again.

"Well, the good news is you simply have to stay alive for another eighteen hours then," Rontego remarked. "But let me caution you in the words of Magaddino, may he rest in peace, 'Beware the dinner invitation from a hungry wolf'."

The Pope took in the advice and nodded his head. Then shifting gears, he shook his head and coughed. "So, two things brought you here, I assume one is to get paid for the Muro thing. Fair enough. But what now can I do for you regarding the other?"

Rontego downed the last bit of scotch in one gulp and declared, "I'm retiring. I want out."

Christian Biela almost laughed, but the sound caught in his throat as he looked at the assassin and realized he was serious. The piercing glare coming from the assassin made the consigliore shift uncomfortably in his seat.

"But why?" he asked.

"Why not?" The assassin asked. "There is bound to be a lot of heat coming down on me after all the work I have been putting in. Also, you and I both know that the Don gets a little bit squirrelly in a crisis. I don't need him second guessing my tenure. What I want from you is a guarantee that no one comes looking for me. I put in my dues. Who knows, maybe this is just a laying low period for me. But as far as anyone is concerned, I am calling it a retirement."

"I see," The Pope said. He turned inward again. After a few moments, he smiled and said, "It's not good business to go after you, Raf."

The assassin stood up and walked towards the door. He holstered his pistol and placed his fedora atop his head. "Good. Just make sure the Don sees things your way."

The Pope got up and followed him towards the door. "But where will you go? What will you do?"

"I think I have a friend to stay with, in Canada." Rafael stepped out into the hallway and turned around. "He has a little cabin by the water. I think I might do a little fishing." The assassin smiled.

"Ah, I think our friend is mutual. I know of a friend of ours who recently made that trip. Tell him Chris says 'Hello.' What of your payment for Muro?"

"Keep it. Keep it as a down payment on your promise." The assassin twirled around and walked past the bewildered guard in the hallway.

"You have my word, Rafael. No wiseguy will look for you," The Pope called out after the assassin, spurring a tiny hiccup of a cough. The Pope shot a glance at the useless guard in the hallway as Rafael rounded the corner of the building. "Next time, do your fucking job."

*

A slight rain began to slip from the mournful and overcast sky that seemed to be perpetually bound to the city of Buffalo, New York. The snow banks absorbed the hint of moisture in a way that created a glistening effect off of the street lamps in the quiet Hamburg neighborhood, a suburb just outside of the city. The soggy lumps of white seemed to get even more amorphous as the rain drops melted the freshest layers of ice and snow.

To make matters worse, Hi-Def's ride didn't have heat. Alex Vaughn and Hi-Def wrapped their jackets tighter around them and rubbed their hands together as they sat outside of Jack's residence and worked up the courage to make a run for the doorway. They parked several doors down so as to not draw attention to a parked car in a dead man's driveway.

Alex always liked coming to Jack's place. The two-story home was built on a brick foundation while the second story was protected by side paneling. It felt like a second home, even if Charlotte hesitated to accept invitations here. Vaughn couldn't blame her though; it was set less than a hundred yards from a large cemetery. They would be putting Jack in the ground, within sight of his home, sometime in the next few days. Alex shook his head and clapped his hands together in an attempt to get circulation moving in his frozen digits.

"Ready then," he declared more than asked.

Hi-Def, uncomfortable, mumbled something in reply, but Alex wasn't listening.

He opened the car door and took off in a jog. In a few moments, he was under the overhang in the doorway and his fingers were feeling along the top of the outer doorframe. He felt some debris which he imagined were the remnants of bugs or bits of dirt until his fingertips slid across the smooth surface of something metal.

Hi-Def came running up behind him and as he exited the rain he asked, "A key?"

Alex brought his hand down and showed the trophy of his find before inserting it into the lock.

The second Alex stepped in the home, a flood of memories wafted over him. Christmas parties, sharing a beer, playing cards, watching football; they all assailed him and for a moment, he felt the loss as poignantly as when it first occurred.

He pushed the memories aside and his reflexive instincts of detection kicked in. Alex searched the house, room by room. The place had been combed over as articles were moved from their original location.

In the living room, just off of the entryway, all of the furniture was moved; the indentations in the carpeting were not in line with the legs of the furniture. That was not unusual, as forensics most likely went over the area looking for hair fibers, blood, anything which could yield a DNA sample.

In the office, the drawers were pried open and the filing cabinets were rifled through. Again, it all seemed normal enough. Detectives on scene would have wanted to know what cases Jack worked on from home. They would have searched his records for any indication as to who was motivated enough to murder a cop.

Through it all, Hi-Def followed Alex like a lapdog. When they were done with the main level, Vaughn had enough of the computer geek and sent him upstairs while he moved onto the basement. At first, Hi-Def thought to protest, but with a death glare from Vaughn, he scurried up the staircase.

As Hi-Def went up, Alex went down. The basement was where Alex and Jack spent most of their time. It was a pure hangout room, built for a man. The leather chairs and wood paneling made the place feel comfortable yet like a camping lodge. Alex was still envious of the sixty inch flat screen mounted on the wall and the complete bar that lined one side of the room. He slid behind the bar and a quiet chuckle escaped his lips as he rested his hands on the wooden rail.

He could hear Jack admonish him, "Now now, just the owner gets behind this bar!"

Alex took a shot glass and grabbed a bottle of rum. He poured a shot of Jack's favorite and set the bottle back down. How many times his friend stood in this very same spot and listened to Alex gripe about his situation at home with Charlotte?

"She just doesn't get me," Alex would complain.

And always Jack would give him that knowing look. That look that said, "I get it, but don't screw it up buddy."

On one such occasion, soon after Charlotte threw him out, he sat on a bar stool across from this very spot as Jack poured him a shot. Alex went on about the righteousness of the job and how important catching the bad guys was.

He declared, "If she can't see how important this work is, then maybe she doesn't deserve to have me around anyway!"

Jack, looked into a glass as he rubbed it dry with a towel, looking the part of a bar keep. "Alex, I am going to tell you something. Don't go getting all blustery when I say it, because believe me, I know how important this job is. But why do you want to go on working so hard when it is hurting your marriage so bad? Alex, there will always be more bad guys to catch. It doesn't matter how many you lock up. Tomorrow, there will be another one. Sometimes that's the one thing I am certain about. While that's great for job security, it ain't so great on a marriage."

Jack put the glass down and grabbed up the rag as he walked around the bar behind him.

Alex was listening with half his heart lingering in the shot glass resting between his thumb and forefinger.

Jack continued as he walked toward the stairs leading upward.

"Tomorrow, next week, there will be some asshole that needs cuffs. But I can promise you one thing, there is one Charlotte. Enjoy the rum. Then go back home, to your wife."

Jack threw the towel across the room as he turned

and walked up the stairs.

Alex, of course, did not go back home.

Vaughn looked at the full shot glass sitting in front of him. He poured the glass out on the floor between his feet.

"Enjoy the rum, Jack."

Alex expected to see the rum pool there on the basement floor. Instead, it trailed off in either direction and then disappeared under the rug Alex was straddling. Vaughn sucked his breath in and crouched to the floor. He flipped the carpet over and pulled it to the side. He sucked in his breath as excitement crept in.

There was a clear outline of a two foot concrete slab. Alex, in an attempt to steady his trembling, told himself it was a place to keep excess alcohol. Vaughn took his pocket knife out of his boot and slipped it into the crevice of the slab. Using it like a crowbar he pried the concrete up and slid his fingers underneath the stone. With a heave, he pushed the block to the side revealing a tiny cubby.

Inside the cubby was a sack and a tiny palm sized booklet, the kind used for taking notes. Alex pulled the notebook up and tried to open up the sack. Noticing the sack was closed tight with plastic wire, he made a slit in the fabric with his knife. As he pulled the pieces apart, Alex almost fell back when he realized its contents.

Money. Lots of money.

Before Vaughn could get a handle on what he was dealing with, he heard the thud of footsteps descending down the stairway. In a hurry, he slid the stone back into place and kicked the rug back over it. Just in time, he tucked the notebook into the folds of his jacket, as Hi-Def came into view.

"Just like I said, nothing."

Alex gave him a smirk and said, "Sorry for

dragging your ass out here. Let's go."

Hi-Def was all too happy to oblige.

Outside in the street, Hi-Def started toward the car, but Alex began to walk through the rain up the block.

"Where ya going?" Hi-Def called to him.

"I just need to go for a walk and clear my head."

Hi-Def hesitated but then got in the car and drove off.

Alex, familiar with the neighborhood having lived in it, walked with a purpose. He needed to see Charlotte and he had to see what was in this notebook. With any luck, it would explain the money he found. One thing kept sneaking to the forefront of Alex Vaughn's mind, no matter how hard he tried to beat it back.

Jack was a dirty cop.

Chapter 24

Rafael Rontego walked down the street, oblivious to the small drops of rain that pelted his hat and trench coat. His hands were stuck in his pockets and his head watched his feet as he strode forward. He wouldn't even be going home tonight. He loved a woman once and he felt like now was as good of a time as any to say goodbye.

Love.

It felt like a millennia since Rontego allowed himself to even think of the word. Hell, Rafael didn't even know if he did love her or if he just thought that maybe he should have. Could a man give his love to a whore anyway? Then again, maybe whores were all a killer like him deserved to love.

If anyone could have seen underneath the brim of Rafael's hat, they might have noticed something that looked foreign on the creased and worn face of the veteran hit man. A natural smile emerged as Rafael thought of that night. He spent five hundred bucks to lure a real looker of a broad as a date to Don Ciancetta's wedding.

At first, Rontego didn't even want to go, but The Pope made it clear that if one didn't go, it would be considered a real insult, the type that would not be forgotten. So Rafael acquiesced and decided to attend.

Then, as if they were sticking it to him, The Pope and Don Ciancetta said they expected everyone to have a date. Something about no creepy lurkers watching people dance. Rafael didn't know any women. Women made you sloppy. They made you weak. But rules were rules and so Rafael made a visit to the local Madame. She had a solution for him and all it would cost him was five hundred bucks.

"Be here at six. She'll go with you to the reception. What you do after, well, that's up to you two."

Rafael handed her the five crisp bills. She smiled

with the satisfaction only a business owner could flash when presented with cold cash.

"Oh and Raf, do be gentle. She isn't tainted yet like all the rest."

"What's her name?" he asked. Not because it was important, but it felt like the right question to ask.

"Elyse."

Elyse.

Oh how it purred off the tongue. You could hold the 'S' just long enough that you could taste it, and then it was gone. Disappeared in the vacuum that absorbed all words ever uttered.

When he picked her up, it wasn't the long legs that seemed to continue forever under her bright red dress that held untold mysteries that caught his attention. Sure, it was the legs too, but more than that it was the eyes, nestled as they were beneath slanting blonde hair that cascaded like a gentle waterfall and hid the brilliant blue orbs from view.

In all his years of killing and fighting battles that almost ended his existence on the earth, Rafael was never as close to dead as the moment he gazed into those baby blues and felt his heart quite literally stop.

They enjoyed an almost perfect evening. He danced with her and he twirled her around like the dainty little thing she was. She laughed at his jokes and he was almost charming in his way. When it was over she invited him up and after they crossed the threshold of her apartment, they were on top of each other.

Rabid animals that reached an unspoken agreement.

He could still feel the smooth texture of her lipstick as she glided over him and he would never forget the sweetness of her perfume.

"Something French", she said.

Rafael looked up from his walk. He was under the stoop that led to her familiar room. By the light in the window, he knew she was awake. She was the only one who kept similar hours to the assassin.

There was something about Elyse that rung true in the assassin. He loved the way that she would take care of him. She even made him lunch a time or two. More important, she was there for him and there were not been many times when a person could be considered 'there' for Rafael Rontego.

The way she made him feel, Rafael felt it gripping him like drugs would an addict. He would lie with her at night or in the early morning and feel contentment he did not know in his childhood. He could watch her sleep and feel at peace. In the end, Rontego wanted to know that contentment to be his own.

He asked her one day, "What if you put aside the whoring business and you let me take care of you?"

It wasn't that she said no, that hurt the worst. It was the way that she scoffed at the idea. "I won't let myself rely on any man, Raf. Men come and go, but I have got me to take care of."

And that was that. She wasn't, at the end of the day, there for Rafael the way he assumed. Life was full of choices. Hers went in a different direction and so, Rafael did what he did best. He continued to perfect his craft and she took a backburner to anything that could advance the hit man in his profession.

At first, they thought maybe they could still play the game together. She would keep on in the whoring business and Rafael would do what he always did, but they would know they were for each other and she never did charge Rontego again.

As time went by, that spark in her eye began to diminish. Life began to reflect in those baby blues and they weren't so baby anymore. He started to resent her for giving away that one of a kind, brilliant type of light she had. As it grew dimmer and dimmer, he felt himself hating her for selling it so cheap.

The assassin climbed the stairs to her apartment and gave the door one loud rap. In a moment, she answered, and she stood silhouetted against the warm and inviting glow of soft lights beyond. She was wearing a pure white nightgown that slit along the leg. It revealed just enough of her thigh.

"Raf!" She said in surprise bordering on delight. It felt almost musical to the assassin after all of these hard years.

Her eyes seemed to catch some of their previous fire in that second, but then it faded away. She shifted her weight and revealed a bit more thigh. Rafael couldn't tell if it was on purpose or not. Eyes were overrated anyway. He took off his hat as he brushed past her and entered the room. He threw his hat on a plush sofa off to the side and turned back around to face her.

"Doll."

"What's going on?"

"I've come to say goodbye."

Just like that, she was upon him. For a moment, Rontego felt like he could still love this woman. But then it flitted away as they fell over one another in search of that instant of ecstasy. That was all life really was, anyway. A series of moments that drifted on too fast; so fast that one could scarce enjoy them before they searched for the next.

They passed out next to each other, exhausted. When he woke up, Rafael took great care not to wake her. He pulled five crisp bills from his clip and laid them on the dresser.

He let himself out into the hallway beyond and whispered, "Elyse."

*

Alex walked towards the north end of the block

199

and stood in front of the doorway to the house that used to be his home. It was a quaint home, two stories tall and built mostly of brick. A solitary bay window overlooked the street. That was the main reason Alex purchased the home.

It's funny sometimes, the small, unnecessary things that remind you most of what a home should be. He passed by the place a few times since Charlotte and he separated.

She was asleep. All the lights were out and somewhere inside, in a crib he built, was his baby girl.

Vaughn felt weary. His head throbbed and he became ever more aware of his disheveled appearance. His jacket was in tatters, parts of it were scorched. His hands were filthy and he could only imagine the layer of film that accumulated due to dust and ash and blood.

Alex turned around to leave. Then, he turned around again and before his courage could leave him, leaning on the door with one hand, Alex lifted the other and gave a sharp knock on the door, once, twice, and a third time.

At first, there was nothing. Alex thought that perhaps Charlotte slept through his attempt at awakening her. But then the house began to come alive. A light in the second floor turned on and Alex almost ran. Then a baby, his baby, began to cry from within. He heard the shuffling of feet inside and then the bolts to locks he installed began to click. All of a sudden, there she was.

The door was open and she was standing before him. She wore a ragged pink robe that he always hated, and her brown hair was tied up behind her head. Sleep was in her eyes and the baby wailed in the background. But there she was. There Charlotte was. Absolute in her beauty.

All of Vaughn's strength seemed to flee from his limbs as he stood there and a moment of silence passed as the two sized each other up. They spoke at the same time,

Alex whispered, "Charlotte."

"Alex!"

He leaned forward and threw his arms around her, having no more strength for words. Charlotte pulled Alex inside, and shut the door.

Fortunately, Charlotte could tell by looking at Alex that the questions would have to wait. For now she just said, "You are going to have to take a shower before you lay down anywhere in this house. You know where the guest bath is. I'll lay out some of your old clothes, but I'm going back to bed. I'll wake you in a couple hours when I get up. Then, you can explain what the hell has happened to you."

Alex smiled weakly at her and walked through the living room to the guest bathroom. As he slid the door shut behind him, he glanced back over at Charlotte who was about to walk up the stairs towards her bedroom, their bedroom.

"Charlotte?"

"Yes?"

"Thanks."

She shook her head as she continued up the stairs, "Of course, Alex, of course."

Vaughn let the warm water wash over him, and felt its gentle sting enter his wounds one cut at a time as the cleansing crept over him. When he was done there was a set of clothes that were all too familiar to him resting on the carpet outside in the hallway. He slipped on the pair of jeans which felt a bit loose to him and a baseball sleeve knit sweatshirt, very much an outfit he would wear on most any weekend.

Alex wanted to go upstairs and look on the face of his beautiful baby, but he didn't want to wake her. So he walked over to the couch and settled in under a hand woven blanket his grandmother made him as a newborn. It just fit over his grown body, but it felt all the warmer for the memories it brought back.

As bad as Alex Vaughn wanted to sleep, he found it difficult to sleep. He kept flashing back to the unopened notebook lying on top of the pile of clothes at his feet. He was dying to know what the contents held, but he was fearful of what they might say about Jack and any extracurricular activities he might have.

It became too much to bear and Alex rolled over to his side and lifted up the red booklet. Besides, what if Jack was dirty? Did it make him any less of a true friend to Alex? The answer was unequivocally no. The two of them grew up together, and time and again Jack proved his friendship to Alex on a very personal level.

Alex decided right then and there that whatever this book revealed, it would do nothing to diminish Jack in his eyes. It was with that sense of resolve that Vaughn flipped the cover of the notebook over on its spiral joint. The first pages scribbled in Jack's handwriting were the words, "Private: Case File Notes."

Alex sucked in his breath. Jackpot. He thumbed through the notebook, page by page, and his excitement faded to amusement and reminiscing as he recalled some of the cases that went back three years or more. It was like a freaking yearbook of Jack's last years on the force. But as he thumbed through the booklet he thought it less and less certain that he would find anything useful. His fears were confirmed when he got to the last page and it was a case from a few months back.

Alex took the notebook and tossed it on the floor. It didn't make sense. Why hide a notebook that contained nothing that should be hidden? Alex sat there for a moment and then picked the notebook back up. He flipped it right to the last page. He ran his finger across the paper and felt its smoothness on his fingertips. Alex noticed that there was a slight indent along the side of the paper.

Perhaps it was just the indent from the pressure of a pen resting on it. But the impression ran along the page vertical, and it ran in to straight of a line.

Vaughn peered more close at it and realized it was not an indentation, but more like the softening of the paper. The detective lifted the pad of paper up to his nose and caught the faint smell of glue. He could feel his heart beat in his ears. Vaughn pulled out his knife and found where the two pages connected up near the top. He slid his knife in between the two pages and brought the blade down around the edges of the paper, pulling the parchment apart. There in front of him was information about the case for sure. But how it fit together, Alex was not so sure. It read:

- $200,000 intercepted from Bonanno crew
- Elliot can be trusted
- 'The Pope' has answers
- Get Alex's help for the meet

Alex was now fully awake. He could trust Elliot, Jack wrote.

If it was good enough for Jack, then it sure as hell is good enough for me, Alex thought.

Alex threw his gun holster over his shoulders and tucked his knife back into the anklet above his boot. He grabbed his jacket and tucked the notebook inside. If 'The Pope' had answers, then that was where Alex was going to go.

Vaughn walked to the mantle and saw his old badge resting atop it, just as he left it. With a quick smile he dusted it off and pinned it to the inside of his jacket. Striding towards the door, Alex paused as he reached the banister. Some part of him pulled at him to run up and say hello to his wife, to check on his baby girl. His heart was up there already. Brushing his fingers through is long brown hair; Alex set his face and forced his feet toward the door.

Chapter 25

Rafael Rontego carried his bag of cash slung over his shoulder and his fedora tilted low over his head as he approached the cashier behind a relic of a wooden desk and a glass window. Rontego found it funny how similar to movie windows train station ticket windows were. A bald gentleman with glasses too large for his face greeted him at the window.

Christ, Rafael thought. *Was this joker really wearing a bowtie? Best to get this over with.*

"I'll take your quickest line to Toronto." Rontego slid his passport under the window.

The geek behind the counter let out a chuckle and said, "Well, that's easy enough, sir. There is only one line from here to Toronto and it departs promptly at three in the afternoon."

Rafael looked over the clerks shoulder and noticed a clock peaking back at him that read 6 A.M.

Nine fucking hours.

The clerk must have noticed the dismay curl out of Rontego's lips because he said, "Yep. You're in for a bit of a wait. May I suggest those wooden benches over there? They are more comfortable than they seem."

Rontego peered out at the little man and asked, "How long do you think it would take to walk there?"

The man chuckled again and his bowtie bounced with his Adam's apple. "Well, you could always take a cab. Or the bus, now that wouldn't be so bad."

Rontego shook his head; he wanted to take the train in, and the people on buses aggravated him.

Screw it. I'm in no rush. "I'll take one ticket please to Toronto."

"Very good then sir. One ticket it is. Would you like that to be first class?"

"Sure."

205

The clerk handed over a ticket booklet and Rafael slid him cash to cover the ride. Rontego took a walk over to the benches suggested by the clerk and laid back down across the bench on his back. He tilted his hat over his eyes and rested his head down on his bag of cash with one hand resting inside of his jacket on a curious cold lump of steel.

If one existed, God forgive the bastard who tries anything funny.

With that thought, Rafael drifted into an uneasy sleep, waking up as each new passenger arrived in the station.

*

Vaughn stepped out of the cab that carried him away from his old neighborhood, in front of a low office building on the corner of First and Franklin Street. A plain white sign with black lettering read Law Office of Christian Biela: Attorney At Law est. 1999. Alex Vaughn knew who The Pope was, and he knew where to find him. The advertisement didn't hurt the search any either.

"Wait right here," he directed the cab driver.

Alex walked from the curb to the building, attempting to evade the cold that seeped in under his jacket. He walked inside to the heat of the building and swung the door around behind, shielding the room from the encroaching cold.

A young receptionist sat in the rear of a small lobby area and held a telephone in one hand and was writing information on a pad with the other. Alex walked past her and headed straight for the door.

She stood up and put the phone down and held up a hand as if to stop Alex and said, "Sir, you can't go in there."

Vaughn pulled his jacket back revealing his pistol

and continued on past her. He pushed open the door and saw The Pope sitting at a desk facing him. He wore a white button down and a red tie. His suit jacket was draped on a sofa to the left.

Vaughn took two steps inside before he heard the click of a gun hammer coming from his back and felt the cool steel of its muzzle pressed against his forehead. Not moving his head, Alex looked to the side and saw a rather imposing man standing off to his side.

Spitting out the one thing that he could think of, Alex declared, "I'm a cop."

"Sure you are," The Pope smiled. "They all are. Let's see the badge."

Alex grabbed the buttons of his jacket and lifted its fold. Revealed beneath, was his gold badge with its American Bald Eagle spread across its breadth.

With a grimace and a wave, The Pope called off his man.

"Mr. Biela, I have something very important to discuss with you."

He started hacking and wheezing as some sort of bug started doing jumping jacks in The Pope's throat.

"Well, what's keeping you, officer?"

Alex was not fond of how The Pope seemed to spit that last word at him.

"I'll make this brief. My friend Jack Benton was murdered three days ago. He was a cop with the Buffalo P.D."

"You don't say."

"Yes, he was. You, sir, were implicated in his personal notes."

The Pope shifted in his chair. "Now I don't know nothing about anything like that."

"I'm sure you don't. But this isn't about whether you pulled the trigger."

Alex pulled his gun out and rested it on the table.

Leaning forward he continued.

"Now I am not here to make things hard on you, though I could, you know. I could be a hassle for you each and every day of your fucking life." He was inches from The Pope's face at this point. Alex straightened up and pulled back, "Or you can answer a few quick questions and I'll be out of your hair. Like I was never here."

The Pope gave a little cough, "What do you want to know? Depending on that, my answers depend."

Alex Vaughn laid it out for him, "Two things. The first is I know who killed my friend Jack. His name is Rafael Rontego and he is a man said to be under the employ of your boss, Leonard Ciancetta. Where is he? The second, why do you suppose my friend intercepted a shipment of two hundred thousand dollars from the Bonanno crime family here in Buffalo?"

Clearing his throat, The Pope closed his eyes as if going through a mental checklist of the ramifications of each avenue pursued from this moment forward.

Finally, he opened his eyes again and said, "Fuck you."

Alex Vaughn snapped. He worked too hard to get to this point to be stonewalled by an antiquated vow of silence. He unhooked his badge and threw it against the wall. Pulling his pistol out faster than he had ever been able to in the past, he cocked the hammer back and pressed the barrel against the lips of The Pope.

"Fuck me? Fuck you!"

Spit flew out of Alex's mouth and his bloodshot eyes watered as he strained keeping himself from pulling the trigger and letting his aggression fall with the hammer launching it into the mouth of this asshole.

"They call you The Pope, well you better fucking have a way forward with God because I swear to Christ you're about to meet him!"

Pressing the barrel forward even more, the steel

grated against the teeth of The Pope. The Pope's eyes were wide, matching the rage in Alex's with the type of fear that comes from something unexpected.

Already holding down his coughing, The Pope went into a terrible coughing fit but he refused to shut his eyes with the steel shoved indelicate between his lips. Alex took a breath, regaining some of his composure but not letting The Pope know he had beaten back the urge to see the color of his brain matter.

"Now are you going to tell me what I want to know, so I can leave here with your face intact?"

The Pope nodded his agreement.

Vaughn pulled the muzzle out of Christian Biela's mouth and walked over to the sofa that held The Pope's suit jacket. He picked it up and used it to wipe the saliva off of the barrel of his pistol.

"I'm fucking waiting."

The Pope swallowed, wetting his mouth, and let out a final cough rasp. "The answer to your first question is he's in a cabin outside of Toronto. If not yet, than he soon will be. Here's the address." The Pope started scribbling an address on a piece of loose leaf paper. "The second is a bit more complicated, but I guess even you cops aren't so dense as to miss the fact that we're in the middle of a damned civil war here. I assume, and again this is just conjecture, that the two hundred grand was a payment from the Bonanno crew for an alliance of mutual benefit with the Falzone crew. I could have heard that somewhere. Why your friend Jack had it, that I do not know."

Alex stood there a moment, taking it all in. He didn't know why, but he believed The Pope. A gun in the mouth has a way of finding truth.

"Alright. See, that wasn't so hard." Vaughn walked over and picked up his badge.

He walked back to the desk and grabbed the piece

of paper with the cabin address etched across it. The Pope, happy to have the ordeal over with nodded his head, but never took his eyes off of Alex.

Alex composed himself and turned to leave, backing out of the room.

"Oh officer? Here is one last piece of advice. Do with it what you will. Don't trust the fucking cops."

Vaughn tilted his head, not sure where to go with that statement. He opened the door and walked out. After he took a few steps he heard The Pope call after him, "Oh, and fuck you!"

Alex Vaughn let a little smile cross his face as he folded the address up and slipped it into his pocket.

Chapter 26

The Pope waited for the officer to leave, then got up and poured himself a scotch from a mini bar in the corner of his office. Dropping two ice cubes into the drink, Christian wondered whether or not drinking before noon made him an alcoholic.

It didn't matter, he decided.

Given what he was going through this week, he figured the alcohol gods would give their blessing to his indulgence. He sat back down, letting a heavy sigh escape his lips.

The Pope looked into his scotch searching for answers. Cops coming to his business, old friends and associates getting gunned down daily, and to top it all off he had to sit down with people most likely intent on killing him. Tonight was the night. Either way, things were going to end tonight.

He fought back the urge to cough again. He was so tired of hacking and coughing. He even went and saw his physician. Damned doctors. All he said was that he must have the flu and he was 'going to run some tests'. All those lab coats were the same. You paid them a hundred bucks just to hear what you already knew—that you're sick.

The Pope thought about what just transpired. *Nosy fucking cop*. At first, Christian thought he should just stonewall the bastard. After all, he took an oath of silence. But there was something unnerving about the look in the cop's eyes. That and a pistol in your mouth was a definite wake up call.

It wasn't the first time The Pope came face to face with a barrel of a gun, but while he was sucking on metal a genius thought occurred to the crafty consigliore. This cop wanted Rafael dead. The Don wouldn't be saddened to see that loose end wrapped up. So if Rontego got taken out, that was fine with The Pope. Conversely, say that the cop got laid low at the hands of Rafael. Well then, there was one less prying cop to deal with.

Win-win situation.

The Pope smiled. If only the prick cop knew how all of this was related. He was glad he withheld that information from the officer. He took down the scotch in one long pull from his glass until the ice cube bounced off of his lips.

He stood up and wiped the wetness from his lips with a brush of his hand.

Tonight. Tonight the house gets put into order.

If not, he would watch it burn down around him. He picked up the phone and called over to Don Ciancetta's at Rumors.

Someone picked up on the other line.

"Hello?"

The Pope recognized the voice as a newcomer to the group, a friend of the Don's son named Ricky Vincenzio.

"Tell the boss that the meeting is a go tonight."

Then The Pope hung up. Just in time too, because he felt another one of his coughing fits creeping up on him.

The consigliore rose and walked over to pour another scotch. Almost as an afterthought, he called to his body man outside the door, "Hey Nuncio!"

He shuffled through the door. "Yes sir."

"Grab the car and shadow our friend who just left. I want to know where he goes, who he talks to."

"How are you gonna get around?"

"Don't worry about me, just go!"

Nuncio did a curt turn and left.

Just once I'd like people to just listen without questioning every little thing.

The Pope shook his head in mild disappointment. He started coughing and had a handkerchief ready this time to catch a wad of mucus that escaped his lips. He looked at the brown-yellow phlegm and wondered if he saw blood in it.

Tonight.

*

Alex Vaughn left the office of The Pope and got back into the cab which loyally awaited his exit; probably because he hadn't paid when he left last time. Alex found out over the years that if you want a cab to wait for you, keep the meter running and don't pay them until you reach your final destination.

Alex Vaughn took out his cell phone and called through the dispatch number that Hi-Def provided him with. An automated voice directed him to enter the 8 digit code to be connected to his party of choice. After a few rings, he heard the familiar voice of Elliot on the other line.

"Elliot here."

"Elliot, its Alex."

"What can I do for you?" His voice seemed distracted or disinterested.

"A lot has happened in the last several hours. We need to talk."

"I'm a bit busy Alex, can it wait?"

"Not really. Listen, I found a large sum of money at Jack's yesterday. That and a notebook that had some leads on it."

Elliot perked up in a hurry. "Christ. Hi-Def told me you didn't find anything."

"Well, I hid it from him. Listen, we can't be too careful who we trust with this thing. I don't know why Jack had all that cash, but it can't be good. If they could have gotten to Jack, then they could have gotten to others. "

"Then why tell me? Jesus, this is heavy." Elliot

didn't seem to like being entrusted with this sort of information.

"Because Jack was my friend and it was his personal notes that said I could trust you. But with all due respect to your men, outside of Ryan Slate, I don't know them. Listen, we need to talk as soon as possible." The warning from the Pope stuck in his head like a damned disc on skip.

There was a moment of silence on the other line and Alex thought that Elliot hung up on him for a second. "Elliot?"

"Yeah, I'm here. Ok, let's meet at the safe house at nine. Can you make it then?"

Alex checked his watch, it was just passed seven. "Absolutely. Oh and Elliot?"

"Yeah?"

"I know where to find Rafael Rontego."

There was a low whistle on the other line and Alex could almost feel Elliot pursing his lips together.

"That's great work. How much money are we talking about over at Jack's?"

"I don't know, but a lot."

There was another moment of silence as Elliot digested the news. "Where is the money now?"

A small warning bell went off in Alex's mind. "I think I am going to keep that to myself, for now."

"Sure, that's for the best anyway. All right, we'll talk more when we see each other."

Alex heard the click as Elliot hung up. Two hours. What the hell was he supposed to do for two hours?

Might as well head over to the safe house.

Alex gave the address to the cabbie and settled in for the rest of the ride. For a moment, he thought he noticed a sedan in the distance, but it pulled down a side road, and Alex let his mind wander.

Chapter 27

Vaughn got out of the cab and tossed the driver a wad of bills before heading up to the door of the safe house. For some reason the hair on his neck was tingling, as if he were being watched. He noticed that the door to the detached garage was open a bit and he slowed down to peer at it. Something in it beckoned to him and he remembered that something was covered by a tarp on his previous visit to the residence.

He took a step off of the main walkway leading to the front door of the home in the direction of the garage, when the front door opened. Ryan Slate, also known as Ricky Vincenzio, came out dressed for the role of his Italian alter ego.

Ryan walked up and grabbed a hold of Alex's hand shaking it in congratulatory fashion. He was followed by Hambone who exited a moment after him, looking large as usual.

"I heard you made quite a few breakthroughs the other day," Ryan said. His face was beaming.

"I got some work done. So I guess Elliot called ahead and filled you guys in?"

Hambone gave a little grunt and said, "Yeah he filled us in." Then the man turned around and walked back inside.

"What's his problem?" Alex Vaughn could feel the ice come off of Hambone's shoulder as he shut the door behind him and went back inside.

"I'd guess he was jealous or something. I think he is just sympathizing with Hi-Def a bit. You should have let him know about what you found. He thinks you left him out to get the credit." Ryan gave him a shrug of his shoulders.

"Oh, well, I didn't do it to leave him out. Just wanted to be careful."

"So where did you stash the money anyway?"

"Somewhere safe. Just until I know who I should turn it into. Maybe I should drive it down to the station." Alex watched Ryan shift from foot to foot. He seemed a bit uncomfortable with the topic.

"You think it will make Jack look dirty?"

"To be honest, I don't know what to think. But I do know that the less people who know about a mountain of cash, the better." Alex let out a little chuckle that was joined in by Slate.

"Alright, well I have to go. Big night tonight. I'm driving Don Ciancetta's son to a sit down. I'll check in with you later."

Ryan walked down the sidewalk and Alex watched him for a second before going into the safe house where Hambone was sitting on one of the chairs wrapping up a phone conversation. The brute abruptly ended the call and clicked his cell phone shut as Alex took a seat in the uncomfortable plastic chair that faced Hambone from across the tiny room.

Hambone cast a stare on Alex and moved a hand to scratch at the stubble lining his cheeks. He was reclined back, his feet stretched out far in front of him. He looked tired, Alex thought. Vaughn could identify with that feeling. The past few nights he slept uneasy at best. But there was something more to the look that Hambone was casting his way, almost as if it were laced with enmity. Alex thought to disregard the feeling but Hambone just kept on staring.

Vaughn was feeling ever more unnerved and could feel his body begin to fidget. Long moments passed and Vaughn got the feeling that the two were sizing each other up. Or at least, he was being sized up. The quiet tick of the clock in the entryway grew loud, a loudness that was muffled by the sound of Alex's heart beating in his ears. Finally, it became unbearable.

Alex opened his mouth to ask, "What's your problem?"

But he was interrupted when Hambone leaned forward in his chair and spit out, "Where's the money?"

Alex, relieved to have the insufferable silence broken, almost told him. But he stopped short of divulging the location.

What is with these people, he wondered.

That was three times in the span of three conversations that Elliot and his crew asked him where the money was. Once from Elliot, once from Slate, and now in his usual subtle way, Hambone.

"What's it to you?" he said instead.

"It's evidence," he said.

Alex was tired of the games. "My friend, my find, my time frame."

Hambone sat there, his eyes were fixed on Alex and his hands were clasped together. The muscles in his arms chorded as he pressed his palms together. This was not a man used to be told to kindly go fuck himself. Alex stood up. Hambone stood up also and blocked Alex's path.

"I'm going to go get some air," Vaughn said, looking square into the chest of the large man. Hambone paused for a moment, and then stepped aside.

"You go do that."

Alex didn't like how he was given permission to go outside, but let it slide in an effort to deescalate whatever bothered Hambone. He took a few steps and cast a wary glance over his shoulder before stepping outside and closing the door behind him.

Vaughn took a look around as he took a deep breath and felt the warm sunlight hit his face. At the same time, a chill from the snow below crept up his legs, creating an odd contrast. Alex thought that it was a somewhat accurate physical representation of what he felt at that moment. He was a jumble of emotions. He couldn't believe he went and saw Charlotte, no matter how brief, the night before. He hadn't the courage to face her, and he guessed, probably still didn't. Last night was an accident of circumstance. The weather, lack of sleep, worry about Jack; all led his feet to her front door.

He didn't have to jet out as fast as he did this morning, perhaps. Charlotte would have told him he was using work to avoid having to deal with his own personal issues. He knew that she would have been right too.

Alex puffed out a cloud of white breath and breathed in deep, letting his thoughts go back to the scene inside and the chaos of the last few days. What was that tension inside all about? Things were much more tranquil out here. He could see how being cooped up inside might start to wear on someone. Still, there was something more to the animosity that Hambone was directing his way and Alex couldn't help but wonder how he offended the man.

As he stood there, his gaze fell over the detached garage and his memory shot to the first time he drove to the safe house just after the explosion that killed Sal. He began to make his way towards the detached garage. It was about twenty feet removed from the house and about fifty feet removed from the road. He stopped and glanced at the windows and at the door to make sure no one was watching him, and then jogged to the garage. With another glance around to make sure the coast was clear, he disappeared inside between the barn-like double doors.

The first thing that Alex noticed was the smell. It was dank in there and smelled more like a musty basement than a garage. There was a hint of oil and gasoline, but the place in general smelled musty. A large rusty pipe lined the roof of the structure and a few shelves that housed various tools lined one of the walls. There was an empty parking space on the left side and some sort of vehicle under a tarp on the right.

Alex remembered the first time he came here and

the tarp being pulled over the vehicle before Alex could get a look. He meant to get that look now. Something called at him to look. Knowing time was an issue Alex hurried over to the tarp and knelt down next to the rear of the vehicle. He pulled the edge of the canvas back; he lifted it just above the license plate where he stopped.

Vaughn could hardly breathe. He knew this car.

Why was Jack's car in this garage?

Alex put his hand gently on the license plate. Touching it made it feel more real. This, all of this, was so surreal. Jack was dead, but his car was here. There was a bag of cash in his basement. Were they working together? If so, then why wouldn't they have known where the money was? After all, Jack said that Elliot could be trusted. Something was not making sense.

When in doubt follow the money, he thought.

He was taught that soon after he earned his shield. The money came from the Bonanno crew. It was intercepted by Jack. Alex reached towards his gun as he worked out the scenario. Elliot and his friends wanted the money. The money Jack confiscated. There was a sound behind him.

Still hunched over the license plate all Alex Vaughn could say was, "Mother Fu-" before he felt the explosion in the back of his head.

He fell to the side of the car, almost blacked out from the pain. He tried to lift his head up off the pavement in the garage, but his body just twitched in response. The blackness started to drift away and his vision came back into focus, just in time to see the laces of a black leather boot swing in and catch him full in the face.

He heard his skin rip just before his old friend, the oblivion, met him somewhere in the recesses of his mind.

*

Fifteen minutes across town, The Pope received a phone call. He listened to the voice on the other line, and then he hung up. He waited a few moments and weighed his options. The consigliore looked at the scotch glass on his desk, then walked over to the bottle and took a swig directly from it. The Pope picked the phone back up and made a call.

His southern accent coming out more with more force, he said to the man who answered, "I need you two to come here right now."

He listened to the voice coming through on the other line. Then he interrupted.

"I know it's going to be hard. But get here anyway. Something's come up."

Again the voice on the line pushed back.

The Pope, irritated, screamed into the phone, "I don't give a fuck! Get your asses over here!"

He slammed the phone down. Just once, he'd like somebody, anybody, to just do what the fuck they were told without questioning every little detail. The Pope felt his blood pressure at a dangerous high level and took a deep breath, holding it in and allowing himself to calm. When he exhaled he didn't feel any different. It did however spur him into another coughing frenzy that left him feeling weak.

He cast a glance at the bottle and opted to cheat in order to bring things back into perspective. The Pope took another drink and then put the top back on the bottle. Taking his suit jacket off of the chair, he put one arm through at a time.

Those bastards better not take too long, he thought.

Chapter 28

Vaughn woke up with a dull ache in his shoulders and a very vivid pain somewhere on his face. As he came to consciousness, he was aware that it hurt most under his eye and pretty much radiated around the back of this head. His ears didn't hurt, though, that was good.

He tried to bring his hand to his face so he could feel the wound and that's when he noticed he was hanging off of the ground with his hands stretched over his head. Alex groaned as he felt the pain throb outward from his eye and he pulled his head back to look at his hands.

There was a rope tied around his hands in a figure-eight twist. The makeshift cuffs were thrown over a hook that hung from a thick steel chain wrapped around the rusty pipe that ran the length of the garage roof.

In a panic, he tried to look around the room, but his eye was almost swollen shut. His breath came out in labored wheezes due to the stretch and weight of his body hanging two feet off of the ground. Catching his attention was a slight scraping sound coming from his left. Unfortunately, Alex couldn't see what was making the noise.

Scrape.

Whatever it was, it was just out of the range of his right eye. He lolled his head as far to his right as he could, and cocked his head at an odd ninety degree angle.

Scrape.

The blood from the wound under his left eye dripped across his lips and Alex could taste the iron of his own blood.

Scrape.

He just registered the taste as he picked up the source of the sound. Hambone was sitting in an old wooden chair in the garage. He held a piece of wood in his hand and a long, curved knife in the other. He was absently shaving pieces off of what looked to be a thick piece of wood that was being pared down. Hambone shot a quick look Alex's way, noticing he regained consciousness.

"Welcome back," he said.

His voice was even and thick. It was apparent that he'd waited there for some time.

Alex decided to get right to the point. "Coward". The blood from his mouth sprayed out with his spittle. "You killed Jack for the money."

He declared it as if it were truth. Vaughn hoped to get whatever information he could now that the gloves were off.

Hambone stood up, tucked his blade into his belt, and stood right in front of Alex, hanging on the hook helpless. Instead of seeing a hint of irritation on the man's face, Alex was surprised when he let out a laugh.

"You really don't get it, do you? I thought you were supposed to be a detective." Hambone turned around as if to go back to his whittling.

Alex didn't know what to make of the situation. He was frustrated and the enormity of his helplessness fell upon him. He began to thrash back and forth on the hook, not knowing what else to do. As he swayed on the hook, Hambone turned around to regard him.

"Calm down," he said. "You'll just make matters worse."

Through bloody teeth and ripped lips Alex's voice came out in a coarse bark. "Cop killer."

Hambone walked back towards Alex. "I have not killed a cop in my life…yet."

"It doesn't matter if you pulled the trigger. You're no better than the rest. At least they can admit what they did, you pussy."

Hambone's face turned red as the sting of Alex's words took hold. The man stood there and unbuttoned the cuffs of his shirt. Glaring at Alex, he rolled each sleeve up and stood less than a foot away from Alex.

"Seems I tagged your face pretty good."

"I wasn't even looking."

The brute scratched his nose with his thumb and gave a little snicker as he looked out at Alex from beneath his furrowed brow.

"Are you looking now, detective?"

With that, Hambone exploded into a burst of action delivering a bruising blow to Alex's exposed rib.

The large fist buried itself into Vaughn's side and sent his air out in a burst. The air rushing out of Alex's mouth brought more blood from Vaughn's throat and sprayed Hambone across his face.

Alex let out another groan and hung there, his lungs gasped for air for his battered body. Hambone walked to a shelf and grabbed a hand towel. He wiped Alex's blood from his face and talked.

"Elliot told me to leave you intact. So unfortunately, we can't keep playing this game."

Vaughn sucked in some air and gathered a bit of his pride as he swayed back and forth, the momentum of the hit still shaking through his body and articulating itself in the momentum of his swing.

"I'm still here, you pussy."

His cracked lips and bloody smile mocked Hambone, who tossed the rag to the floor. "You really think you're a tough guy, don't you? Well, I guess I can go one more round before Elliot gets here."

He strode forward and curled his arm back to deliver another hit to the rib. But Alex was ready this time, and using his momentum on the return swing, curled his foot behind his leg and snapped his knee up, bashing it square into Hambone's nose just as the large man swung his own momentum forward to hit the detective.

It resulted in a satisfying *POP.* It was Hambone's

turn to gasp for air as his normal means for breathing was temporarily caved in. He stumbled backward with a shout of surprise and bent over about four feet from Alex, whose momentum carried him back and forth yet again.

For a moment, Hambone stayed there, doubled over, watching his blood speckle the garage floor and felt his smashed nasal cavity. After a moment, he pulled the blade from his side and ran at Alex. Before Vaughn could react, the man pressed the blade against his throat and was pressing it forward.

The two were eye to eye and the anger in Hambone's eyes was apparent as the glare bore into Alex's resigned eyes.

Hambone pressed the knife against his throat a bit hard and Alex felt its ridges bite into his flesh. Vaughn felt like this was the end. He wasn't going to give Hambone the satisfaction of seeing even a moment of fear or regret in his eyes. He locked into a stare with the man and dared him to do it.

"Fucking do it, you coward."

At that moment, the door to the garage swung open and Elliot and Hi-Def walked in. Elliot, gathering a sense of the scene before him, held up a hand as Hi-Def came in behind him. Hi-Def stopped and looked in and a mask of horror crossed his face as he looked at the two men nose to nose in the garage.

"Go into the house and wait there," Elliot said.

Hi-Def, not needing to be told twice, walked out of the garage and shut the door behind him.

Elliot came forward into the room and laid a hand on Hambone's arm pressing the knife into Alex's throat and said, "Go sit down."

Hambone sent a glare at Elliot, but retracted the blade.

"Sit down," Elliot repeated.

With a frustrated shout, Hambone hurled the knife

at the corner of the room and walked out of the garage snapping, "I'll be right outside if you need me."

Elliot walked back to the garage door and pulled it shut. He then grabbed the chair that Hambone sat on and put it under Alex's feet. Backing up, he stood between Alex Vaughn and the exit. He pulled his pistol and held it out as a reminder to Alex to not do anything rash.

Vaughn caught his footing on the chair and asked, "Do you mind if I pull my hands off of this hook and sit down?"

"Not at all, just remember who has the gun."

Alex nodded his head and brought his hands forward off of the hook. At once, he felt the relief in his stretch joints and felt the cartilage release from his overextended shoulders. Elliot watched him with his lips pursed together as if contemplating what to do.

Alex faced the man and accused him, "You killed Jack."

He jumped off of the chair and stood in front of it.

Elliot looked shocked by the accusation. "I most certainly did not."

Vaughn couldn't believe that the man had the gall to lie to him. Face to face, he still wouldn't tell the truth.

"Enough of the games!"

Elliot rolled back from the force of the shout and held the gun up again to remind Alex who was in charge here.

Regaining his composure, the detective sat down on the chair, and asked point blank, "What the hell is going on here?"

He stood there a moment, as if he were deciding what to do. Elliot said, "Fair enough Alex. I'm going to level with you here. You're a dead man and there is nothing I can do about it. Jack's dead, and there isn't anything I can do about that either."

Alex wasn't as surprised to hear that he was a dead

man as he would have supposed he might. It wasn't often that one got his face kicked in and hung on a hook and had a knife put to his throat and the intent was not to sooner or later kill the guy being abused in such a way. But he was confused.

"So why tell me, if all you're going to do is kill me anyway."

"Because Alex, I am not a dead man, yet. I need that money."

Alex brushed his bloody and matted hair away from his face. "Well, I'm not going to tell you where the money is unless you tell me why."

Vaughn was resigned to the fact that he was not getting out of this.

Elliot laughed. "No, I think you will tell me Alex." Here he waved his gun over his shoulder as he spoke. "You see there are those in our little group that feel if you don't tell us, we might have to make a visit to your family down the road."

Alex lunged forward and yelled, "You son of a bitch!"

Vaughn wanted to rip this man's lips off of his face and choke him on them.

As he came forward though, Elliot brought the gun around and placed the barrel at Vaughn's head, halting his momentum.

"Sit back down."

Vaughn inched backwards and sat back down on the chair.

Keeping his gun leveled at Alex, Elliot pulled a finger up to his lips and stood there for another moment before continuing, "I don't *want* to hurt your family, Alex. This business has gotten messy enough. But understand this; I will do what I have to do to survive."

Alex met Elliot's gaze and looked at him mustering as much nerve as he could.

"Tell me what is going on, and I will tell you where your money is. Why did you kill Jack? That's all I have wanted to know this whole time. Why is Jack dead?"

Elliot scratched his head and looked at the ground for a moment before snapping it back up and declaring, "Deal." He paused and took a breath then continued, "Jack is dead because one of his informants alerted him to a shipment of cash coming from the Bonanno crime family in New York City. That money, Jack was told, was supposed to be delivered to Falzone, the underboss of Don Ciancetta. It was going to bankroll a major switch in allegiance before the war started."

Alex shook his head. "Confiscations happen all the time. No outfit is going to kill a cop for intercepting cash and locking it up in the evidence ward. It's the price of doing business."

"Ah well, you see there's the problem. That money that was going to bankroll the switch was supposed to be delivered by me and my team."

Vaughn almost choked. "You've been working for them this whole time?"

"Well, I wouldn't say we have been working for them," Elliot said. "More like we make the monetary transactions between the families and we take a cut. We tax it. Listen, this money was going to be delivered with or without us. At least we can make a few bucks on the side."

Alex's face went flush and he felt anger welling inside of him. "I don't believe it. Jack would never..."

Elliot cut him off. "Jack. Good God, no. Have you ever even met the man, Alex? That guy is straight through and through. No, Jack wouldn't give us the money no matter how many times we told him we were the deep undercover unit on the case. Never mind the fact that we *are* assigned to watch the family's relations."

"So then why, why was Jack even there night?"

"I guess I bear the responsibility for that. Unfortunately, the one way I could get the money to be delivered was to convince Jack that it needed to be delivered for our undercover mission. Jack was to make the exchange and pay off the man who was supposed to switch sides."

"Only Jack didn't bring the money."

"Only Jack didn't bring the money." Elliot repeated. "Also, Rafael Rontego wasn't the type to be bought off. Even if he didn't have the money, like you said, they would never just kill a cop. Threaten him? Kidnap him? Extort him? Sure. But a cop who was paying somebody to eliminate the mafia hierarchy, well I guess they made an exception."

Vaughn's head was swirling. He could never have guessed how deep all of this went. He flashed to the scene that night. Jack lying on the pavement. Rontego disappearing around the corner. The white van. The cigarette. The white van.

How had he not pieced it together before?

"You were there that night."

Elliot arched an eyebrow. "Well done, detective. Yes, we were there. We watched helpless as Jack was shot. We even saw you run up the alley. That was a surprise to all of us. Frankly, we had no idea that Jack reached out to you. In fact, we had no idea how to deal with you or what to make of you until you, quite fortunately for us, fell right into our lap. When you called Ryan Slate, it all seemed too perfect for us."

"Christ. Ryan too?" Alex felt depressed now.

Was there anyone in this fucking city who was who they said they were?

"Relax, Alex. Ryan is not that involved in all of this. He's undercover. I was his undercover liaison. You wanted to reestablish your cover, so the rest naturally worked itself out." Elliot put his lips together and glanced down at his watch. He cocked the hammer on his pistol. "If you don't mind, I need to know where that money is."

Alex was growing more and more desperate. He knew that the money was his only bargaining chip. A chip he would be forced to throw on the table to protect his family. But he was going to hold onto that chip as long as he could.

"So this whole thing was all about one man's greed. It makes me sick. Two hundred grand is a nice chunk of change. I admit it, but it hardly seems like enough to kill for. What is two hundred grand divided by three of you anyway? A year, a year and a half of salary?" Vaughn spit on the ground and looked at Elliot. "You make me sick."

Elliot grimaced at the verbal assault and ran a hand through his hair. Then he chuckled. With a hint of regret he said, "I wish we were getting this money. No, we won't see a dime of it. Unfortunately, the Bonannos want their money back. I can't say that I blame 'em, we did fail to deliver the cash and we were turned down in our overtures in any case. We have until six tonight to return this money or we're dead men; me, Hambone, Hi-Def, dead. This, all of this," he waved his pistol around the room, "it's a self preservation thing."

Alex sat there, the ropes biting into his skin, his eye pulsating from the wound under it and the cut along his neck burning; and took it all in.

"Now, the money."

Vaughn closed his mouth, knowing what would come once he let Elliot know.

Elliot walked around behind Alex, and placing his mouth next to Vaughn's ear whispered, "For your family, Alex."

Alex Vaughn hung his head in defeat. "It's under the floor behind Jack's bar. It's in the basement."

Without saying a word, Elliot walked to the front

of the garage and waved Hambone over. "Give me twenty minutes to collect the money. Once I have it, take care of this."

Hambone shook his head in understanding.

Before Elliot walked out he turned and regarded Alex Vaughn as if getting one last look before he said goodbye. "Sorry things couldn't have been different. But life is a goddamn shit storm and all of us are trying to fit under the same little piece of cover."

Alex could just watch, helpless, as Elliot closed the garage door behind him with a clang of finality, and left Hambone and Vaughn alone.

*

Rafael Rontego snapped his head up with a start. He'd dozed off. With a cough, he swung his feet off of the wooden bench and sat up. Pinching the corner of his eyes with his thumb and forefinger, Rafael rubbed the sleep out of them. He glanced at the bag still resting at his side and gave it a pat.

"Oh it's still there lad. Not many people seem to be lining up for the train today."

Rontego looked to his right at the edge of the bench and saw an older gentleman seated just beyond the perimeter of where his slumbering feet had lain. The man clutched the handles of a plaid bag with both hands. He was hunched over in the fashion of most eighty year olds and his thin grey hair seemed to have faded away with the years of his life.

God no.

The old timer slid over on his corduroy pants until he was seated right next to Rafael. He could smell the man's World War II musk and caught a slight hint of what appeared to be peppermint on his breath.

It was confirmed when the man asked, "Care for a

mint?"

"No thanks."

Rafael looked careful at the man's lips as they moved but found that he was noticing the rather clean shave that was broken up by a single patch of stubble where the old-timer's eye sight must have failed him.

"Just as well. Sugar is no good for you anyway. My doctor says it's not good for me. Oh well, at this point what is good for me?" He flashed a grin that was manmade.

Rafael could only clear his throat in response and he stared straight ahead at the empty tracks.

"I couldn't help but notice your hat," he went on. "I used to have one just like it, years ago."

Rafael glanced over at the man out of the corner of his eye. A slight twinkle developed there as Rontego thought how odd it was that this man was shooting the shit with him. It'd been sometime since anyone talked to Rafael about anything other than business. The old man looked at Rafael and the assassin realized that he missed something.

"What was that?"

"I said, where ya heading, son?"

Rafael glanced at the departures screen. "This is the train to Toronto, isn't it?"

"Oh yes, but I suppose what I mean was, are you seeing family, friends?"

"Friend."

"Ah, friends are good. Me, I'm going home. I just got done visiting my great grandson. Now I'm heading back home to the missus. She doesn't let me stay away long, no sir."

The old man began shuffling in his plaid bag and with a triumphant smile pulled out a little wallet. Humming a tune Rontego didn't recognize, he flipped through several items inside of it until he came to what he was looking for. He held a small photograph in front of Rontego. There was a picture of an infant lying down in a pink blanket covered to the neck and sporting a pink wool-knit hat.

The old man cleared his throat and pronounced, "Cute little fella, isn't he? It's a boy, never you mind the pink. That's what they get for keeping things a surprise. Molly, that's my wife, she knit the cap there. Yes sir, great grandson number three. Thirteen grandchildren in all."

"That's all?" Rontego noticed the surprise on the man's face and let a smile past his lips.

The old man chuckled and pointing to Rafael's ring finger said, "Big talk from a man who isn't even married." The old-man chuckled again seeing the surprise switch over to Rafael as the dig took a hold.

"Not even a contender then?"

"Oh, I don't know. Perhaps there was once upon a time."

"Once upon a time, eh? Well, the thing about fairy tales is they only come true if you will them to."

Rafael laughed. *Was this man really trying to impart wisdom on him?* "Perhaps. But that ship sailed long ago."

"I never understood that statement. The ship has sailed. People say that like you can't just turn the ship around again."

Rafael sat there for a long moment. His thoughts shifted to the evening before and his rendezvous with Elyse.

"Sometimes it's best to see what else the world has to offer."

"Fair enough."

The old man popped a mint into his mouth and seemed to retreat inside of himself.

The assassin looked over at the man, an odd moment of thoughtfulness creeping up on him. "You think a man can rewrite his history?"

The old-timer thought about it for a moment and then shook his head.

"No, I don't believe you can. History, that's done. Ain't no changing it. Set in stone it is, sir."

Rafael Rontego dropped his head, realizing the truth of the man's words.

"Now, your future son, that's what's to be decided. Your future, that's a thing written in sand. It can change or even disappear with a strong gust of wind."

The assassin looked up at the old man who flashed him that artificial smile that felt all of a sudden very real. He accepted his pat on the back and felt something he hadn't felt in a long time. Rafael Rontego felt hope. He felt alive. He felt like there was the business of living to attend to. For the first time, he felt like he was the captain of his own ship. The past; that was the past.

Hell, most of those fuckers got what they had coming to them.

But that was life by a different set of rules. That was survival, not living. Rontego smiled as he thought about life on his terms, about actually *living*.

Chapter 29

Vaughn lay down on the pavement as Hambone instructed. Time seemed to have gone much quicker than any other twenty minutes Alex ever knew. As he lowered himself to the floor, he was keenly aware of his various aches and pains. The cut under his eye burned as drops of Alex's nervous sweat infiltrated the wound. The gash on his forehead pulsated with his heartbeat and the razor thin tear along his neck itched but Alex's bound hands couldn't scratch at it with any authority, even if Hambone afforded him the time.

The more he thought about it, the more he wanted to dig his nails into his neck and scrape of a layer of skin; anything to stop the itch. Alex let out a little groan as his bruised ribs protested against his body stretching out on the floor. It reeked of gasoline and the smell became more poignant as Vaughn lay his face down onto the cool cement.

"Why make me lay on the floor?"

"It's less messy. Ever try to clean brains off of a wall?

Alex didn't know what else to say. He forgot about the discomfort of his neck as he couldn't dislodge the image of his brains sliding down a wall. Vaughn closed his eyes. He didn't want that to be the last image in his mind as he exited the world. He forced his mind to think of other images.

Her smile. He concentrated on Charlotte, he thought of how her face looked. Every memorized crease along her lips, the whiteness of her teeth. Despite the lone crooked tooth in her under bite, the smile loomed supreme to Alex.

He concentrated on Ella. Her wide eyes. Alex could see them learning. They gobbled up everything that her gaze fell upon and they did so without judgment.

Simple regard, acknowledgment, and wonder filled all her vision. Her baby picture was still tucked in his boot. At least if it was too messy, they might be able to identify him by the picture in his shoe.

Alex thought about what Charlotte scribbled on the back of it.

The creation of Charlotte and Alex Vaughn.

The cut under Alex's eye grew moist and stung with the salt that the new moisture left behind. He thought of all of the things he wished he said. The things he knew he should have said. He didn't want Charlotte to become someone he used to know. He didn't want to become someone Charlotte used to know.

Vaughn thought to get up and make Hambone earn his kill. He wanted to fight. He wanted to make it messy to clean up, but he thought about Ella. He thought about Charlotte. He lay still. He could never endanger them.

The tears continued to melt through the creases in Alex Vaughn's eyes. Not tears of fear, but tears of bitter, salty regret. They flowed unabated as he felt Hambone stand over him. Alex willed himself back to images of Ella, to Charlotte.

He heard two explosions. Alex's body clenched as every muscle contracted in unison. His neck still itched. The tears still stung his wounds. Alex breathed in.

He breathed.

Still prostrate on the ground, Vaughn opened his good eye and heard some shuffling. He saw two sets of boots.

"Hey Garducci." Alex knew that voice. It continued. "Now don't do that. I said don't do that."

The detective rolled over and saw Hambone sitting down and propped up against the far wall of the garage. His body leaned at an odd angle, hunching forward towards the ground but trying to maintain an upright posture. A bullet scorched a single hole through the side of his neck.

Smoke drifted between Hambone's fingers, which explored the new cavity.

One explosion accounted for.

Vaughn swung his head around in a daze and saw the garage door swinging on the hinges back and forth, tapping the wall beyond in an obtuse and eerie sort of rhythm.

Explosion two.

Hambone tried to stem the flow of blood from the gaping wound on his neck with one hand. The other still clutched his pistol and he alternately gripped it, tried to bring it to bear and dropped his arm back to his side. Tom Coughlin advanced on Hambone while Jimmy Jacks pulled Alex to his feet.

Hambone tried again to raise his pistol, but Tom Coughlin gave it a kick and the firearm slid across the floor. Tom, his gun leveled at Hambone, looked over at Jimmy with a questioning glance. Jimmy, with his arms around Alex, just offered a shrug of his shoulders in reply.

With that, Tom Coughlin turned around and regarded the man at his feet. He drifted further down the wall as his energy left him, but Hambone's eyes gazed at Tom, confusion seeping from them. Tom shrugged his own shoulders and pulled the trigger.

Alex winced as he caught sight of the results of the blast. Hambone's head snapped back and bounced off of the wall. At the same time, a splatter of blood and brain matter sprayed across the enclosure. The smell of gunpowder filled the room, followed by the hint of charred flesh. Tommy turned around, a look of disgust at the scene before him still registering across his face.

"Tom, look at that mess. What'd you do that for, he was dying anyway."

"Shut up, Jimmy. I don't have time to wait for this prick to bleed out. Let's go."

"Glad to see us, Vin?" Jimmy shot Alex a wink.

"Yeah, Jimmy. Yeah." Alex took a step but his knees felt weak. He stumbled and Jimmy Jacks turned just in time to catch him.

The trio exited the garage with Jimmy holding Alex upright. Tom Coughlin led the way to a dark sedan with tinted windows parked on the side of the road. Alex noticed that the motor was idling.

When they were about halfway there, Tom stopped and ordered, "You two wait right here." He walked towards the car, and looked left and then right. He pulled opened the door and disappeared into the back seat.

Jimmy gave Alex a grimace and stayed by his side helping him stay on his feet. After a long moment that seemed like an eternity, Tom Coughlin reemerged from the automobile and signaled Vaughn to come over. Lifting himself off of the support Jimmy Jacks was providing, Alex half limped and half dragged his body over to Tommy.

"Big man wants a word with you."

Alex nodded his head and opened the door to the sedan. It was dark inside the vehicle and as Vaughn sat down on the leather seat and closed the door behind him, his eyes took a moment to adjust to the gloom.

"Hello Vincent. Or should I say, officer."

Vaughn looked over and almost jumped out of his skin.

"Yes, I know now who you are."

There in the car next to him was Christian "The Pope" Biela. The detective shook his head. The Pope must have known that Jimmy and Tommy worked for Falzone. Yet here he was and there they were. Alex winced as he thought back to his antics earlier that morning. Vaughn felt even more vulnerable as he noticed his gun and holster and knife sitting on the seat between them.

"What to do with you detective? You know, I came here to kill you along with those," here The Pope dragged out the 'S' lacing it with contempt or trying to hold back a cough; perhaps both, "cops. Those pig fuckers, those two-faced bastards. I've been wanting to deal with them for a long time. It made my day when I thought you were with 'em. But, you're not." He started coughing and held up a finger telling Alex to wait while tears rolled down the consigliore's cheeks. When he composed himself, he continued, "There's a geek's body in the kitchen that led us to that conclusion just moments ago."

Alex could just nod his head in silent accord.

"So back to the question. What. To. Do. With. You. "

"All due respect sir, but I'm confused. I thought these two worked with Falzone."

The Pope raised a brow, and glanced at Alex. "I forgot that you spent time as Mr. Garducci. I'm not mad about that by the way. A man doing his job. Besides, any hindrance to that group is ok by me. As for Tommy and Jimmy…" The Pope let out a wry chuckle. "It amuses me that the police think they are the only ones that plant people. I mean, we show them time and time again that we can get people inside their very organizations, yet still, they assume they are the masters of infiltration."

Vaughn was aware at this point how adept the gangsters seemed to be at penetrating organizations.

"But you sent Rafael to Wizeguyz to bring the place to the ground."

"Well, yes. Perhaps others view it as coincidence that Tommy and Jimmy weren't there when that went down? Interesting."

He paused for effect and pulled a cigar from his jacket. It was rolled tight and Alex wondered whether or not it was a Cuban. He never smoked the things but he figured, by the way The Pope slide it under his nose and soaked in its aroma, that it must be a good one.

"Me? I don't believe in coincidence. Take you for example. This, this is no coincidence. That's why I'm not gonna kill you." He grimaced and took another look at the cigar and then tucked it back into the folds of his jacket. "You have unfinished business to attend to. I sympathize. But let me ask you one question. Who did you see here today?"

Vaughn knew where this was going, and given his day, he was fine with playing along. "No one."

"Well then, I guess there's no reason to kill you. Let us just call it honor amongst thieves."

"Honor amongst thieves."

The Pope held out his hand and Vaughn clasped it, grateful.

After a brief moment, The Pope gave Alex a nod and said, "Now get the fuck out of my car."

Vaughn stepped out and shut the door. The car started forward and then stopped. The window rolled down and Alex heard The Pope. "You might need these." Alex walked up and grabbed his pistol and shoulder holster and switch blade.

"Thanks."

Without saying a word, The Pope waved the driver forward and rolled the window up. Within moments, he disappeared down the block and around the bend.

Before Vaughn could take stock of what just happened, Jimmy ran towards another car that Tommy must have pulled up to the curb. "Get in Vinnie!"

"Hurry up, you two!"

Tommy was inching the car along only just waiting for Jimmy and Alex. Having no other way out of the place, and not wanting to linger around the scene, Vaughn hobbled into the backseat of Tommy's car. As they peeled out of the neighborhood, Alex realized the reason for their rush. Smoke billowed up behind them as the safe house burst into flames. Jimmy Jacks turned around in his seat and watched the smoke recede behind them; his eyes alight like a child on Christmas morning. They rode along in silence. After a while, Vaughn felt the need to cut through the quiet.

These men saved my life. As much as he hated it, he felt indebted.

"What a day," he stated.

"Day ain't over yet." Tommy stated.

"Look, I just wanted to thank you two for earlier. You saved my life."

Jimmy flashed him a toothy grin, but Tommy said, "Just following orders."

Vaughn accepted the statement. After few more moments, when they were safe beyond the area of the fire, Alex had Tommy drop him off at a diner not far from the baseball stadium where a minor league team played. With a wave, Alex said goodbye and stood alone on the street corner. The cold air felt good on his battered body and he found a patch of pavement free of snow courtesy of some well-placed salt by an employee of the diner.

Flipping open his cell phone, which somehow survived in his coat pocket, he dialed Ryan Slate. He needed to gauge the truth of Elliot's statement that Ryan was not working for them. Alex needed someone he could trust. If Elliot wasn't lying, then Alex needed to warn Ryan. He had to warn him about Elliot, and about the fact that the Garducci cover was blown.

After a moment the call connected. "Hey, Vincenzio here."

"Ryan, its Alex. I need you to meet me at a bar downtown. Meet me at 76 Pearl Street."

"I'm a little, involved, at the moment."

"Ryan, it's a matter of life and death. You need to get your ass over here."

The silence echoed on the other line. "Okay. I'll be there in twenty."

Alex hung up the phone and then went inside to sit down and wait. His stomach rumbled. It felt like forever since he enjoyed a warm meal.

*

The hum of the tires lent a rhythm to The Pope's musings. Nuncio drove him through the city streets towards the bar that had been the epicenter of the consigliore's life for the last twenty years. He let his eyes drift into the alleyways they passed as they drove and somewhere in those catacombs, he found his own mind hidden in the maze of side streets.

Christian Biela—he'd been called that in a previous life. Sure, people still used his name, but what they were thinking, what they were all thinking, was *this is the fucking Pope.* He roomed with a close cousin of Don Ciancetta's as an undergraduate.

Back then, The Pope was a scrapper and won more bar fights with his new college roommate than he could count. It was amazing the kind of bond that could be forged through common blood and bruised knuckles. His roommate was long since gone. His throat was cut in Vegas. But he introduced him to his cousin, a man named Leonard Ciancetta.

The Pope cupped his chin in his hand. Most people might be angry how it all worked out. But The Pope had a sense of loyalty that the Roman Legions would be hard-pressed to instill in its soldiery. His eyes darted back and forth amongst the passing avenues as he saw his past playing out right in front of him. He could see their faces as clear as if they were being cast on the walls of the buildings by a movie projector. They were younger then, but their roles in each other's lives were steady, and remained unchanged.

Christian hadn't been able to pay for the law

241

school he got into. He remembered bitching about it to Leonard while they were searching for some cheap college pussy on Quarter Beer night. It was offhanded, and Christian needed an ear to hear his gripes. Imagine his surprise when he found fifty thousand dollars in cash sitting on his pillow when he got home.

They were friends, but more than that, Don Ciancetta was a benefactor to the lawyer. Since that day, The Pope, as he was now called, made every move he could in order to help his friend the Don.

It's the least I can do, he mused.

To The Pope, every player in this game of life was just a pawn devoted to the protection of The King.

The Pope felt a cough coming on and brought his handkerchief. He paused for a moment, wondering if he could hold back the explosion. His body ached from all of the hacking. He couldn't, and he caught the air and spit onto the piece of fabric, glancing at its contents before folding it over and sticking it back into the folds of his jacket.

Blood.

He noticed a bit of it and wondered if it was from the constant coughing rubbing his throat dry or if it was from something worse. It would have to wait either way. In a few hours, he would know whether or not it even mattered.

The Pope ran his fingers through his hair. It was dark, his hair, but used to be darker. He wondered if the hair was thinning out. He couldn't be sure though, these changes happened so gradual.

Everything changed. This whole war, it was about fighting against the tide of change. If they won, it would just stave off change until the next guy wanted a poke at the top spot, or they all got arrested. It was the way of this world.

The Pope, though, he built a reputation of being

able to protect the family from within the confines of the law. Sure, he stepped over on more than one occasion, but reputation—reputation is everything. For instance, he didn't *know* what happened in that garage. He could well imagine, but he didn't *know.* Sometimes, that was enough.

He let that cop go. Most people would have killed him. The Pope wasn't playing games when he said he respected the fact that the officer was doing his job.

Maybe if more people just did their job this country wouldn't be such a cluster fuck.

There was also opportunity there. When the cop stuck that gun in The Pope's face, Christian felt pretty sure about the cop's desire to kill Rafael Rontego. Either way, it was better for the family and better for Don Ciancetta.

Hell, and if the cop gets the best of Rafael, then we might be able to strong arm the pig to our advantage, he mused.

"We're here, sir" Nuncio declared.

The Pope came back to the present and realized they pulled up to the curb in front of Rumors. Nuncio got out and slammed the door beside him. The Pope put on a pair of dark sunglasses even though it was overcast and threatening to snow outside.

A moment later and Nuncio opened the back door and The Pope was sliding out of the car. A few of the fellas hanging around the outside of the bar stopped what they were doing and shuffled closer to watch The Pope enter the building. It was all slicked back hair and leather jackets from the small throng of men that cloistered around the consigliore. It was all about respect and The Pope meant to see to it that, after tonight, respect for the hierarchy would no longer be an issue.

Chapter 30

Alex Vaughn sat in the booth in the back of the bar and sipped on some water. He picked this seat because it was close to the rear exit and afforded him a view of the front door. The bartender was kind enough to rustle up some chicken fingers and Alex was devouring them when Ryan Slate made his way into the hole in the wall bar.

At first, Vaughn couldn't tell who came in. The dwelling was so poorly lit that when the door opened, the sheer whiteness from outside blinded the detective. After a moment though, the silhouette of Ryan Slate became clearer and Alex waved him over.

Alex could tell that Ryan was not pleased to have been called out of action. If there was any doubt from the scowl on his face, it was gone once Ryan started talking. His voice took on the gruff edge of a New York City cab driver.

"This better be good. I have a lot going on today and I can't even get a hold of Elliot or … Jesus Alex, what happened to you?"

Alex studied Ryan for a moment. He took a sip of water to buy time as he was unsure how to proceed. He wanted to trust Ryan. He hesitated, and then decided to tell Ryan everything. Just like the first time the two spoke after Jack's death, everything flowed out.

He told Ryan about how Elliot and the guys were after the money and why. He told Ryan about the torture and how the very people saved him he'd been sent to take down in previous investigations. Finally, he told Ryan of how he knew where Rafael Rontego was. When he paused for a breath, he recognized the look that crept on to Slate's face. It was fear.

Fear of what though, Alex wondered.

"Christ. You know I have been feeding them information on the Ciancetta crew for months now? If they were working with Falzone and the Bonannos then I could have been inadvertently helping to provide intelligence for God knows what."

Slate's face looked ashen and a layer of sweat beaded on his forehead despite the bar's chilly atmosphere.

"To be honest, I don't know what to do Ryan. Elliot is out there running around. We have dead bodies down the street. There's a guy who killed my best friend in Canada for crying out loud. I mean, we're fucking cops, aren't we?"

Ryan swallowed hard. "Well, I think its real simple. We gotta go to the captain."

"He assigned Elliot to organized crime."

"So we bring the Internal Affairs guy, Billy, with us. Either way, this is too much for us."

Vaughn bit his lower lip and gave the back of his neck a reassuring rub. "What about Rafael?"

"What about him? Alex, you gotta ask yourself, what are you doing all this for? What are you after?"

"I'm not even sure anymore." The realization was painful. Vaughn's cracked lips tried to smile but the pain brought them back down into a stoic grimace. Alex, seeing that Ryan was hoping for more of an answer, changed the subject. "I don't think you should go back to Ciancetta's. It's too dangerous with Elliot running around town knowing your identity."

Slate chuckled. "I suppose not." He leaned back in the booth. "So shall we go see the cap'n?"

Alex gave a half smile to the part of his face that didn't hurt. Slate wasn't going to let him off the hook. "Ok, but can I ask a favor?"

"Sure."

"Can I have a ride?"

Ryan Slate started laughing. It was such a spontaneous laugh that for the first time, Alex felt like things might be all right. It was pure and came from the man's toes. Vaughn knew he placed his trust in the right guy.

*

The Pope sat across from the Don's mahogany desk and studied his old friend's face. Everyone else called him the Don, and even Christian called him that in front of the men. But here, when it was just the two of them, he was Leo.

Leo looked tired. His face was gaunt and his angular features looked even more angular. Maybe it was dehydration. The Don ran his fingers through his hair over and over again—a nervous tick that The Pope came to recognize over the years. The Don's fingers stroked hair that had once been jet black but was now littered with patches of grey. He grew a bit of grey stubble that set in, which was odd for the fanatically clean shaven boss. His eyes, which boasted a green hue, were bloodshot and darted back and forth with a look common to that of a caged jackal. He was worried, and the consigliore didn't blame him.

Don Ciancetta picked up a cigar and cut off its tip, then inserted it between his teeth. "So everything is ready then?"

The Pope looked at his friend and nodded in the affirmative. He felt sorry for the man; it was tough sometimes to get what you wish for. Everyone gunned for the top spot.

The Don caught the look and gave his friend a small smile. It was an attempt to reassure the consigliore.

"I'm okay. Don't worry about me."

"I know Leo, I know."

"Christ, we've been through worse, you and me. Remember how we got here? To this position? Now that was a scary time."

It was The Pope's turn to share a smile and, despite himself, he couldn't help but recall the success fondly. He helped navigate a series of wars and triumphs at his friend's side over the years.

No time for old glories, he thought.

"Leo, everything's in place. Everyone knows their role." The Pope felt his chest seize up and knew that another cough was on its way. He held up a finger as it hit him and he coughed so hard that his eyes began to water and his body ached. "That one hurt," he allowed as the Don tossed him a bottle of water.

"I been telling you, you ought to get that checked out. I ain't no doctor but it don't sound good."

The Pope took down the cool liquid and felt it creep into the crevices of his throat. He swallowed hard and felt as if his throat muscles were pushing down a Cadillac. "Eh, what's the point? If tonight doesn't go well, then it won't matter."

The Don stood up and looked at The Pope with eyes searching for a hint of a joke before his voice took on a shrill pitch that was new to the consigliore.

"Jesus Christ! Tell me that's a joke. It isn't funny but it better be a joke. I mean what the fuck Chris?"

"Relax, relax. All I'm saying is that I'll go get it looked at tomorrow. Tonight will be fine. It's my job to worry. So I worry about everything."

The Don sat back down and took a deep breath. "You surprised they're coming?"

The Pope let his mind wrap around the question for a few moments then shook his head. "Not really. What other choice do they have? Sure, we took some losses, but they took more. Sure, we lost some money, they lost more. Muro's dead. They don't know Rafael is halfway to Canada. Sitting down, trying to negotiate, it's their one chance."

"What if they got a little surprise for us?"

"Then we'll be ready."

Chapter 31

Rafael Rontego grabbed up his bag and made his way towards a tiny gift shop in the rear of the train station. It wasn't much; the place seemed to first and foremost sell bubblegum and magazines. A middle aged woman, rather unremarkable other than a small mole on her left cheek, greeted him with a wave.

Rontego stared at the collection of crap and shook his head. He'd always been told it was rude to not bring a gift when visiting a friend. He had no clue whether or not the Cleaner would be there yet, but Rafael thought a small token of his appreciation is what normal people might do.

He was about to leave, deciding that the place had nothing to offer, when he glanced at the checkout counter and saw a stack of lighters and magnets. The magnets were ordinary enough, one said "I love Buffalo", and another had a picture of Niagara Falls on it. But what caught the assassin's eye was a lighter in the shape of a gun. It was about the size of derringer but it looked real enough.

Perfect.

He pulled out ten dollars and told the clerk to keep the change.

*

Ryan Slate took a drag on a thin cigarette and the pull caused the ember to flare in the encroaching dusk as nightfall began its hurried wintry descent. The two of them huddled against the wall outside of the station and Ryan was laughing, which caused smoke to puff out of his nose and mouth in tiny clouds of smoke and steam. Again, his chuckle was a bit infectious, and Alex allowed himself a smile.

Ryan's mirth defied the seriousness of the situation they just, somehow, emerged from unscathed. Slate shook his head, his eye twinkling in either amusement or amazement, Vaughn couldn't tell.

"I have no clue what just happened in there." Slate breathed in on his cigarette and his usually excitable voice was steady, as if he were viewing things through a different prism.

Truth be told, Alex certainly was.

Standard procedure dictated that Alex Vaughn should have handed his badge and gun to the chief until such time as an investigation as to his role could be concluded. At first, everything seemed to be going in that direction. While Alex told the story of the last few days, beginning with Jack's death and ending with the deaths of two dirty cops in an urban safe house, the chief's face just got redder and redder. By the end, his garnet colored face outshone the brass name plate that said "Wilcox" on his desk.

A moment of silence followed that left Alex sitting back in the chair, facing the chief's desk, his face muscles twitching as he braced for the eruption. Still, the silence continued, and all the while the chief's face held its garnet hue. Alex wished the man would just speak, if only to relieve the pressure from his head and so that Vaughn wouldn't get shafted for a cleanup detail when it exploded.

When Chief Wilcox did speak, Alex was forced down into his seat by the sheer volume of the voice flying at his face. He glanced over at Ryan Slate, who was pressed back into a corner of the room behind him. There was no help coming from that direction, though. Ryan just looked on with wide eyes.

Alex didn't even know what the chief was yelling at him. All he heard were snippets of words that had larger meaning. Words like "protocol" and "chain of command" slapped Alex across the face and would have left a sting if he were not so hypnotized by eyes bulging out of their sockets, protruding from a mass of unorganized flesh.

Teeth and eyes were amplified by a pure flesh background, as the vein-addled forehead of the chief had no end. With no hair to interrupt the flow of his face, Vaughn could see the vein from Chief Wilcox's jaw bone run up and along the side of his face and disappear somewhere beyond the imaginary hair line.

The tirade continued for several minutes and was only interrupted by several downcast glances that teamed with worry and concern, shot Alex's way by the Chief.

In those moments, he would shake his head and mutter, "What am I to do? It's a disappointment really. A disappointment."

Those words hurt Alex worse. The Irish temper that flared out from the Midwestern accented Englishman raised in an Irish home didn't bother Alex as much as disappointing the man who had as many different nationalities in his lineage as an Olympics opening ceremonies.

As tough as he was, the man was always someone Alex considered to be fair. That was why Alex wasn't going to make Wilcox ask for his badge and gun. He knew it would kill the old man to have to ask for them, but he would have to. So Vaughn took his gun and badge and laid them on the desk, halting the chief's berating.

Silence.

The chief looked Alex in the eye and put a hand over the gun and badge, his hand trembling with the adrenaline still coursing through his veins.

Then the door to the office swung open. The chief glanced up, his eyes snapping with a dangerous flare. A slight man shuffled in. His shoulders were rounded and a pair of glasses hung from the tip of long nose. He held a file that he was bent over even as he walked, allowing those in the room a good look at the handful of hairs that adorned the crown of his head. Despite the sparse, chaotic arrangement of his hair, he found a way to part them and comb the strands over from one side of his head to the other. A long, gnarled finger was planted into the book and moved in unison with the gentleman's eyes as they scanned the file.

William Spence, Billy, shuffled in and momentarily dislodged his eyes from the file in his grasp and saw the Chief's hand resting on Alex Vaughn's badge and gun. He snorted and looked back at the file resting opened in the palm of one hand. He raised the other and waved off the Chief.

"That isn't necessary. No, not at all."

The Chief, stood statuesque and breathed, "Bill, what are you talking about?"

"Sir, we have been conducting an, um, well, an audit on Elliot Craft for the better part of three years. Detective Vaughn's assessments are correct and consistent with our investigation."

Wilcox closed his eyes and held them shut for an extended moment. A normal color began to ease itself onto his face, "Why was I not told about this investigation?"

Billy peered up from his file and looked at the Chief from just above his spectacles. "Internal Affairs business, Chief Wilcox. Surely you understand that we are very careful with who knows what. At any rate, Detective Vaughn, who no doubt deserves a reprimand, probably shouldn't be forced into resignation. Wouldn't you agree Mr. Wilcox?"

The Chief let go of the badge and scratched the back of his head. He let out a deep sigh, and grabbed the gun and badge and started sliding it towards his end of the desk.

"Perhaps it would still be prudent to have an inquiry."

Alex was unsure what was going on and he looked around the room searching for some sort of answer. He looked first at the Chief with his face that was still deep pink, and then looked at Ryan who was still sitting it all out in the corner of the room. Finally, he turned his head and looked at William Spence. The I.A. officer peered back at Alex Vaughn and Alex could see his jaw clench. Something was resolved in Billy's mind.

William Spence slammed the folder shut and straightened his hunched shoulders as much as his bent frame would allow. He took one hand and pushed his glasses more secure onto his face and lifted his chin so that he was looking at Chief Wilcox square in the eye.

"How?"

"Excuse me?"

"Chief Wilcox, how is it prudent? What I mean by this is how is it prudent to take the only man who knows the location of a known cop killer off of the case? The only man who is a witness to crimes committed by officers of this very department?"

The Chief placed both hands on the dark mahogany desk separating him from the Internal Affairs officer.

"I'm not sure I follow you. The protocol is…"

William Spence took two steps forward and placed the file on the desk. Interrupting, he waved his hand yet again.

"Bah. I'm saying that you are the Chief of Police. How do you think it will look to the politicians? How do you think it will look to the voting public? The politicians answer to the public. You answer to the politicians. If you take a detective who has *witnessed* corruption, who has the location of a cop killer due to his investigation, no matter how unorthodox, and sit him on the sidelines…." Spence lifted his glasses and pinched his nose between his thumb and forefinger. "Well, naturally, the question will come up."

"What question is that?" Wilcox's face was

gaining a red hue again. His voice trembled but whether or not it was from fear or agitation, Vaughn had a hard time telling.

"What question? Well, who are you protecting, of course? Yourself? For political reasons or for criminal reasons? The corrupt officers? To what end? What dirt do they have on you?"

Wilcox glared at Spence and his fists curled into balls on the desk. Alex could see the pressure building up there as knuckles turned white. Evidently, William Spence saw it as well and attempted to diffuse the Chief's mounting anger. He did another casual toss of his wrist and picked up his file.

"However ridiculous the questions, they will be asked."

The Chief sat down. The color drained from his face and he glanced down at the gun and badge. He pushed them across the table toward Alex Vaughn.

Alex pulled his tattered jacket around to stave off the cold that threatened to seep through the folds. He rubbed his hands together generating friction in order to create some semblance of heat.

Ryan was still grinning and he muttered something about "lucky bastard", as he rubbed out his cigarette out on the brick wall of the station.

Alex smiled at Slate's assessment but doubted the truth of the words. If luck was having a buddy who was dead, a wife who couldn't bring herself to love him anymore, a daughter he only just knew, and a body so battered that every ounce of his fiber ached; well then yeah, Alex felt lucky.

Alex felt his gun dig into his hip as he leaned against the wall. He couldn't believe he so casually offered up his gun and shield. As he watched the back and forth between Wilcox and Spencer, the whole thing struck him as out of place. It was as if he was watching a movie about someone else's life. But the whole time, he looked at the shield. There was a time that he would have cut off the fingers of anyone that tried to take that badge from him. It was a thing of honor and symbolic of a tradition of service that extended far beyond the life and times of Alex Vaughn. But now, and in Wilcox's office, it just didn't seem to shine as bright as it once did.

"So not only are you not fired, but now you have a date with the Marshals and the Mounties to go and grab up Rafael Rontego? Man, this bust will be huge. We get him, ain't nobody safe in organized crime." Ryan Slates eyes shone with a hint of admiration.

Most people would have basked in it, but Alex turned his head and looked out into the cold night sky.

Ryan caught the shift and after studying Alex's face for a moment asked, "What? And don't say nothing 'cause it is definitely something."

Vaughn watched his breath run away; it dissipated in to the world around him. It was so important, air. For a moment, it was everything, quite literally, that one needed to survive. But it didn't matter how much you needed it. Eventually, your body would let it go.

"You know I don't want to go. I think I would much rather just go to Charlotte's."

They were probably having dinner right now. She used to make the best lasagna and this garlic bread that would just melt in your mouth. Maybe she was under her quilt at this very moment, the one her grandmother knitted for her as a child.

"So what are you going to do?"

Alex hung his head and watched the ground between his feet. Without saying a word he started towards the parking lot.

Ryan Slate called after him, "Alex! Alex what are you going to do?"

255

Without breaking stride Alex Vaughn continued forward. "Do what I always do. I'm going to finish it."

Chapter 32

Rafael Rontego took a look around at the platform as he grabbed the rail that guided him into the belly of the train. The steel on his hand felt cold and slick. He looked at the sleepy train station and felt a wrenching in his heart as he gazed at the few people shuffling around, the wooden benches, and a blue sign with white lettering that said, "Welcome to Buffalo, New York."

He studied everything he saw in that moment and he realized it might be his last look at the place he called home for so very long. He felt the weight of the place bearing down on him so hard that he thought the ceiling would collapse on him, and he took a step backward and into the train. The weight followed him as he walked along the aisle and found his seat. He was pushing his bag under the chair in front of him, and it felt like someone was standing on his shoulders trying to push him into the fabric of the cloth seat.

A porter walked up to Rafael as he struggled to shove the bulky bag under the seat in front of him. He was wearing one of those ridiculous hats that had a white strip around the perimeter and carried a dark navy blue on the rest of it. The hat hung back on the porter's head and seemed that it would fall off at any moment. He was a young fellow, maybe just over eighteen.

"Can I help you secure your bag sir? I can put it in the overhead compartment."

Rafael leaned back in his seat without looking up at the porter and kicked the bag under the seat in front of him. Still leaning back in his seat, he pulled the brim of his fedora down over his eyes, dismissing the young man. He would have said something, tried to make nice, but the infernal weight threatened to swallow him whole. He couldn't breathe, let alone speak. He sat there, hiding under his hat, as the train whistle blew, announcing departure.

The piercing sound didn't even register as the assassin was exercising every bit of control to keep from hyperventilating. He hadn't expected this. The gears on the train ground and he felt it jerk forward. As it picked up speed, the pressure seemed to lift off of the assassin. His labored breathing became more regular. He found a measure of control in himself once more.

Sitting up in his chair, he glanced out the window as snow covered buildings shifted to mounds of white dust and evergreens, until finally, the train was racing past small frozen ponds and scattered cloisters of trees that seemed to have grown snow in absence of leaves.

All the while, Rafael Rontego continued on his path to normalcy. The weight seemed to fly from his shoulders with each mile left behind him. He took off his hat and ran his fingers through his hair slicking it back. A tiny smile curled out of Rafael's lips and they trembled with the unfamiliar movement.

*

The Pope and Don Ciancetta sat in The Pope's sedan outside of a house in a Hamburg suburb. Nuncio was manning the front seat, while the two power brokers sat in the rear. The lights to the sedan were off but the car remained on so that the heat could keep the biting cold at bay.

The tidy rows of houses looked like something out of a snow globe or a Norman Rockwell painting. The nice brick pathways were all equal in distance apart and shoveled of snow. Smoke drifted upward through chimneys that gave off the fresh scent of burnt cedar. Snow fell in swirls in the black sky and blotted what was left of the starry night from view.

They sat several houses down from a foreclosed

home that sprouted a worn and battered "For Sale" sign in the yard. Snow was piled half a foot on the wooden crossbeam that held the sign above the ground. The car was parked along the gutter to another foreclosed home so as to not draw attention to the vehicle in front of an occupied home.

Even though the heat was sufficient to keep them warm, Don Ciancetta kept rubbing his gloved hands together. His eyes darted back and forth, but the fear that was there earlier seemed to be replaced with calculating eyes that judged the wind in equal measure with the innocuous movements of suburban life.

The Pope opened his mouth as if to say something reassuring, but was interrupted by the glare of headlights slicing through the snow up ahead. The car pulled against the curb opposite the mobsters, in front of the foreclosed home down the way. The lights went out and the area fell back into gloom, as a solitary streetlight hung off in the distance casted an ominous pall over the new vehicle as several silhouettes emerged from the car. One held open the door for the other. When he emerged, the shadowy figure that held the door open draped a coat over his shoulders. Two more men sat in the car, the driver and another larger fellow. The two shadows shuffled across the yard walking up the pathway of the house, then disappeared inside, while the other two remained inside the car.

The Pope watched it all and glanced over toward Don Ciancetta.

"You ready?"

Ciancetta gave his friend a tight grin and nodded.

The Pope tapped Nuncio on the shoulder and leaned forward in his seat, his heart beat echoing in his ears as the adrenaline flew through his veins.

"Alright, let's do this."

Chapter 33

Alex Vaughn turned up the heat in the Crown Victoria that Chief Wilcox issued him for his trip across international borders. The unmarked squad car was a luxury vehicle compared to Vaughn's Ford Taurus. The fact that it wasn't rusted out and had steady heat set it apart, but Alex wasn't enjoying the ride.

Vaughn's thoughts were directed inward as boarded up, ramshackle industrial complexes passed by his window and dilapidated buildings watched his progression towards the Peace Bridge which joined Canada with the United States.

On the other side, there was a U.S. Marshal who would oversee the American part of the arrest and a few Canadian officers who would do the direct takedown. Alex was still unsure what his role in the event would be, but positive identification on a ghost like Rafael was scarce. The only one who was still alive who saw a picture of him, no matter how grainy, was Alex Vaughn.

Alex stared at the road in front of him. Water traveled past him on either side as he drove up and onto the Peace Bridge. The Niagara River was a murky grey and brown this time of year; there were stretches of the river that were iced over. Lake Erie pressed her frozen lips against the river and its effects trailed outward along the shoreline.

Ryan was right. This bust had the potential to be a game changer. If this guy was a murderer for organized crime leadership, his testimony could blow the lid off of everything. But testimony meant a deal. A deal meant this guy would get to go on living.

Vaughn gripped the steering wheel and his knuckles turned white. He punched the accelerator and weaved in and out of cars on the bridge. Alex slid past the pack of cars and found some room.

"You gotta ask yourself, what are you after?"

The question rattled through Alex's brain. Over and over again it tap-danced across his consciousness. Jack bleeding out on a city street.

"What are you after?"

Explosions, gunshots, hidden money.

"What are you after?"

Power struggles, favors, almost resigning from the force.

"What are you after?" "WHAT ARE YOU AFTER?"

Alex let out a yell. It came from the floor boards and rumbled along his spine until it escaped from his cracked lips. It lasted a moment but it stopped the incessant question from ricocheting across his temple for just a moment.

Alex sighed as he slowed down. Up in front of him was the border and cars were lining up to provide passports for the custom agents allowing access into Canada.

As he brought the car to a full stop, he couldn't help his lips from whispering, "What are you after?"

*

The two mobsters exited the car. They pulled the cowl of their trench coats close around their necks and obscured the bottom half of their faces from view. The larger of them took the lead and strode up to the door of the foreclosed home.

In better times, this place might have been considered a decent place to hang one's hat, but now, parts of the front stoop were in various degrees of disrepair. Several loose bricks were scattered beneath the white powder that covered the walkway. An old mailbox bolted to the masonry near the front door rusted loose and hung at an angle. There was a faded black square where a sticker labeled the previous owner of the home, but had long since disappeared due to the elements.

The two walked under the entryway. The snow started to descend and grabbed at them in spiraling claws of frozen moisture. The slight triangular overhang offered little protection from the snow that reached for them from multiple angles. The lone window stuck above the red door was covered in a grey layer of film that did not allow for a view to the interior of the house.

The mobsters looked at each other. A knowing look was on both of their faces. They knew that beyond the door was the endgame. This was another in a series of moments that would make or break them. The smaller one pulled aside the flap of his trench coat where one hand rested beneath the fold. It was gripping a small snub nosed revolver and its silver glint reflected in the gloom. The larger mobster patted his own trench coat and nodded his head. They paused. Their breath came out in a slow vapor.

The smaller mobster opened the door.

Chapter 34

Vaughn pulled up to the border agent allowing access to Canada. He pushed a button on the door and lowered the window. A woman strolled up to his window decked out in a set of navy blues. She looked innocent with large wide set eyes that matched her brown hair, but the gun hanging at her hip told the truth. Another agent hung back inside of a small booth alongside his lane. He was looking at a monitor and Vaughn could guess what sort of capabilities existed in the art of detection. Mission by mission, he had seen a lot of cool shit the techies put together. The Patriot Act after September 11th opened up a whole new world as far as security was concerned. Alex knew, they could be x-raying his balls at this very moment.

With that on his mind, the border patrol agent came alongside him and requested his passport. "Where you heading, sir?"

Vaughn pulled out his badge instead and was satisfied when he noticed her demeanor shift from one of control to one of curiosity. "I'm meeting a United States Marshal here. We're supposed to be linking up with some local Mounties?"

"Your name, sir?"

Alex liked that she called him sir. He let himself smile as he stole a second peek at the beautiful browns on either side of her nose. "Vaughn. Detective Vaughn."

"Oh yes," she said as she skimmed his badge and identification. "Agent Johnson's been expecting you. He's inside the office. When you get past the gates, just pull over to the side." She waved over at a low rectangular structure about fifty feet off of the highway.

Alex nodded his thanks and rolled the window up. As he pulled over to the structure, he saw several cop cars in the parking lot but they were emblazoned with a red and blue swoosh along the side; the crowned seal of Canada imprinted just back from the front fenders.

A black SUV with tinted windows pulled alongside the curb and a large vehicle that looked like it might be armored rested nearby. The wheels were huge and looked like they could drive over the squad cars like matchbox toys. The box on wheels had a rectangular shape intermittently broken up with holes that looked perfect for the muzzle of a gun. Although unmarked, there was little doubt that that piece of machinery was used for transporting a group of people more deadly than your casual cop.

Vaughn stepped out of the car and stretched his legs. They felt stiff from the cold and the exertion he put them through over the last few days. The lights from the border crossing assaulted his eyes in the dusk as the lighting played off of the dancing snowflakes that threatened to turn the entire world white. Alex squint his eyes to shield them from the light and the motion pulled at his healing skin. He felt the scab under his eye crack with a lack of pliability. He pulled his hand to his face to make sure that there was no blood escaping from the wound. Glancing at his fingers, Alex was happy to note that he hadn't reopened the gash.

A single doorway stood sentry to the rectangular structure and Vaughn figured that was where he was supposed to go to meet the Marshal. His feet left imprints on the fresh snowfall behind him as he made for the warmth of the building. Just as he grabbed for the door-handle, it swung inward and two men came out.

The larger one wore a black outfit with various straps and containers hanging off of his hips and chest Kevlar. He wore a black military style cap with the letters ETF emblazoned on the front and based on the armored vehicle behind him, Alex figured he must be the Canadian version of SWAT.

The gentleman next to him wore suit pants and

wore a suit jacket slung over his shoulder in one hand. His white shirt sleeves were rolled up even in this brutal weather and he seemed to disregard the elements. A badge rested on his hip that read U.S. Deputy Marshal along a gold star. Both men sported pistols strapped to their hips.

While Vaughn regarded the men, the brown haired Marshal with youthful features and a slight build studied Alex's face for a moment, making the detective uncomfortable with the battle scars that stood out.

After a moment he stuck out his hand and announced, "Deputy Marshal Johnson. You must be Alex Vaughn."

Alex cleared his throat and his eyes flicked back and forth between the large Canadian and the Marshal.

"Good memory for faces Marshal?" He clasped the Deputy's hand and noticed it was firm but not obnoxiously so.

"Not so much that, but with a mug like that your either a criminal or a cop. Looks like you've been doing a little brawling lately."

Alex brought his hand up to his face and brushed the cut with the tip of his fingers, feeling the rough texture.

The Canadian next to Deputy Marshal Johnson gave a little cough, drawing the attention of both men in his direction. The deputy blushed as he regarded his own impropriety and planting a foot in the ground introduced the man next to him.

"This is Corporal Renaud. He is in charge of the Emergency Task Force group assigned to conduct the takedown of the target."

Alex extended a hand and caught the grasp of a crushing hand that seemed ready to break stone into dust.

"Detective."

Renaud had a French hint to his voice that caused him to hit his consonants hard and prompted Alex to take note.

"From Quebec Corporal?"

"Oui." The Corporal smiled and tilted his head in acknowledgement. "But based out of Toronto now. Don Mills to be exact."

Alex nodded his head. He heard of the training facility in that area of Toronto. It was quite a complex complete with its own barracks, rifle ranges, rappelling towers and a garage that housed a fleet of vehicles designed to handle a variety of possible engagement scenarios.

The Marshal interjected, "So, your superior filled you in on your role here?"

Alex nodded his head again.

"Good. You will be presenting a positive identification on the suspect. Once he is affirmed, Corporal Renaud and his boys will be initiating the takedown. The reason for the arrest will be that the target is an unwelcome visitor in Canada. At that point, they will turn over custody to me as the liaison for the United States. Once we cross the border, I will hand custody to you as the arresting officer. You can hold him for up to forty eight hours while you wait for the judge to get an arrest warrant into your hands. At that point, gentleman, it's all paperwork."

Corporal Renaud gave a curt nod and stepped away from the group. He mumbled something into a radio mounted on his shoulder. Whatever it was Alex couldn't hear but it appeared to be an order of some sort.

Almost immediately, the door to the building opened up and half a dozen men in similar black outfits and carrying varying types of weaponry ran towards the black armored vehicle. The first two pulled a set of double doors on the back apart while the other four jumped in. Corporal Renaud walked over to the passenger door and stepped inside. One of the two men that held the doors open for the rest of the crew jumped inside and pulled the doors shut behind him. The other ran alone to the driver's side door and jumped in.

"I know they're Canadian, but these guys carry a serious whoop-ass stick." The Marshal's eyes were alight at the activity and he nudged Alex towards a car that waited for them.

A police cruiser, considerably less dramatic than the armored van, waited on them. A constable exited and opened the doors for the two Americans as they approached.

As they took their seats, Alex thanked the Marshal for setting up the arrest. International arrests had to be at least incrementally more difficult than domestic ones.

"Eh, don't worry about it. To be honest with you, it's always a lot of coffee and computer screens at my office. This is worth staying on the clock for." The Marshal flashed a grin as the cruiser peeled out and followed the armored ETF van in front of them. The lights flashed on the two vehicles and sirens blared out pounding Alex's head just behind his eyes. Catching Alex's wince, the Marshal leaned over and yelled above the screeching, "Don't worry, once we get close they'll turn the sirens off and we will approach the target on silence, lights out!"

Alex Vaughn pinched his nose and closed his eyes, trying to turn the sound off and focus. He thought he would be more excited at the prospect of bringing down Jack's killer, but instead he was just tired. He would give anything to just crawl next to Charlotte and hold Ella in his arms and sleep for eternity.

The caravan sped along the highway at over one hundred and forty kilometers per hour and the lights flicked between blue and red. Alex's vision scattered for a moment with the strobe lights and Marshal Johnson's face alternated between red and blue as his skin reflected the piercing light. The sirens wailed in unison with Alex's heart, a discordant lonesome wail.

The detective cracked his neck and reset his eyes. "One more step." He said it aloud.

"What's that detective?" Johnson hollered.

"One more step!" Alex struggled to raise his voice above the din.

"Fuck yeah baby, that's the spirit! Rock and roll, boys!" The Marshal leaned back into Vaughn. "This here is what we call the rebel yell, detective!"

He rolled down the window and screamed into the wind, a horrible howling of a scream that seemed to harmonize with the mournful siren. A scream that brought back visions of Sal Pieri burning with his sins. A scream that echoed in Alex's soul.

*

The mobsters eased in through the open doorway and could hear a couple of voices talking in hushed tones at the back end of the home. One voice was withered with a cracked whistle to it that they both recognized to be Aldo Marano. His cadence was broken up by the inhalation of smoke and was studded with moments of breathing the toxins out.

"They'll be here. These younger guys, they don't have the balls to do what they should do. If they did, we wouldn't even be here right now."

The next voice was crisper. There was a bit of worry along the edges and his breathing accentuated the end of his sentences. A slight tremble irritated his inflection.

"It should never have gotten to this point. I've known Leonard since he was a boy." It was Falzone.

The mobsters stopped their stealthy walk and paused and glanced at one another. They gave each other a silent and affirming nod.

Aldo's voice wheezed in between exhalations, "This thing, it's all business Joe. Just business."

There was a wheeze that seemed like it must have come from Joe Falzone himself. "I hope you're right, old friend."

At that moment, the two mobsters flung open the door to the kitchen and stepped in. They paused. There was a moment where Aldo and Falzone had surprise etched on their faces. Then it became one of recognition.

Falzone spoke first, "What are you two doing here?"

Falzone was dressed in his Sunday best, suited up in a dark Armani. His grey hair was slicked back just above his bulbous nose. He sat behind a brown wooden kitchen table next to Aldo who held a lit cigarette that rested between his fingers. Behind them were old yellowing cabinets that might have once been white.

Aldo eyes looked at the two men. No emotion flashed there, just a knowing twinkle. "Angelo Della Morte." He grinned.

Then the two mobsters pulled out their pistols. The smaller one had his snub nose out in an instant, gripping it in his left hand. The larger one pulled out a black .22 caliber pistol and carried it aloft in his right hand. Side by side, they squeezed the trigger and the muzzles flashed.

It seemed as if there was an eternity of no sound. Just the repeating flashes of the gunpowder explosions. Aldo's body twitched left and then right as metal pounded into his flesh from multiple angles. He fell backward over his chair and lay on the ground. At the same time, Falzone took two bullets in his chest and tried to stand, kicking his chair backward. Another bullet burrowed into his belly and he hunched over the table. Blood flowed onto the wooden structure and the old man tried to catch it in his fingers as he stumbled forward onto the table. Then, he fell to his knees. He tried to grab the table to hold him upright but there was no strength left and he slipped on his own blood and fell to the floor.

One of the mobsters walked over Falzone who lay on his back next to Aldo's still lit cigarette, smoke drifting upward from the floor. He spit on the man where he lay.

"You traitor fuck."

He pulled out a long curved knife and knelt next to Falzone. He lifted the blade and slid it into Joey Falzone's chest, sending a spray of blood across his knuckles. A dozen times he sent the thirsty blade forth and plunged it into the thousand dollar suit. A dozen times he cursed Falzone as a traitor. When Falzone's feet stopped their twitching, the mobster stood up.

"Come on Jimmy; let's get the fuck out of here." Coughlin spit again on the broken body.

"Sure thing, Tom. Sure thing."

Chapter 35

The Pope watched as several pops sounded in the vacant home a little more than a hundred feet away. They were muffled and Nuncio rolled the ignition on the car several times causing it to screech in protest. They waited in silence, as time seemed to stand still and drag on indefinite.

After a few heartbeats Don Ciancetta, who was still rubbing his hands together, asked, "You think we should jet?"

"In a minute. We gotta make sure of who leaves that building. You ready just in case, Nuncio?"

Nuncio flashed his black steel revolver with a wooden handle in reply.

"Good."

A few moments later, and two silhouettes eased the door open and shuffled their way towards the empty car waiting outside the foreclosed lot. As they made their way along the frozen path and back to the vehicle, Nuncio inched the sedan forward, one hand on the wheel, the other pointing his revolver at the door facing the silhouettes. They closed the gap in a hurry and as they approached the two mobsters, The Pope rolled down his window and looked at the men to discern their identities. A smile crept across his face as the car drifted by Tommy Coughlin and Jimmy Jacks.

"Alright, let's go." He rolled up the window and looked over at Don Ciancetta. "War's over."

The Don let out a relieved laugh that seemed to drop a dozen years off of his frame. He leaned over and put a hand on his consigliore's face and pulled him in for a hug.

"I can't thank you enough." He pulled his face back and looked at his friend eye to eye. "What you do for me, every day, I can't thank you enough."

The Pope smiled back. "What are friends for?"

Don Ciancetta flashed another smile. Then his eyebrows crinkled up as a thought struck him.

"What about the guns, the car, the evidence?"

"In thirty minutes all of that will be compacted down at the yard. Jimmy and Tommy are pros, don't worry about it. All that the cops will have are the bodies of a few gangsters, and no one to point the finger at." The Pope held his hands apart, making himself look clueless.

"Something tells me they'll still point the finger."

"Welcome to America. God bless the judicial system that requires a little thing called evidence, my friend."

The Don leaned back in the leather seat and pulled out a cigar, slicing off the tip. He crunched the tobacco leaves between his teeth. The consigliore pulled out a Zippo and lit it for the Don as he pulled the smoke through the packed tobacco and puffed it out in a perfect circle. "Welcome to America."

The Pope smelled the sweetness of the cigar wafting through the sedan. It smelled delicious. It smelled of victory. Then, unannounced and unasked for, a coughing fit took him. The burn in his chest ate away his smile and drove the tears back into his eyes, with a cheese grater.

The Don studied him for a second and then waved his cigar at his friend. "You ought to get that checked out."

*

The windshield wipers crashed left and right, throwing small mountains of snow from the front of the police cruiser. The sound they made as they snapped one way and then the other was the only sound other than the slight crunch as the tires moved through the snow and the hum of the engine as it propelled the cruiser behind the armored ETF vehicle. The sirens turned off, along with the emergency lights. The spiraling snow fell down as if shoveled from the tops of the clouds by strong armed angels. They were forced to keep the headlights on as they made their way through a small dirt road that lead to the address listed on the piece of paper Alex carried from The Pope. They reflected now, off of the plummeting heaps of frozen precipitation.

To Vaughn, the reflections looked like a myriad of twirling eyes gazing back at him and judging his very existence. He wanted to put a bullet into Rafael's face for what he did. It would be justice after all, wouldn't it? He knew that the man who killed Jack was this monster, this assassin. The oldest laws on record allowed—no demanded—an eye for an eye.

He could do it, too. He knew he could, and he wouldn't even feel bad about it. He could watch the life drain from this son of a bitch and it wouldn't even give him so much as a bad dream. No sleep would be lost.

Alex looked over at Marshal Johnson. The young man was tapping his finger on the ledge of the window and his knee shook as the adrenaline struggled to manifest in a body constrained to sitting. Vaughn pushed his hair behind his ear and glanced down at the badge hanging from the Marshal's hip. His badge seemed brighter than the one that Vaughn placed on his Chief's desk just a few hours earlier.

He remembered how eager he'd been when he first joined the force. He believed so much in the ideal back then. Other cops, they had something to prove, or had nothing better to do. Vaughn, though, believed in the concept behind the badge. To him, "To Protect and Serve" wasn't a motto. It was a way of life. The Marshal glanced over and caught Alex's stare on the badge.

"It's beautiful, isn't it?"

"Yeah, I was just thinking, yours looks a little shinier than mine."

The Marshal looked down at the star and smiled.

"The thing about a badge is it's only shiny so long you keep it polished." He raised his eyebrows as if it proved his point and then looked back out the window.

Alex took the cue, and looked out his own window as the car bounced along the uneven road and threatened to throw their foreheads into the roof. He watched the woods as they grew thicker around the dirt road and seemed to close in on the small caravan from all sides.

Branches were scraping at the windows like hands reaching out to them, wanting to pull them into the forest forever. The night sky blocked out all but the nearest trees and Vaughn could see his ghostly reflection in the glass. He looked like shit. His eye was swollen and the various bruises on his face shone with a yellowish tint. The cut along his forehead and under his eyes looked like they scabbed over something infected and were white along the edges. His eyes looked vacant and hollow. Alex barely recognized them.

It was as if someone who looked like him was staring back, only Alex could tell he was an imposter. The detective let his eyes trail out into the forest. Alex tried to look past this other view of himself.

Chapter 36

They found a clearing about a hundred yards from the house, Alex was told, though they couldn't see it through the dark and the cloistered evergreens. The moment they exited the cruiser, the wind seemed to pick up a bit and Vaughn could feel the cold whip in through the top of his jacket and work its way down along his back. The men in the armored ETF vehicle jumped out and one group of two took off towards the left and another duo of men ran right, their destinations known before they arrived.

They had flashlights affixed to their semi-automatic weapons. The beams of light cut several feet into the night before the snow extinguished it. A fifth officer carrying a large rifle, with a scope on it about the size of a soda can, took off down the center. He had some sort of contraption on his face that looked like binoculars, and Vaughn realized they must be night vision goggles. He carried some sort of sharp metal objects in his hands and Alex watched him as he disappeared into the darkness.

Corporal Renaud hopped out of the ETF wagon and took long strides over to Alex. "He is going to climb higher for a better view."

Vaughn nodded. "So how are we going to proceed?"

Renaud waved a hand to the left. "I have four men taking up positions, one on each corner of the house. Constable Demarais is going to be up above watching us like an eagle." The Corporal pointed upwards and in the direction of the man with the night vision. "As for you and me, we will go together, through the front door. There, you will make the identification."

The Marshal gave a little cough and set his feet. "What about me Corporal, what would you like me to do?"

Renaud gave the Marshal a toothy grin and patted the air with his hands.

"You stay here and watch the vehicles, Marshal, along with the Constable. This is a Canadian issue until we get the suspect in custody."

Marshal Johnson stood still for a second casting a stare at the Corporal, then shuffled his feet and took a step back, "Of course, Corporal."

"Very good then." He handed Vaughn a small ear piece and said, "Put this in, it is linked to our man with a visual of the interior. Detective, would you like to take a moment, and then join me. We will draw this to a satisfactory conclusion." Captain Renaud turned around and unclipped the safety on his side arm and again began to talk in hushed tones on his shoulder mounted radio.

Alex Vaughn inserted the ear piece and stole a glance at the crestfallen Marshal and clasped his shoulder as if to say, "I'm sorry."

The Marshal just mumbled, "Damned Canadian sovereignty."

Alex Vaughn walked off past the Marshal and towards Corporal Renaud. He too, decided it would be best if he were to approach the situation with the safety off of his gun. He felt it click with a push of his thumb. He felt the click reverberate through his body.

Game on.

Corporal Renaud and Alex Vaughn walked side by side through the snow in the direction of the cabin. The evergreens continued to grope towards Alex with their wooden fingers and the sound of their boots packing the snow beneath their feet greeted his ears each step of the way. Vaughn felt like they would be uncovered at any moment. To Alex's surprise, Corporal Renaud began speaking to him, though Vaughn thought it best that they remain as stealthy as possible.

"This man, Detective, he is very dangerous, no?"

"Yes."

"What makes a man more dangerous than others?"

Alex looked over at the Corporal, who was staring into the gloom. "Excuse me?"

"Take us for instance. Are we not dangerous, too?" He patted his sidearm as if to emphasis the point.

"I suppose we are." *What the fuck is his point?*

"Ah, but we have rules, you and me. Do you think that makes us more dangerous or less so?"

Vaughn thought about the question for a moment as the crunching of their feet ate into the silence. "Maybe less dangerous tonight, but more dangerous tomorrow."

Renaud stopped walking, prompting Alex to stop too. Vaughn looked into the darkness and saw the shadowy shape of the cabin less than thirty yards away, nestled between two large masses of trees. Light poured forth from the windows and faded back into darkness, less than fifteen yards from where the two of them stood. But Renaud wasn't looking at the cabin. Alex felt him watching him and turned to regard the Corporal.

Renaud nodded his head. "There you have it then."

"There you have it."

The two of them continued walking towards the cabin. A single flash of light came from their left and then another from their right.

"They are in position," Renaud said as they continued their march.

It didn't take them long until they were just a few strides from the wooden structure, the trees opening up around it in a ring. It looked as if it were made of log, with rounded beams stacked up until it reached a metallic roof, made possibly of tin. It wasn't large and boasted a single chimney that released thin grey smoke into the black sky. At least a foot of snow settled on the roof, and didn't seem to have a mind to move at all. Two steps led up to the door and that was where Renaud and Alex paused. Renaud placed his hand on the door, and he tried the handle. It rolled over, and Vaughn could tell it was not locked.

The ear piece came alive with a voice that informed them, "There is one suspect inside. His back is to the main doorway, he is about ten paces from the door."

Renaud held up his other hand, his gun now resting in his grip and mouthed, "On three."

Alex nodded.

"One…"

He felt his adrenaline spring through his heart and into his throat.

"Two…"

Alex Vaughn pulled out his Beretta. Snowflakes nestled on his shoulder.

"Three."

Corporal Renaud flung the door open and entered the cabin, his gun raised in front of him and cupped in one hand as he moved in and to the left of the frame. Alex Vaughn followed, his gun cradled in both hands and hanging at the side of his hip.

The first thing he saw was a man with his back to him. He hadn't the time to remove his jacket, and wore one in black leather. He wasn't very large and he had dark hair with a bit of grey coming around the base of his crown. He was standing at a counter and looking out of a window that peered into the woods behind the cabin.

The cabin was one big, open space other than two doorways that led into other rooms. A couch and a couple of chairs covered with plastic decorated the room. The place didn't appear to be used much or often. To the right of the assassin were two hooks. A black fedora hung from one, while the other one supported a double holster made of leather. Two pistols with silencers attached to them hung there.

"It's him!" Alex said.

Renaud walked further into the room. His voice

seemed to boom as he addressed Rafael Rontego.

"Mister Rontego, I am Corporal Renaud of the Toronto Emergency Task Force. We are to take you into custody as an unwelcomed visitor across our borders."

Alex noticed that the assassin's head dropped a bit lower, but otherwise he didn't move. Vaughn moved further to the right, positioning himself in the path of the killer and his weapons.

Renaud continued, "Mister Rontego, do you understand me? Mister Rontego, show me your hands."

Still, the assassin barely moved. His shoulders moved up and down with his breathing and Alex was pretty sure the man was trying to figure out his next move.

Vaughn jumped in, "There is nowhere to go; the building is surrounded."

The Corporal nodded his approval as he moved to the left, putting more distance between himself and Alex. "Come now, let us end this peacefully."

Vaughn was now almost directly to the side of the hit man and could see the side of his face. He noticed the man's eyes were closed and his breathing was erratic, his breath was coming in short bursts as if he were preparing himself for something. His lips moved as if he were speaking to himself.

That was when Alex noticed it.

The man was clutching a small gun in his left hand pressed against the counter. At that moment, everything happened at once. The killer spun around and his hand stretched out towards Renaud.

Alex screamed, "Gun!" and dropped into a crouch.

He swung his hand upward and fired off a shot. Renaud crouched down and attempted to squeeze off a round when a single bullet exploded through the window, shattering tiny reflective pieces of glass into the room along with bits of ice and snow. Pieces of glass whipped across the Corporal's face and his shot went wide of the assassin, striking the wall behind him.

But both the sniper's bullet and Vaughn's found their mark. Vaughn's struck him in the gut and the sniper's hit him in the center of the chest. He fell backward against the counter with a thud. A splash of blood sprinkled the window behind him and a streak of it followed the murderer's body as he slid down until he was sitting on the floor. The sniper's bullet left a burning hole in the assassin's jacket and smoke trailed upward out of it. Vaughn's bullet tore into the belly and blood oozed through the fabric of his shirt, so dark that it almost looked black where it poured out the most. The gun fell from the man's grasp as he sat against the counter and fell to the floor at his side.

Renaud spoke into the radio on his shoulder, "We need medical help in here. We have a man down."

Vaughn paused for a moment as he struggled to interpret the scene. Alex noticed the man staring past the room and his left foot kicked from side to side as if he were trying to walk.

This is all wrong.

He ran forward towards the assassin and slid on his knees along the wooden floor. He pulled the man onto his back and pressed his hand against the wound in his stomach, where the blood seemed to be seeping out the worst.

"Don't you die you son of a bitch. You have to answer for what you did to my friend!"

The assassin lay on his back and blood trickled out of his mouth. He stared up at the ceiling and Vaughn could see his eyes roll as he struggled to bring them into focus.

"Who's your friend?"

"Jack Benton!"

The killer coughed and a smile made more of blood than of teeth flashed at the detective. "Never heard of him."

"You fucking prick! Don't you lie to me! Don't you lie to me!"

Alex felt a rage in his soul that traveled to his very fingertips and he wanted the assassin to feel it too. He pressed his fingers into the wound in the man's stomach and the killer thrashed as the pain registered across his brain.

"Say it! Say it!"

The assassin turned his head and coughed, his blood pouring out of his mouth as his lungs filled with blood. He started laughing, as if it was all one big joke.

"Say what?"

"Say you knew Jack Benton!" Alex pressed his fingers into the wound even harder and again the assassin kicked out from the sheer agony.

Renaud spoke from behind him. "That's enough Detective."

Still Vaughn dug his fingers into the man's stomach.

"I knew him! I knew Jack Benton!" He screamed out the words as his body convulsed and Alex couldn't tell anymore if it was from pain or from death throes.

He looked back over his shoulder as the Corporal stared in shock back at Alex. Several men started to flood into the room, followed by the Marshal and Vaughn felt the blood rush out of his face as his own actions came into focus.

He rolled over next to the assassin, and looked down at his hands. They were covered in black blood and his shirt was speckled red from drops of spray. He heard a low laugh to his side and looked over at the assassin.

He tried to say a few words, but then he laughed again in a death filled delirium. His lips were moving and he was staring at Alex. Vaughn couldn't make out what he was saying so he lowered his ear next to the assassin. Still he couldn't decipher the sounds coming from the man.

When his ear was almost to the man's blood covered lips he heard him.

"This, all of this, is per niente."

"What?"

"Per niente. For nothing."

Then he started laughing again and Alex could see the man's fingers twitching against the wooden floor. Blood was all along his arm and Alex wondered whether or not any part of the world was free of the red liquid. As he sat there watching the assassin struggle for life, he wished that it could be so. He wished that some piece of the world was free of the stain.

The assassin gave one last gasp that heaved more blood than air into his lungs and his body gave one last kick and then was still.

Renaud walked over to the detective who sat there staring into the vacant eyes of the killer. "What did he say?"

"He said this is all for nothing. I don't get what he means."

"Perhaps this is why." Renaud crouched down and showed the pistol to Vaughn. He pulled the trigger and a small flame leaped from the barrel of the gun, and stayed there.

"A lighter?"

"Oui."

Alex's dehydrated lips pulled on one another and his mouth fell open.

"You couldn't have known."

*

Alex Vaughn rubbed his eyes as he tried to focus on the snow streaked pavement flashing under his tires along with the partially obscured yellow lines that raced past the wheels. The adrenaline wore off during a marathon session of answering questions and helping the local Mounties fill out their paperwork and the weariness seeped into every cell of his body. From there, it was just going to trickle down.

"As if I didn't have enough paperwork already," lamented Marshal Johnson when he viewed the gruesome scene moments after the assassin stopped moving.

Alex tried to stifle a yawn but it escaped between his fingers despite his best efforts. No doubt he was going to have to file a report too, and it was always better to fill it out while things were fresh in the memory. He glanced over at the gun holster with a twin set of pistols lying on the seat next to him. A black fedora rested on top of them and off to the side and it quivered with the vibrations of the car as if an invisible hand was shaking it back and forth.

"You might need these to put some pieces together. Perhaps for other investigations." Renaud handed the items to him as he clasped him on the shoulder. "You know, real gun or not, you still acted to save my life. Thank you for that."

The man looked him in the eye and held him there for a moment. Nothing else needed to be said, Alex felt that same way when two mobsters sprung him from the clutches of one of his corrupt brethren just several hours earlier.

How do you put a price on tomorrow?

You don't care how you got it, you're just happy that you have a tomorrow, today.

Jack once waxed philosophical with Alex, as he often did after a few drinks. The two of them were reclining back on some cheap lawn furniture, smoking cigars, while a woman Jack was dating and Charlotte were inside talking about the pregnancy. Alex just found out that it was going to be a girl, and Jack brought these cigars that were wrapped with a pink band that proclaimed, "It's a girl!"

"How do you feel, old pal?" he asked as his eye caught a twinkle with the setting sun. His bushy eyebrows seemed to shade his eye just enough to keep it open and to reflect the light in a way that made Alex think Jack knew something he didn't. It was often that way with the two of them.

"I feel alright. You know, I thought, for sure I thought, I would feel a bit down if it wasn't a boy. But I just feel different. Instead of thinking football, I'm thinking dances and boyfriends I have to keep away. Different, but still really, really good."

Alex felt a tranquil smile creep up and meld with the relaxing sun as it began its ritual downward slope. The warmth of it spread across his face and he closed his eyes, feeling the gentle heat.

"Well, if you have any trouble with the boys, you send them over to Uncle Jack for a talking to." He put the cigar between his teeth and clasped his hands behind his head, taking a long look at the purple and red streaks sliding out from the center of the orange ball of flame. He puffed on the cigar sending bits of smoke trailing from the corner of his mouth. "Is it a funny thing?"

"Is what a funny thing?" Alex rolled his head over to better regard his friend.

Jack's lips curled in a slight smile and he cocked his head to the side, as if he found it amusing that Alex hadn't caught on yet.

"To realize that you're living for someone else's tomorrow rather than your own today?"

Vaughn studied his friend. Jack's eyes were closed now and a half-smile splayed across his face. He raised a hand to his mouth, catching the cigar between his fingers and bringing it down to his side.

"I don't know, I guess I hadn't thought."

"Well, you better start, old boy. You better start."

For the first time, Alex Vaughn was thinking about

what that meant. He looked at the road, his eyes alert now. The paperwork would have to wait.

Home beckoned.

He put the Crown Victoria in park and grabbed the holster and fedora and trudged up the walkway to Charlotte's. He thought his heart would be heavier, that there would be more trepidation to confront her. He didn't feel that sense of anxiety. Perhaps it was because he knew that all that stood in their way before was him.

A gust of wind almost knocked Alex over and he jogged the final steps to the door. It was after 2 a.m. again, but he didn't feel bad about coming home this late. Better late than never.

Alex Vaughn pushed in the doorbell and heard the familiar chime behind the door. He pulled his tattered jacket taut with his free hand, trying to make himself look presentable and he brushed his hair back behind his ears. He noticed his shirt and the dried blood that caked it, and he glanced down wishing he changed it, or stopped off at his apartment first.

Before he could settle himself, she was easing the door open. Her brown hair was pulled back in a bun and she had on that pink bathrobe again and Alex couldn't help but smile at the shocked expression that leaped off of her soft features.

"It's been a long day."

She continued to look at him, her mouth agape. "Your clothes, your face! My God, what happened to you? Every time I see you there's less of you!"

Alex couldn't help it, he tried to hold it back but his lips trembled and he laughed. His eyes began to tear up, he was laughing so hard. Then it wasn't laughing tears that began to stream down his cheeks.

"Baby, I want to come home."

She moved across the threshold in that subtle and

shifting way that Alex thought so perfect, it appeared mystical. She draped her arms across his shoulders, blood and sweat and tears and all, and she pulled him close.

"Oh Alex, don't you know that's all you ever had to do?"

The tears dropped off his cheeks and landed on the shoulder of her robe, and Alex tried to firm his jaw, but it just trembled all the more.

"What?"

She pulled him inside and shut the door.

"All you had to do was come home."

The next morning Alex woke up just after noon, to a little girl waddling across his bedroom. She was all of two feet tall and every few feet she stumbled and grabbed a hold of something to keep herself upright, but she made her way over to the bed and put her face right next to Alex.

She looked him right in the eye and he looked at her and said, "Good morning beautiful."

She didn't say anything back, but Alex felt sure, just by looking into her eyes, that she knew what he was saying, that she knew him. Vaughn picked her up and walked down the stairs, feeling her tiny fingers grab his finger and hold on with a trust he hoped to earn over the years.

The smell of fresh coffee wafted up the stairs and entered his nose. Charlotte was up. He put Ella down on the carpet and held on to both of her hands. Her unsure legs wobbled towards the kitchen and she used Alex's hands to guide her to her mother.

Charlotte was drinking a cup of coffee at the table and her rose colored cheeks turned upward and into a smile as Ella let go of Alex's hands and ran forward. She scooped her up and gave her a bear hug while little Ella squealed in delight and buried her face in her mother's neck.

"She was sleeping next to you when I came down stairs. She misses her Daddy." She gave Ella a kiss on the cheek. "Would you mind grabbing the paper from outside?"

Alex Vaughn looked at his wife. His lips were helpless to do anything other than to smile at the two of them, his beautiful women. With a laugh and a wave, he turned around and walked towards the door. He felt more complete in this moment than since before he could remember. Last night, the end of it anyway, was as close to perfect as he could remember. He put on his shoes and walked outside. The cold whipped at him, but the sun fell on his body and kept the cool air from washing over him. The newspaper lay on top of the snow at the end of the driveway. He made his way towards it, as last night came more into focus.

Charlotte brought him upstairs and he dropped the gun holster and the fedora on the nightstand. She pulled him close and said over and again how glad she was that he decided to come home.

He held her in his arms and said, "I am done with this job. I need to be here, I need to be with you and Ella."

He thought for sure she would be ecstatic with joy, but instead she pushed herself away from him, separating the two of them while he still held her in his locked arms.

"I want you home, but only if you are doing it for you."

"Baby, I'm doing it for you and for Ella and for me. Don't you want that?"

"Of course I do! But you have to do it because *you* want it. You can't do it and then a week or a month from now decide I made you. I won't have our child resented by her father." She started to tear up and the little pools of brown threatened to spill over. "And I won't have my husband resent me." A single tear meandered down her cheek onto her chin.

"I'm doing it for me, Charlotte. I'm doing it for me."

Alex Vaughn pulled her back in and kissed her lips. Rose colored, tender lips. His lips. He took his bruised and battered hands and wiped her tear off of her cheek and told her he loved her in every way he could imagine. They lay down together and she lay in his arms and they fell asleep together for the first time in a hundred years.

Alex picked up the paper. The plastic that covered it was damp from the snow and he brushed the water off of it as he looked around. The driveway needed to be shoveled and the sidewalk needed salt. There was something on the street, just off of the curb.

Several somethings.

Vaughn worked his way over. They were tiny, but there were five or six of them. He edged closer. They were black. Vaughn knelt down and picked one of them up between his thumb and index finger and he almost threw up. He looked around left and right down the street. All sound seemed to stop and his eyes darted back and forth. There was nobody. He leapt up and sprinted up the walk, the cold air filled his lungs, but he didn't notice. He ran into the house and locked the door. He ran into the kitchen and threw the newspaper down along with his new discovery and sprinted towards the stairs.

"Alex?" Charlotte called after him. "Alex!"

He bound up the stairway two steps at a time and ran into the bedroom. He looked at the nightstand and stopped. Images of the cabin flashed through his mind.

The soft sound of footfalls came up behind him and Charlotte asked, "What's wrong Alex? Why did you bring this filthy cigarette butt in the house?"

Ignoring her question, Alex felt the blood drain from his face. The cold from outside clung to his bones and his heart seemed to stop beating.

"Charlotte, did you move the gun holster and the hat off of the nightstand?"

"No baby, why?"

Look out for the next Upstate New York Mafia Tale,
coming soon.

About the Author

Nicholas Denmon studied English at the University of Florida. He started story telling from the moment he could talk and has spent a lifetime perfecting the art.

His life has been varied, giving him no shortage of material. Some of his unique experiences include growing up with a schizophrenic mother, having six brothers and sisters (of which he is the middle-younger child), a perfectionist father, an evil step-mother, a college life to rival Tucker Max, and working for politicians on the Presidential as well as local stage. He has been, at times, a devout Catholic, a closet atheist, and an honorary member of the Jewish tribe.

Nick's joy of art knows little in the way of limitations, as he loves unique paintings, music, acting, film, and of course writing.

Made in the USA
Las Vegas, NV
15 July 2021